PLUTO

TOR BOOKS BY
BEN BOVA

PLUTO

Ben Bova
and Les Johnson

TOR

TOR PUBLISHING GROUP

New York

PLUTO

A Tor Book
Published by Tom Doherty Associates / Tor Publishing Group
120 Broadway
New York, NY 10271

www.torpublishinggroup.com

Tor® is a registered trademark of Macmillan Publishing Group, LLC.

EU Representative: Macmillan Publishers Ireland Ltd, 1st Floor, The Liffey Trust Centre, 117–126 Sheriff Street Upper, Dublin 1, D01 YC43

The Library of Congress Cataloging-in-Publication Data is available upon request.

ISBN 978-1-250-29665-8 (hardcover)
ISBN 978-1-250-29666-5 (ebook)

Our books may be purchased in bulk for specialty retail/wholesale, literacy, corporate/premium, educational, and subscription box use. Please contact MacmillanSpecialMarkets@macmillan.com.

First Edition: 2025

Printed in the United States of America

10 9 8 7 6 5 4 3 2 1

To the Baron Peter von Kill IV, good buddy
and
To Rashida Loya-Bova for her passion to continue
Ben's legacy

Lo! Death has reared himself a throne.
In a strange city lying alone
Far down in the dim West . . .
  —*Edgar Allan Poe, "The City in the Sea"*

CHAPTER 1

Gazing out across the always dark terrain of Pluto, Aaron Mikelson, PhD, saw what the average human could see—a surprisingly smooth icy plane, mostly black and a ruddy orange—but he was able to view more than a human eye. Viewing the scene with the infrared part of the electromagnetic spectrum, Mikelson determined that there was hardly any temperature change over the surface. He also noticed a lack of radiation discharges aside from cosmic rays infiltrating the wispy nitrogen atmosphere and minimal amounts of carbon monoxide and methane within it. When observed through the infrared all the way up to x-rays and gamma rays, Pluto looked relatively tranquil.

As he rolled across the cold and soulless surface, stopping occasionally to scan an interesting formation or odd radiation glint, Mikelson's four wheels gave him sure footing, despite the ice, allowing him to focus on collecting scientific data rather than surviving the inhospitable world. He could hear the radio traffic from the *Tombaugh* orbiting above, their feeble calls to stop and return to the ship as well as their near-continuous data transfer across the light-hours separating Pluto from Mother Earth.

Mikelson pitied his crewmates, still wedded to their organic bipedal forms. They would never be able to see or hear as he did; never experience, physically experience, the cold vacuum of Pluto as he experienced it. They were still fully human. Mikelson was something more. Something he would never have imagined had it not been for the accident that nearly killed him on Titania, Uranus's largest moon.

The explosion in the Titanian habitat severed his legs and arms and induced third-degree burns over his remaining torso. In the midst of intense pain, he didn't remember agreeing to be merged with the experimental artificial intelligence; had he known then what he knew now, he would have readily agreed. He was so much more now. Liberated from his body, he was encased in a carbon fiber–wrapped superconducting memory core and only recently installed in the XA-1 rover. He and the rover were much more than simply the merger of two. Natural humans would never truly understand, and that was a pity. If they were able to do what he could do, then they would have found what he was close to finding. The only thing he would change, if he could, were the memories of the accident and the pain. With his new electronic memory storage, no memory dimmed with time and that was both a joy and a curse—especially when something triggered memories of the accident.

Mikelson's crewmates' chatter annoyed him, and he grew bored of their entreaties to return to the ship. Had Marlene, the AI with which he had been intertwined, survived the merger, then he would have at least had someone else to speak with, but she hadn't, leaving him alone with his thoughts. Mikelson was looking for something, he didn't exactly know what, but, based on the evidence, he knew enough to believe it would be revelatory. He wasn't planning to leave the surface of Pluto until he found it.

Unconsciously, Larry Randall leaned slightly forward in his contoured command chair, squinting into the eyepiece hanging in front of him. The image he saw was magnified, digitally enhanced, and completely boring. In short, Larry could see nothing but the flat, open plain of Sputnik Planitia. It was vast, dreary, and dark as the soul of a devil. The sky was black, this far from the sun, with only Charon casting a pale radiance across the almost featureless plain. Even the gleaming stars strewn across the sky seemed far away, aloof, uncaring.

Larry stared at the icy tracks left by the missing XA-1 and again wondered why anyone would choose to go AWOL on Pluto, forcing the Space Force to come to the rescue. This Mikelson guy would have hell to pay when this was over—if they could bring him back alive. They had no reason to believe Mikelson was dead. He had radioed his ship, *Tombaugh*, a few times, none recently, and they tracked his rover's path across the surface well enough to identify a good spot for Larry and his team to land and attempt a rescue, or retrieval, whichever the case turned out to be.

The scientists aboard *Tombaugh*, conducting orbital and surface studies at Pluto for six months, were beside themselves and ready to move on. When it was time to pack up and leave their surface base, everyone did as directed and returned to their ship. Everyone except, of course, Dr. Mikelson. No, he decided to go solo and remain on Pluto despite the requests, admonitions, and outright threats from the ship's captain and his colleagues. After a week, Captain Blackstone contacted Space Force for assistance. As was official policy after the Windward Disaster a few decades ago, a Space Force cruiser was required to be within a two-week high-energy burn of any research vessel or large cruise ship in the solar system. Small, private ships were exempt; there were now simply too many of them, and such ships flew at their own risk. No one wanted another Windward mass casualty event, and the Space Force used up a huge chunk of its budget to provide ready rescue should it be needed. Fortunately, it was not needed that often.

The tank-like vehicle Larry drove was officially called a Landing Craft, Vehicle and Personnel (LCVP), a massive machine, mounted on studded tracks that crunched across Pluto's icy surface like a metallic worm. He and his crew called it the "Beast," and they were in it following the trail left by the wayward XA-1. Larry headed the Beast's crew of four, and for this mission, it was outfitted to traverse icy surfaces. On board *Aurora*, circling several hundred kilometers above, was Beast's sister, Beauty, similarly customizable; the two could be outfitted to traverse the surface of virtually any moon or dwarf planet in the outer solar system.

Larry had guided Beast from orbit to a spot less than a mile from the XA-1's current location and set out in pursuit. He would have preferred to set down within eyesight distance of the rogue scientist, but the ice formations near Mikelson looked precarious and he did not want to land on an icesheet that could not bear the weight of the LCVP. Caution dictated they drive, paying close attention to each ice increment to make sure it was safe. Though once it looked like Mikelson cleared questionable ice, Beast could use its thrusters to ballistically hop closer, taking only a fraction of the time, but it would have used precious fuel—fuel he might need in an emergency or, worst case, series of emergencies. Driving was slower, but safer and more prudent.

What he couldn't understand was why Mikelson had gone rogue. How much more could one learn about this remote and desolate place that you couldn't gather in half a year? And how long could any human stand not seeing a blue sky, green tree, or body of water larger than the ship's swimming pool? Mikelson was now solidly beyond asking why. He had made that clear when he cut off communication with his colleagues aboard *Tombaugh* and refused the answer hails from *Aurora*. No, this was now a retrieval mission. Larry's orders were to follow Mikelson and the XA-1, rescue him if necessary, and bring him back to *Tombaugh* regardless.

Aurora was now in Pluto orbit with *Tombaugh*, a research ship staffed with a few dozen scientists and crew, on its charter to explore Pluto—one of the least studied bodies remaining inside the Kuiper Belt. It was Larry's second long-term deep-space deployment, and while he felt a bit restless for home, he also never tired of seeing the black starry skies of space and other worlds. He was where he was meant to be. Most of the crew of *Aurora*, though not all, shared his outlook. Mikelson's refusal to return to the ship bewildered Larry, though he could kind of understand it emotionally—Pluto was beautifully desolate.

But Major Larry Randall, United States Space Force, took his job seriously and wouldn't waiver in his assignment to return the errant scientist safely back to *Tombaugh*. Retrieving Dr. Mikelson was his job, and he was bound and determined to do it well.

We could die out here in this frozen wilderness, Larry knew. For some reason, Tennyson came to mind:

"Forward, the Light Brigade!"
Was there a man dismayed?
Not though the soldier knew
Someone had blundered.

Someone had blundered, he repeated silently to himself. And we've been picked to find out why.

Theirs not to make reply,
Theirs not to reason why,
Theirs but to do and die.

Larry repeated the lines to himself a few times as he kept the ungainly vehicle trundling forward, following the faint, barely discernible tracks of the wayward XA-1 and its radio beacon.

Into the valley of Death.

Sitting slightly behind Larry's right shoulder, Dr. Abigail Grigsby peered anxiously into the vision-enhancing eyepiece hanging before her face. She was the only woman of the LCVP's four-person crew. Female scientists outnumbered the men aboard *Tombaugh* by practically three to one, but the inverse was true on the *Aurora*—a fact she found intellectually interesting, but of little consequence. When *Tombaugh*'s Captain Blackstone asked her if she would join the Space Force retrieval team, she readily agreed. She would have agreed to almost anything to get back to Pluto's surface. Blackstone thought she would be the person best able to convince Mikelson to return. She suspected that was because she was one of the few who didn't completely ignore him. It was not easy or comfortable to have a conversation with a disembodied person, especially the arrogant Dr. Mikelson.

Stepping away from the eyepiece and standing up, she murmured, "Nothing in sight."

From behind her, Mitsui Arashi, the crew's avionics engineer, offered a dry laugh. "Just kilometers of ice. The closest bird to us is four hundred million kilometers away." Of average height with a lean, athletic build, Mitsui had dark, expressive eyes reflecting his determination and intelligence. His jet-black hair was often kept short for practicality, and he took pride in wearing the uniform of the U.S. Space Force—always impeccably pressed and adorned with the various badges and insignias marking his accomplishments.

Beside him, Bashar al-Salam, their engineering tech, slowly shook his head. "His tracks are still visible. This is a foolish mission."

"Those were the orders—foolish or not," returned Larry.

Al-Salam made a sour face. "As you say, Major."

The Beast trundled along in near silence. Within the

heavily insulated cockpit, the crew couldn't hear the constant crunch of their vehicle's treads on Pluto's surface. As they continued across the endless ice, Larry wondered if Mikelson would allow himself to be rescued. The XA-1 had not reported back to *Tombaugh* for eight days. He must be okay since his beacon was functional and reported the XA-1 making slow progress across the ice ahead. At their current travel rate, the Beast would catch up to the XA-1 in a matter of hours.

CHAPTER 2

As the nineteenth century drew to a close, astronomers were puzzled. The newly discovered planet Neptune was not in the position their calculations showed it should be. Something tugged at it, a gravitational pull nudging that world out of the position it should be in. Faced with a difference—ever so slight—between their calculations and their observations, they trusted the calculations.

The hunt was on.

Pluto was finally discovered in 1930 by Clyde Tombaugh at the Lowell Observatory in Flagstaff, Arizona. At that time, it was thought to be the farthest object in the solar system.

Named after the ancient Greek god of the underworld, Pluto was—and is—a bleak world: cold, dark, inhospitable. Increasingly fine examinations of Pluto eventually revealed that it was slightly less than twenty-four hundred kilometers in diameter, approximately 70 percent the size of Earth's Moon. *New Horizons*, the first spacecraft to reach and study Pluto, revealed it to be a world with a million-square-mile nitrogen glacier at least two and a half miles thick, covering what many scientists believed may be a vast liquid water ocean beneath.

Ongoing studies of the outer solar system eventually proved that Pluto was merely one member of the Kuiper Belt, a vast ring of rocky and icy bodies stretching from the orbit of Neptune to more or less twice that distance. In 2006, to the disappointment of children everywhere, the International

Astronomical Union reclassified Pluto as a dwarf planet. Several other dwarf planets were discovered in the Kuiper Belt, some larger than Pluto. For more than a century after *New Horizons* provided the first detailed glimpse, there were few follow-up missions. Humanity's expansion into the solar system primarily focused on its inner worlds, with only a few scientific outposts and tourist destinations near the outer planets of Uranus and Neptune.

As the twenty-first century drew to a close, entrepreneurs, scientists—and nearly everyone else—viewed Pluto as a mere curiosity.

In the middle of the twenty-second century, the world's space agencies decided it was time to revisit Pluto and learn more of its geography, composition, and history. Led by the United States, they commissioned a refitting of a deep-space cruiser renamed *Tombaugh*, staffed it with an experienced crew and competitively selected its complement of scientists for a one-year mission reminiscent of the nineteenth-century voyages of discovery back on Earth. Among the scientists selected was Dr. Aaron Mikelson—who had compelling credentials and a highly rated scientific study plan. However, unbeknownst to the selection committee and everyone else, Mikelson was a renegade, made more so by his accident.

CHAPTER 3

"I can see the rift." Abigail broke the cabin's silence. "over to the left, close to the horizon."

Larry leaned forward and peered into his eyepiece. Off in the distance, near the horizon, a sinuous dark line snaked across the icy plain. The latest orbital survey revealed the rift in the ice sheet, which appeared to be relatively new, perhaps not more than a few years old—or maybe a thousand—or ten thousand. Who knew? They had been tracking toward it for quite some time and had hoped to overtake the XA-1 before reaching it. A rift meant ice movement and instability—and that meant risk. Larry didn't like risk. Unfortunately, the radio tracking indicated that Mikelson's XA-1 was dead ahead, tracking parallel to the rift and much too close to it.

Larry began turning their cumbersome vehicle in that direction.

"The rift is long, over a hundred kilometers," she announced in her calm and seemingly never ruffled voice.

Al-Salam added, "If he gets too close to the edge, he'll topple in."

"Or maybe the edge will collapse beneath his bus's weight," Arashi suggested.

"We should be so lucky," added al-Salam.

"Enough of the negative talk. So far, there's no indication that he is in any sort of trouble. It looks like he's stopped. Unless we see a reason to do so as well, we should reach him in forty-five minutes, give or take," said Larry. Sometimes the crew relished trying to outdo one another in dire predictions but as a practical matter, they were among the best, and when faced with a task, tackled it with a can-do attitude. Negative chatter was their way of blowing off steam.

Larry followed the tracks, keeping at least fifty meters from the edge of the rift, no matter how close Mikelson's trail edged toward it. He and his crewmates fell into a guarded silence. They could hear the air recirculation fans and the occasional creak as the Beast's metallic frame encountered uneven terrain.

"There he is," Abigail pointed out. "He's near the edge but looks to be okay."

In his viewer Larry saw the bulbous metallic shape of the XA-1, sitting like a giant worm near the rift's edge, far closer than Larry was willing to go. He stopped fifty meters behind and close to the same distance away from the edge.

"Arashi, let *Aurora* and *Tombaugh* know we've found him and turn on the laser beacon so they can get a precise marker of our location for some imaging. Ask them to use the SAR. I want to know where the danger zones are within that rift and under the ice surrounding it," said Larry. Without the laser beacon and multiple spacecraft placed in orbit by *Aurora* acting as relays, it was next to impossible to get precise positions for surface objects from orbit, even with their not-as-directional radio beacons fully operational. With their exact location pinpointed, the ship could activate its ground penetrating radar to see deep into the nearby ice and identify any loose ice ledges along the rift that might be a problem should they have to get closer.

"Copy, sir. Mikelson is on the comm," announced Arashi, lightly tapping the implant above his right ear to adjust the volume.

"So, the good doctor decided to speak with Space Force after all. Put him on speaker," ordered Larry.

". . . you are here. I could really use your help." Mikelson's abrasively loud voice jolted everyone in the cabin.

Larry asked, "How are you, Dr. Mikelson? What's your condition?"

"I'm fine. I've been waiting for you to find me."

"So, nothing is wrong? Are your systems functional?"

"Yes. I'm fine. The rover's fine. We're all fine," snapped Mikelson, not even trying to hide his impatience.

"Then, why didn't you return to the base camp at the rendezvous time?" Larry asked. "More importantly, why are you wasting not only the time of your fellow scientists on *Tombaugh* but also of a U.S. Space Force cruiser?"

"Wait. What? Who the hell is this?" asked Mikelson, as if he were just joining the conversation.

"This is Major Larry Randall, United States Space Force, assigned to the cruiser *Aurora*. We received a call for help from *Tombaugh*, something to do with a rogue scientist—you—lost and possibly in trouble on Pluto. We diverted from our current mission to render assistance. I'm here with some of *Aurora*'s crew and one of your colleagues, Dr. Abigail Grigsby, to lend that assistance. So, you had better be stuck, injured, or otherwise disabled in a way that would explain why you didn't communicate with or return to your ship, justifying a call to the Space Force, or this will be a bad day," stated Larry in his most matter-of-fact tone.

"Why would the fools do something like that?" asked Mikelson.

"Because they were not going to leave you here. Now, what is the nature of your emergency?" Larry asked again, making his voice sound intentionally impatient.

"I've found something, and I do not want those boffins screwing up my discovery or claiming it as their own."

"Discovery?" Abigail asked, unable to contain her innate curiosity.

"I found an anomaly."

"Please continue," Larry said. "We are all curious as to what anomaly could be so important as to warrant you going rogue."

"A neutrino source under the ice," Mikelson replied. "Strong enough to be seen against the natural background and distinguish it from the flux from *Tombaugh*'s reactor. I first picked it up halfway around this ice ball of a planet."

"A neutrino source?" Abigail leaned forward to make sure she heard correctly. "How could anyone have missed *that*? We scanned this planet with every instrument available and at every base camp. I don't recall any anomalous neutrino sources being reported."

"I don't know why we didn't see it earlier. The signal is weak, but not that weak," Mikelson granted. "I detected it after we started breaking camp. I do not believe it was there before. That's why I wanted to check it out."

"And why are you only now reporting this? If you had informed your ship, they might have been supportive of investigation and sent help," intoned Larry.

"I didn't tell them because I don't trust them," Mikelson retorted dismissively, muttering a few words under his breath that Larry couldn't make out, and then added, "My only focus is finding the source of the radiation."

"Dr. Mikelson, you're sure the neutrinos are coming from *within* the ice? From what I know of neutrinos, don't they pass through mass as if it wasn't there? Could they be solar neutrinos?" He added the honorific to show respect, something he knew Mikelson seemed to value very highly.

"Well, maybe, if the spectra I'm seeing were different, that would be the simplest explanation. But the decay spectrum is very unusual. It does not match what we see from the sun or from cosmic ray interactions with the pathetic atmosphere around this ice ball. I did find a close match in the database, but I don't know if I am ready to go there yet."

Abigail motioned for Larry to cut off the transmitter.

"I've got it too," Abigail shared. "Once we stopped, I began a directional scan and I see what he's seeing. It's weak, probably coming from something deep under the ice, but it's there."

"Have you pinpointed the source's location?" asked Larry.

"No. But if we combine our data with Dr. Mikelson's, we should be able to get a good fix."

"So, he is not lying. Thanks for the heads-up," responded Larry as he reactivated the transmitter.

"Dr. Mikelson. We've also detected the radiation. Have you determined its source?"

"As a matter of fact, yes. It's coming from the rift. Two kilometers down. I'm not sure exactly where. I can't pinpoint it with the data I'm getting from here and my remote. If you could share your data, I can determine its location."

Larry looked over his shoulder at Abigail. She nodded her head in affirmation.

"We are sending our data now. Let us know when you get a better fix," Larry requested as he turned off the transmitter.

"This obviously wasn't something we expected. I need to call Colonel Ruiz to figure out our next steps," Larry said to his crewmates.

"We had no idea," Abigail said quietly.

"I realize that. No one did. The situation here has gone from search and rescue to something else. I need to confer with the colonel and figure out what he wants me to do."

"Dr. Mikelson, this is Major Randall. We need to talk," Larry asserted as he reestablished contact with the XA-1. Colonel Ruiz and Captain Blackstone had both monitored Larry's conversation with Mikelson and decided that bringing him back to *Tombaugh* could be put on hold until they knew more concerning the anomaly. They instructed him to help the annoying doctor in his activities as long as they placed no one in danger.

"I'm here," announced Mikelson.

"Have you located the source?"

"Yes. I believe my drill should be capable of getting through the ice to where it ought to be situated. As I don't have the necessary appendages to perform the task myself, I'm hoping you can set up the drill I have on board to retrieve it."

"We are permitted to assist under two conditions: The first is safety—we are waiting for a radar assessment to determine whether or not the ice is stable. If it is secure, then the second condition is that after we find the source, you will agree to return to *Tombaugh* without further delay," replied Larry.

Mikelson was quiet for a few moments before replying with only one word: "Okay."

The radar results were encouraging. The ice around the two rovers was stable with no voids anywhere nearby. By the time they received the data, it was too late to do anything with it. The Beast's crew had been on duty and working for over twelve hours and it was time for a meal and some sleep.

Mikelson, who no longer needed sleep, was not happy with the delay, but had to accept it. The problem was the perceived passage of time. While biological humans rested for eight hours, he was wide awake and processing thoughts at a pace that made their sleep time seem like weeks. All the extra time available at first seemed like a blessing. Mikelson had used it to study, read journal articles on topics that he might never otherwise have prioritized and read, and write original research papers of his own at a pace no other scientist could possibly match. His academic output soared, even while at the edge of the solar system exploring this nearly pristine world. But it also left him too much time to ruminate. Ruminate on the loss of Marlene, his accident, and the life he might have had if his body had not been ravaged beyond repair.

Mikelson was a scientist. Analytical. Practical. To give him focus, and a life purpose that would help him not dwell on the past, he decided to be the best scientist he could possibly become—to push back the boundaries of knowledge as far as he could push them. He newfound abilities amplified that capability beyond what he could have imagined before the accident. From the external world's perspective, he had been stupendously successful. His papers were being read and cited. His peers throughout the solar system were reaching out to ask for his opinion and seeking him as a co-author on their research proposals. Inwardly, he felt empty. He tried to fill this emptiness by working yet harder; while he waited this time, he decided to complete the paper with Dr. Padilla describing the scaling laws of ablation waves in Pluto's ice fields. It was a stimulating, but ultimately unsatisfying, task.

At 8:00 A.M. sharp, the LCVP's radio crackled with the sound of Mikelson's voice. "Good morning people, are you ready to get to work?"

Larry and the rest of the crew had been awake since just after six, eaten a good breakfast, and had done their morning workout and rover systems' checks. They were ready to go when Mikelson's call came in.

"Good morning, Doctor. Yes, we're here and ready to go. But it seems that Dr. Julie Bridenstein, one of your colleagues, would like to have a word with you before we begin," answered Larry.

After a few seconds' delay, Mikelson sighed heavily. "If I must. And I would hardly call her a colleague. Spare me, please. She was put in charge of this mission as a consolation prize for losing the vote to chair the academy and is clearly out of her depth. She has not published a paper worth reading in over a decade. I would rather she space herself to put us all out of our misery. Will she call me directly?"

"No, my captain wants us to be part of any discussions

between you and the scientists aboard your ship. Arashi will patch him in on this channel."

"Very well, but I think it will be a colossal waste of time."

Larry looked at Abigail, who responded by rolling her eyes.

Three minutes later, Julie joined the call.

"Mikelson, you found something. Most of us gave up on you, but you were actually onto something. We've been up most of the night looking at your data and comparing it with our earlier surveys."

"And?" asked Mikelson.

"It was there. The signal was weak and buried in the noise from our reactors and the sun. We didn't think to look for it because it was not something we expected to find. We compared the neutrino spectrum with known sources and found that it's a good match to . . ."

"Antimatter annihilation," Mikelson interrupted.

"Yes, antimatter annihilation. Which should not be possible," added Julie.

"Nonetheless, it's down there," replied Mikelson.

"You know we have to get to the bottom of this, right? I've spoken with Captain Blackstone and Colonel Ruiz, and we can give you whatever you need."

"I think we can handle things here. Larry's team seems to be capable enough," replied Mikelson.

"We have a lander prepping who can probably be down there within six hours . . ."

"No. We have this covered." Mikelson's tone became aggressive.

"Dr. Bridenstein? This is Major Larry Randall. Before you send anyone down, let us see if we can access the source. Between our surface team and Dr. Mikelson, I think we have everything we need. If we have problems, we'll let you know."

After a pause, Julie replied, "All right. Stay in touch.

Whatever this is should not be here. Get us more data." She then cut the connection.

"'Get us more data,' my ass," snorted Mikelson. "A few days ago, she wouldn't give me the time of day, now she implies that the data belongs to 'us.' No, it belongs to me."

Larry listened quietly to Mikelson's rant, waiting for him to get it out of his system so they could plan the next logical step in getting the requested data, regardless of who ultimately got credit. But first, as he tried to digest what he had heard, he began to worry.

"Dr. Mikelson, did you say antimatter? Isn't that dangerous?"

"Well, yes, in large quantities. Actually, in small quantities it is as well. It's probably the most dangerous substance in the universe," he replied.

"Then, why . . ."

"Didn't you tell me you have a PhD?" asked Mikelson.

"No, I didn't," said Larry. "But it sounds like you have done your research on me, and you are correct. I have a doctorate in planetary science. I also have a bachelor's in mathematics, and I graduated from high school with honors. Is there anything else you would like to know?"

Mikelson ignored Larry's retort and continued, "Then you know what antimatter is—normal matter, like a proton or electron, but with an opposite charge and something different regarding its spin state. What's important is that when a bit of normal matter comes into contact with its antimatter counterpart, it goes boom. All the matter gets turned into energy. That's what makes it dangerous."

"And you think this antimatter source is buried under the ice below us," noted Larry.

"I believe so, yes."

"Do you know how much antimatter is in whatever it is that's emitting the neutrinos?" asked Larry.

"I cannot tell you exactly how much antimatter it contains, but I can say it is a small amount. The annihilation rate is very slow. Unless that changes, the emitted radiation is well below anything for normal humans to be concerned with."

Normal humans. By that he means us, thought Larry, not him.

"Don't worry. I'll monitor the neutrino flux and let you know if anything changes long before there is a threat," Mikelson said, then added, "Probably."

"Probably?" asked Larry.

"Well, we don't know how much antimatter is in the source. If there's a lot, and it were to all be released at the same time, then it could be an unbelievably bad day."

"Can you elaborate, please?"

"One gram of antimatter would produce an explosion comparable to the atomic bomb dropped on Hiroshima, Japan. A few grams would alter the landscape of Pluto."

"Oh," was all Larry could say. That's great . . .

"We'll find out more when we learn more about the source. Let's stop talking and get to work, shall we?"

"It will take us some time to get suited up and out there. Please be patient." Larry knew that preparing to leave the warmth of the lander and spend hours on the surface of one of the coldest planetary bodies in the solar system shouldn't be taken lightly. Granted, the scientists on *Tombaugh* had half a year of experience doing so, but that made the process riskier. Most accidents were born from familiarity. "I've done this a million times safely, I'm sure I can do it again without a problem." A mindset that often precedes tragedy.

Pluto was so far from the sun that it received only one-tenth of one percent of the sunlight that Earth receives. At minus 375 degrees, Larry and his crew had to make sure they didn't become permanent frozen features of this desolate world. For this reason, they religiously followed their

EVA checklist, making sure every part of their vacuum suits worked properly, with margin. It took nearly an hour before Larry, Abigail, and Bashar opened the airlock and began their attempt to drill down to whatever was exciting all the scientists. Arashi would remain in the rover.

As the outer airlock door of the LCVP opened and Larry stepped onto the frozen surface, he thought he could feel the cold reach all the way to his bones. A glance at the heads-up display in his helmet confirmed his suit's systems all worked normally, and he attributed the cold feeling to be purely psychological. But he still felt it.

"Let's get started, shall we?" intoned Mikelson, with his customary impatience. Larry wondered if Mikelson's disembodied state, or perhaps his merger with his AI, had warped his perception of time.

"All things in good time, Doctor. If one of us gets injured, then the delay will be even longer," said Larry.

They made their way over to the XA-1 and accessed the cargo section near the rover's front. Larry looked at the hatch and paused while he tried to find the access panel so he could open it.

"I'll get it," offered Abigail as she reached for a small panel to the lower right of where they were standing. "I've set these up so many times in the past several months that I think I could do it with my eyes closed." Moments later, the hatch swung to the side, revealing the drill.

The three wrangled the drill from the compartment where it was stowed after its last use a few weeks ago and, with Abigail's guidance, had it set up and ready to go within an hour.

"Thanks for the OJT," quipped Larry.

"OJT? Is that some obscure Space Force acronym?" asked Abigail.

Larry smiled and replied, "On-the-job training."

"Of course. Well, let's keep the OJT going then." She smiled.

Larry felt a slight tug at the way Abigail's eyes crinkled as she smiled, which he immediately suppressed. He was also impressed with her quick recovery and, he had to admit, he really didn't know all that much regarding this particular drill and how it operated.

Abigail pointed to the uncoiled portion of the assembly. "The rest of the drill assembly is expandable and flexible and we'll keep it coiled inside the XA-1's stowage compartment, ready to be rolled out as needed for reaching depths as far down as two kilometers. Given that we will be drilling through frozen liquids and gases, this particular drill uses a complex heating and venting mechanism to remove to the surface what it drills through, where it will then rapidly re-condense into ice. The bore-hole diameter can expand to as much as two meters at the barrel's full diameter. We haven't needed to do that so far. We usually stop at a little over one hundred meters. I don't think we've ever had the need to go further."

Stepping well back from the spindle, Larry gave the signal for Mikelson to begin.

As the process started, a cloud of what looked like steam rose from the bit's contact with the ice, somewhat obscuring it. As the barrel moved downward, they knew that the process was working—all in an eerie silence. Larry heard his own deep breathing and felt a deep vibration beneath his feet. At the rate things were progressing, they should reach the source's depth around noon.

As the time passed, they alternated between checking the status of the hardware, monitoring each other's suits and vitals, and gazing at nearby Charon, which filled a good portion of the sky. No one said much.

For Mikelson, drilling was like learning how to ride a bicycle for the first time. He extended his sensor network into the head, feeling the temperature variations as the superhot bit sank deeper and deeper into Pluto's outermost layer and, despite having been merged with the XA-1 rover for nine months, marveling at how he could actually experience the process. It reminded him of the thrill he felt as a young man when he would leap from the pool's high dive and pierce the cold water. He could also see the hole being created, thanks to the visible and infrared optics embedded in the drill head. So far, other than a cloud of vapor and seemingly endless ice, there hadn't been much to see. His other sensors, however, those monitoring the neutrino flux, told him he was getting close to the source. He began to detect secondary radiation characteristic with what one expects from energetic electrons and positrons coming from a nearby matter/antimatter annihilation. It wasn't much, slightly above what might be considered the natural radioactive background back on Earth, but it was well above the natural background of Pluto.

Abruptly, they broke through ice into a void and Mikelson quickly, within milliseconds, shut it down.

Larry saw the barrel stop.

"Dr. Mikelson? Is everything all right?" Larry asked.

"Yes. The drill entered some sort of void, right where the data says antimatter source should be. My IR sensors say there's a small thermal hot spot, and I'm waiting on the vaporized ice that leaked into the chamber to settle so I can see what's here . . . yes. There is something. A cylinder. A cylinder, by God! It's over a meter long and maybe thirty centimeters wide. Maybe metallic? It's hard to tell in this light. I don't have a spectrometer on my head so I can't get any more specific. I'm sending you a visual," proclaimed Mikelson.

Larry switched his heads-up display to what Mikelson was relaying. He could see what appeared to be an irregularly shaped void in the ice, perhaps four meters in height and maybe half that in width. Mikelson's description referred to the object at the bottom center. Definitely cylindrical and exceptionally smooth. Clearly artificial.

"It's not natural," observed Bashar.

"No, it's not. I'm contacting Captain Blackstone to ask him to stop all unnecessary communication with Earth. We don't want word of this to get out until we know what we're dealing with," said Abigail.

"Do it," agreed Larry. "Dr. Mikelson, I assume you concur?"

"Yes, of course."

"Major Randall, Dr. Bridenstein is on channel three, she says it's urgent," said Arashi, interrupting them. "I've got her on hold."

"Patch her through," said Larry.

"Randall! We've been watching and can see that thing. Whatever you do, don't let Mikelson disturb it until we get a full team down there. We can't risk contaminating the site until we characterize everything we can possibly learn of it," Julie admonished.

As she spoke, Larry noticed changes in the barrel, which began to glow a dull orange and expand, causing more vapor to rise from the bore hole.

"Dr. Mikelson, what are you doing?" asked Larry, already knowing the answer. He was expanding the hole to bring the cylinder to the surface.

"You know what I'm doing, and you can tell that glory-seeking bureaucrat that I will retrieve this artifact no matter what she says," replied Mikelson.

"What's he doing? Stop him!" implored Julie.

Larry looked at the glowing barrel and replied, "Dr. Bridenstein, I couldn't stop him if I wanted to. It's too dangerous to interfere with an active drill."

"I'll take this to your commanding officer," replied Julie.

A third voice came into the conversation. "You won't need

to do that, Dr. Bridenstein, I'm monitoring the situation and I concur with Major Randall. He's on-site and making the decisions. If he says it's too dangerous, then it's too dangerous." The voice was that of Colonel Ruiz, *Aurora's commanding officer.*

Larry silently pleaded for Mikelson to remain quiet. He didn't get his wish.

"Bridenstein, butt out of this and mind your own business. All you do is micromanage your people and add your name to the papers they publish. You haven't done any original work since you were a graduate student, and I wouldn't be surprised if half the scientists on the ship wouldn't agree."

Larry activated his private comm channel back to the lander. "Arashi, please cut Dr. Mikelson's audio feed from the other channel."

Seconds later, Mikelson was no longer part of the conversation.

"Yes, sir. I'll oversee Dr. Mikelson, as best I can, and make sure we do not violate any safety protocols as he tries to retrieve this thing," Larry assured both Colonel Ruiz and Dr. Bridenstein, as well as the rest of his team.

"Very well, I understand, but I don't like it. If your colonel agrees, I'll send down recommendations from the full science team, and we would appreciate you considering these moving forward," said Julie.

"I would expect nothing less," agreed Ruiz. "You're the experts—scientifically speaking. But when it comes to the safety of Major Randall and his crew, science is subordinate. Are we clear?"

"Yes, perfectly clear," said Julie.

"We'll keep the feed open as things progress. Let us know if you want us to do anything specific," offered Larry.

Half an hour later the drill activity stopped once again. The barrel had expanded to its full width of two meters and began to cool down. The gases still circulating in the void blurred the view from the drill-head camera.

"There it is," exclaimed Bashar.

"I'm going to use the manipulator to try and grab it," said Mikelson.

A thin, multi-jointed manipulator arm with three articulating fingers at its tip extended from the drill head. Larry watched with growing anxiety as Mikelson directed the pincer-like claw across the void toward the cylinder. After two failed attempts, the fingers grasped the rod and slowly lifted it from the bottom of the chamber. Larry puffed out a breath he hadn't realized he had been holding.

"He's got it!" Larry announced for all to hear.

"Locking on," said Mikelson. Then, "Hauling it up." For the first time, Mikelson's voice was tight with concentration instead of indignation or anger.

As the drill rig retrieved the extended barrel, it deflated and rolled back onto the dispenser inside the XA-1. Larry suddenly realized how hungry he was. They had been out on the surface for just shy of eight hours, and though he had remained hydrated, he hadn't taken any vitanutrient from the suit the entire time. He turned his head and put his mouth on the straw, simultaneously activating the system to produce a somewhat tasty, and ever-so-healthy lunch—if one could get over sucking it through a straw.

It took a little more than an hour for the drill rig to raise the cylinder to Pluto's bleak, frozen surface. A few minutes before the cylinder exited the bore hole, Larry and his team retreated to their rover and behind it, watching the final exit on their displays. Mikelson stopped the drill's motion so that the cylinder dangled from the pincers, barely a meter above the icy surface.

"I want a full scan of the object before anyone goes near it," said Larry. If that thing is leaking antimatter, then it's a hazard until we determine otherwise. Doctor, do you copy?"

"I hear you. I've already run the scans. It's safe. The emissions are still there, but barely above the background. It hasn't changed since my first scans," he replied smugly, no doubt proud of the fact that he could think faster than a human. "The rate at which this thing is converting antimatter into energy does not pose a risk," he added.

"That's assuming we don't do something to cause however much antimatter remains in it to go boom," uttered Bashar.

"Well, I don't know about you, but I will take a closer look," said Larry as he walked toward the cylinder and the XA-1 rover.

The three astronauts, illuminated by the bright beam of their headlamps, circled the mysterious cylinder. Larry ran his gloved fingers along its surface and shook his head.

Mikelson mused, "If it's been under the ice as long as I think it has, then it could have been here for a few thousand years, or tens of millions."

Larry's eyes widened. "That's a long time."

Abigail stepped forward and pointed at the cylinder. "If this thing melted away the ice with its heat, then it might not be that old . . . how can we know for sure?"

Mikelson replied, "We can't. At least not yet. But from what we can tell, the cylinder isn't emitting that much heat. It would need to have been a lot hotter at some point in the past for it to have sunk that far into the ice."

Suddenly, Abigail raised her eyebrows and asked, "We're ignoring a big question . . . what is this thing?"

Larry shrugged. "What do you mean?"

The eerie silence of the alien planet was broken only by the sound of Abigail's voice as she asked, "What is it? How did it get here? Who placed it here and for what purpose?"

"The Uranians?" Bashar suggested in a hushed whisper.

Abigail shook her head. "The remains found in Uranus weren't this advanced, were they? Antimatter power is pretty sophisticated and the few remnants of the ancient civilization at Uranus scientists found don't match with a culture that has that capability. All they found were simple metals, right?"

"You're correct. What was found on Uranus was much more primitive than a civilization capable of harnessing antimatter. This thing might have been left by those who destroyed them, however. Whoever wiped out a civilization so completely that only a few pieces of metal could be found on the bottom of its atmosphere would need access to energy similar to what it takes to create and store antimatter," stated Mikelson.

Larry shivered, glancing anxiously at the dark sky, then back at his colleagues. From what he could tell, they were all ready to retreat to the safety of their rover and rest their tired minds and bodies.

"I think it's time we call it a day," said Larry. "We exceeded our usual EVA time limit and I, for one, could use some shut-eye. I suspect I have at least two hours of meetings ahead of me with the captain and the rest of the scientists before I can even think of my head hitting a pillow."

Larry looked at his colleagues and could see that they were not upset at the suggestion of returning to the rover to wind down and rest.

"I'll continue examining this thing and let you know if I find anything," Mikelson volunteered as Larry started walking back toward the Beast.

"Thanks, Doctor. Please do that." replied Larry. "In the meantime, we're heading back to the rover to get some supper and long-overdue sleep."

After removing, cleaning, and storing their EVA suits, the crew of the Beast shared a small snack, chatting between bites as they discussed the events of the day and what they'd found. Soon, they tired of speculating, but not before Larry took interest in some of the ideas that had been put forth by Abigail.

"So, Dr. Grigsby, what was the primary focus of your research here on Pluto?"

"It's rather detailed," she began and then momentarily stopped speaking. "Wait. You're a scientist, right? Dr. Mikelson brought that up earlier today."

"I am. I earned my bachelor's in physics at the Space Force Academy and my PhD in planetary science at the University of Arizona."

"Arizona is top-tier. Where did you do your postdoc?"

"Out here. In Space Force. They paid for my doctorate and now own my soul for the next several years."

"Have you been able to publish much?" she asked.

"Not really. Space Force doesn't ascribe to 'publish or perish.' They need me for my on-the-jobsite walking-around knowledge; they don't really care if I do any original research and advance the state of knowledge."

"Do you ever regret that? I mean, to do all the work necessary to get the degree and to then not use it as a working scientist must be difficult."

"Maybe, sometimes. Who doesn't think about the road not taken and what their life might be like had they taken it? But then again, most planetary scientists do all their work remotely. I get the best field experience anyone could possibly have." At least that's what I say in my self-talk, he thought.

"What about your colleagues on board the ship? Are there many other scientists among the crew? I have no idea."

"Space Force is very selective, and a majority of the crew have at least a bachelor's degree, mostly in some form of engineering. There aren't that many scientists and very few PhDs."

Larry knew that many of his fellow guardians looked at his PhD as something he earned because he didn't want to, or, worse yet, couldn't make it in Weapons School. Technically, Space Force viewed both career paths equally, but the culture still held biases. Larry had been promoted to major on merit and Space Force requirements, but he wondered if the culture would interfere with his ability to be promoted in the future.

Larry smiled. "But that's enough about me, I'd like learn more about you and your research."

"Well, okay. I attended a small college in Oregon for my undergrad. I majored in philosophy of all things. I then worked for about two years in odd jobs here and there, none really amounting to much, until I read an article about Saturn's moon Enceladus. I was enthralled. The next thing I knew, I was reading every popular science book I could find about the planets and began taking math and science night classes at the local community college. My goal was to apply to grad school and study planetary science, which I then did. Arizona didn't accept me, but Northwestern did. So, here I am."

"And your research? Why Pluto?"

"My primary interest was to better understand the formation of Hekla Cavus, the big depression near the equator to the west of Sputnik Planitia. My goal was to determine if the mechanism of its formation resulted from subsurface deflation or something else."

"Did you think cryovolcanic processes might have been involved?" Larry asked.

"Well, as a matter of fact, I considered that when I planned our site visit. I brought . . ."

Arashi looked at al-Salam, rolled his eyes, and nodded his head toward the other side of the lander.

Al-Salam nodded. "Dr. Grigsby, Major, I'll let you two talk science while I get ready to talk to my dreams. If you'll excuse me?" He and Arashi rose and quietly departed.

Larry barely acknowledged al-Salam's comment. He was far too caught up in sharing ideas with Abigail to spare more than a moment of his attention, afraid he might miss some technical detail essential to understanding her findings and conclusion.

Their discussion continued quite a while until Abigail glanced at the wall chronometer. "Oh my, it's getting late. We'd better get some sleep, or we'll regret it tomorrow."

"I didn't realize. Thanks for taking the time to share some about your work, Dr. Grigsby. I'm impressed."

"Please call me Abigail. You gave me some ideas that I hadn't considered. I should thank *you*."

"I'll certainly do that in the future, Abigail. And you should call me Larry. I'll let the rest of the crew stick with 'major.'" Larry grinned.

"Deal. Have a nice rest."

"You, too." Larry moved to get himself ready for bed and realized that sleep might take some time to come. His mind was racing, his curiosity running in high gear. He hadn't had that sort of intellectual banter since before his current deployment. He missed it. It was a perfect way to end a day of discovery on Pluto.

CHAPTER 4

Larry groaned as he awoke to see the message light blinking. His stomach ached with hunger and he had to go to the bathroom, but he first needed to hear what Dr. Bridenstein had to say.

"Good morning, Major Randall. You did outstanding work yesterday, even though I might have been a bit too controlling when it came to the recovery of the artifact. I know you are on the ground, and I am not. Dr. Mikelson consented to send us all the data he collected studying the cylinder yesterday and overnight. Our assessment is that there is little danger in bringing it aboard a rover or *Tombaugh* so long as we monitor its neutrino emissions for any changes. Be aware, however, that there may be other risks involved. The object should be retrieved and stored in your sample containment box—assuming you have one—and brought up to the ship for analysis. We will treat it as a possible biohazard and take every possible precaution so as not to put *Tombaugh* at risk. Let me know if you need help or have any questions."

Larry had reached the same conclusion while drifting off to sleep last night, yet he still wasn't sure how Mikelson would react when they returned with it. Bringing up the object was their only option if they wanted to learn more; leaving it on Pluto was an unacceptable solution. He knew it was time to take the artifact and get back to *Tombaugh*, although he didn't know what lay ahead.

During a meal more satisfying than what they slurped the previous day, Larry filled the crew in on his plan. As usual, Arashi and Bashar remained negative about Mikelson's probable response, postulating that they might have to take the artifact from him using physical force. Abigail was more optimistic. She thought he would readily agree and be eager to integrate himself back into his personal ambulatory device, or PAD, which allowed him to roam freely on the ship and actively participate in more detailed analysis of the findings. Larry simply had no idea how the eccentric doctor would react. So far, he had been a wild card.

"Good morning, Dr. Mikelson," Larry began as he initiated the call.

"How kind of you to call. I trust you've taken care of all your bodily needs?" replied Mikelson. The comment drew a grunt from Bashar.

"Yes, we slept well and had a great breakfast, thanks for asking," Larry retorted. *I will not let this man get my goat . . .*

"Hmph. Well, in any event, you will be pleased to know that there was no change in the artifact's status overnight. The neutrino emissions remained constant and everything else remained the same—according to the fidelity and capabilities of my instruments."

"We're bringing it up to *Tombaugh*," Larry said. His firm tone sounded far more confident than he felt.

Mikelson responded, "Are you sure that's a good idea?"

"We don't have a choice," Larry replied. "It's the only way we can learn more."

After a long pause, Mikelson said, "I guess you are right. I'll help you load it onto your rover. You can take it to the ship. I'll join you there to make sure those idiots don't blow it up."

"Doctor, do you think that's a serious risk?"

"Not really. Neither of our bosses are real scientists, and

they have no idea of the implications of this find. I'm convinced there's more out here and I'm sure the scientists on board *Tombaugh* will agree, even that fraud Bridenstein. Ask her."

Larry didn't reply as he watched the XA-1 lumber over to the Beast and lower the cylinder onto the LCVP's sample containment box. Once it was secure, the XA-1 backed away and then began driving northward along the rift.

Larry informed both captains of their status as he and his crew completed their pre-launch checklist. To his credit, Blackstone didn't issue any edicts or commands, he just said he would take it under advisement and consider options. On the open mic, Colonel Ruiz simply gave Larry the authority to make tactical decisions. On their private channel, he commended Larry for his management of the situation.

As they lifted from the surface for their brief flight back to *Tombaugh*, Larry couldn't shake the feeling of unease. He knew that they took a risk by bringing the artifact aboard *Tombaugh*, but he also knew that they couldn't pass up the opportunity to study it. The cylinder might hold the key to understanding a presumably long-extinct, or at least very distant, alien civilization.

The flight back to *Tombaugh* was uneventful. As usual, crossing the boundary from outside the ship to inside caused momentary disorientation and, much to Larry's dismay, more than a little nausea. Transitioning from Pluto's low-gravity environment to weightlessness in space—plus the excursion in the Beast—was something his body had gotten used to. Making what felt like an instantaneous shift from weightlessness to the one-gee gravity of *Tombaugh* jarred him. As he recovered, Larry thought about what it must have been like for those early space explorers to venture forth to the Moon and Mars on voyages lasting months to years before the advent of the localized gravity field generators. Pity they required too much power to be installed on all the rovers and smaller craft. Having them on landers would make landing and ascent much easier.

Once on board, and before the docking bay repressurized, a service robot rolled across the floor, retrieved the box containing the artifact, and placed it in yet another sealed box before rolling across the floor and out of the area—presumably taking it to one of the labs for study.

Larry mentally went through his action-item checklist: The sample was on board and in the hands of the scientists—*check*. Mikelson was on a flight back to *Tombaugh*—*check*.

Larry knew he should feel satisfied with the outcome, but instead, he felt uneasy. He didn't like the fact that Mikelson violated protocols, placed himself and others in jeopardy by going AWOL, and diverted *Aurora* from its station to retrieve him. Granted, finding an alien artifact, of all things, could be considered a mitigating circumstance, but in Larry's mind, Mikelson deserved punishment despite the breathtaking nature of his discovery. *The end does not justify the means.*

Larry decided he didn't have the time to worry about Mikelson. Instead, he and his team needed to return to *Aurora*, stow the rover, and prepare their after-action reports. Captain Blackstone would decide what to do with the rebellious scientist, not him.

Abigail removed her belongings from the rover and said her goodbyes. Larry didn't want to see her go. He enjoyed discussing planetary science with her—and hoped he would have a chance to do so again soon.

By the time Larry, al-Salam, and Arashi returned to *Aurora* and completed their task list, the usual dinner hour had long since passed.

The three of them trudged to the galley and sat for their delayed meal. Larry only felt mildly hungry and picked unenthusiastically at his dinner. Bashar and Arashi had no such inhibitions. The conversation mostly focused on items unrelated to the events of the last few days until Arashi broached the subject about which they had all been thinking.

"What is it?" he asked.

Al-Salam shrugged. "I think it's junk that the alien visitors left behind. Some spare part they threw overboard from their ship when they left."

"Alien garbage," remarked Arashi. "How glorious."

But Larry shook his head. "I don't believe that aliens who could cross interstellar distances would have thrown out their garbage so carelessly."

Arashi stared at him. "Then what . . . ?"

"It might be a signaling device. It might be sending something back to the aliens who left it there," suggested Larry.

"A signaling device?" Arashi sneered.

"The aliens came to our solar system thousands to a few million years ago, destroyed whomever they found on or around Uranus, likely scouted Earth, and from what we can tell didn't leave anything there, then came back out to Pluto solely to dump a piece of garbage? I don't buy it. And why would it still be active?" Larry offered.

"I don't know," Arashi said.

Bashar picked up the narrative, "So they left our solar system, but maybe placed a signaling device to report on anything new, and it activated when it detected us nosing around?"

"Now that I think about it, I don't buy that either. This thing was buried under a lot of ice and has no obvious sensor of any kind. It emits barely enough energy to keep from getting colder than a few hundred degrees below zero. If it was here to monitor and report something, then it likely failed. What could it see to report on? And how? All we could detect from the surface was its neutrino signature," said Larry.

"A signature that might not have been there a few months before," reiterated al-Salam.

"If the scientists missed it before, that implies something changed to cause it to start using energy and emit neutrinos. The only 'something' was us. And that implies it has sensory capabilities of some kind that we cannot discern," Larry concluded, taking his last bite of mystery meat.

"They left the device out here on Pluto, waiting for us to get smart enough to come out here and find it." Bashar looked at his fellows as if seeking confirmation.

Arashi shook his head. "You're building up a whole theory on one flimsy piece of evidence. That's a lot to swallow. And why us? Was it placed here before or after when the Uranians were alive and kicking?"

"That, guardians, is a question for another day," announced Larry as he rose from the chair and carried his mostly uneaten food to the recycler. "Maybe I'll better enjoy this food when it comes back as steak and potatoes," he said as he pushed the food-filled tray through the recycler's orifice.

"Keep thinking that what we eat is made from recycled food, and you'll be good," advised Arashi. "And try not to think of everything else that we recycle into it."

"Today's coffee is yesterday's coffee," quipped Larry.

Though it was a common joke, given that virtually everything aboard the ship was recycled into something else at one time or another, including the organic waste no one liked to dwell upon, joking about it still elicited a groan from all three men.

Larry left the room and quickly made his way back to his cabin, where, before doing anything else, he sat down and checked for messages. One was there. The weekly message from his wife, Athena, waited. It had arrived two days ago and though he could have watched it while he was on the surface in the rover, he decided to wait until he had returned to the privacy of the ship.

He activated the message and Athena's 3D form took shape

in the screen. Her long brown hair, lightly salted with a few gray hairs, framed the face he remembered and loved as she spoke.

"Hello, Liebling," she said. "I wish you only the best while you are out there, wherever you are. I hope you can tell me where you've been and what you've done when you return. I hate it when you can't, but I understand. I still love you and miss you. It's been a busy week at work, the company lost two sats from orbital debris and we're scrambling to patch the gap in coverage. It turns out that the replacement sats won't be ready to launch for another few weeks and the CEO is concerned that Malaysia won't renew the contract if the gap lasts too long. But you probably don't want to hear my work woes, I'm sure you are more interested in the kids."

The mention of his two children, Caleb and Joshua, now aged six and four, brought a smile to Larry's face.

"Caleb is being Caleb, loving school and doing everything he can to drive me crazy when we get home and begin the evening routine. Last night after dinner he offered me my favorite dessert, Oreos and milk. Only he replaced the Oreo filling with toothpaste. I could have killed him! Not because it tasted bad, but because I was so looking forward to my milk-dunked cookie and it caught me by surprise. He laughed until he went to bed!"

Larry smiled. *You gotta love him . . .*

"Joshua is his usual compliant self, though I am worried that he is too often trying to copycat his brother. A few minutes after I spit out the poisoned Oreo, he came to Joshua with a new plate of cookies and another glass of milk. The poor little guy didn't have time to find the Oreos, so he spread the toothpaste on the shortbread cookies from your library. Of course, I had to hold my breath and eat one so I could react again like I had just minutes before. He tries so hard to be like his big brother. And both of them try to be like you," she added.

Larry's smile turned into a look of melancholy. He missed them terribly and wondered how long this deployment would be. Already at five months, he suspected it would be at least that long before he was able to return home.

After filling him in on the latest news from the neighborhood, including the problems they were having with the upstairs neighbors who somehow always managed to get loud when the kids were ready to go to bed and sleep, depriving Athena of much-needed alone time, she wished him well and blew him a kiss.

He activated the camera and began composing his response. He was used to not being able to reveal where he was or what he was doing, but that didn't make it any easier. He desperately wanted to share the excitement surrounding their find, but he knew he couldn't. He also wanted to tell her about some of the scientific discoveries made by *Tombaugh*, but he really couldn't do that either. Athena was not a scientist and though she tried to be a good listener, he knew that most of what he might say would likely not be fully understood or appreciated by her. She was a good egg and showed interest in his scientific endeavors, but he knew she did that out of love, not genuine curiosity. Instead, he provided generalities regarding his day-to-day activities and asked more questions about the kids. When he signed off, he already looked forward to her next message.

CHAPTER 5

As the latest model in the growing Space Force fleet of deep-space cruisers, the *Aurora* was built primarily for rapid transit, search and rescue, and to project force, when needed. The Chinese, Russian Federation, and even India had begun to tout their abilities to extend Earth-based geopolitical military rivalry into the heavens. Seven hundred feet long, the ship didn't look like much from the outside.

Unlike the new deep-space cruiser liners, *Aurora* didn't need to be sleek in order to appeal to the aesthetics of potential customers. Instead, it was the definition of functional. The habitable part of the ship was rectangular, thanks largely to the introduction of the recently developed gravity field generator, which allowed the crew to live in a ship environment not dissimilar to ocean-going ships back on Earth. The designers optimized the interior volume for manufacturability and the ability to interface with the complex systems required for long-term deployments in deep space: propulsion, power generation, life support, and radiation shielding, among many others. Bolted to the outer skin were numerous communication and radar antennas, laser emitters and receivers for secure optical communications, and massive radiators needed to remove the waste heat generated by the ship's fusion reactor and drive system. The bay holding the LCVP and intership transfer craft (ITC) lay on the port side, and the locking clamps used when in space dock were starboard.

Then there was *Aurora*'s armament. After all, a United States Space Force deep-space cruiser needed to not only be able to sprint to the location of those needing rescue but also to rapidly deploy anywhere in the solar system where lethal force might be needed. The ship used long- and short-range missiles, mostly designed for catastrophic damage, taking advantage of their kinetic energy; a few were capable of carrying nuclear weapons. Sticking to traditional U.S. policy, the U.S. would not confirm or deny that any of its deep-space ships, including *Aurora*, carried nuclear weapons. It was nonetheless widely assumed that they did.

The ship also had a selection of nonlethal missiles, including those designed to deploy electronic countermeasures (ECM) and offensive EMPs. For close defense, should the ship get into actual combat, there were kinetic launchers that would project a wall of ball bearings in the path of incoming missiles to detonate them far from the hull of the ship. Finally, the lasers used for optical communications were not the only lasers on the ship. On the "top" of the ship, the side that would be above the crew as they traversed the near-normal gravity interior of *Aurora*, was a hemispherical turret containing a frequency tunable, one hundred megawatt pulsed laser, capable of blinding sensors across the optical spectrum and actually burning through the hull of any ship foolish enough to choose close-range combat. It did not have a rapid or sustained rate of fire—the power requirements and immense waste heat made that impractical. After only a few minutes, it had to be shut down for at least twenty minutes for the capacitors to recharge and the ship's radiators to syphon and disperse the heat.

No, *Aurora* didn't look sleek, far from it. *But* it was highly functional—and lethal.

Fortunately, with the exceptions of the Sino-American conflict forty years ago and an occasional act of space piracy, the Space Force primarily fired their shipborne weapons for testing and live-fire training. However, the threat remained. After the conflict, China, Russia, and India expanded their space capabilities and began deploying ships of comparable lethal quality to *Aurora*. Many believed it was only a matter of time until another major conflict erupted. Everyone hoped it wouldn't result in as many deaths as the previous one. The U.S. slowly rebuilt Portland while China had largely abandoned its reconstruction of Yantai, though neither country seemed eager to resume active conflict. Great power competition remained alive and well, playing out on Earth and in space.

Larry replayed the events of the last few days in his head, including last night's dinner discussion, as he awakened before his alarm. They had a mystery. One that was now out of his hands to solve, or even participate in solving, now that *Tombaugh* had the artifact. Still, he couldn't get it out of his head.

What was that thing? Why was it on Pluto? And what was it doing?

Larry resumed his normal daily routine, including his time in the ship's gym and in the sim of the day—a search and rescue in the Jovian system where they had to navigate a complex gravity well. The ship's AI was particularly good at creating simulations with seemingly no-win scenarios, and the crew often found that out the hard way. Sometimes they beat it, but Larry wasn't sure that was because they achieved their goal due to their actions or because the AI knew that if it always won, the crew might stop trying. Today was not one of those days. Not only did they lose the crew of the stranded vessel in orbit around Amalthea, but also severely damaged *Aurora*. The other ship's fusion drive had vented, resulting in a radiation dose far in excess of safety limits for *Aurora*. No immediate loss of crew, but many would be dead before the ship made it back to Earth or Earth's Moon for medical help. He suspected Colonel Ruiz would rerun this sim to see if the crew could find a better outcome. Larry didn't look forward to it.

When he had some quiet, or at least, some alone time, Larry's thoughts returned to the conversation he had with Abigail late that night in the lander. *How would my life have been different had I not joined the Space Force and instead entered academia to do research? Would I have liked it? Would I have been good at it?* He knew there was no way to really answer these questions, but he couldn't help but think about them and imagine what life might have been like had he taken that path. *Would I still have married Athena? Would she still have fallen in love with me?*

He had been out of yet another sim for mere minutes when the comm on his left wrist alerted him to a message from the colonel.

"Report to my office at sixteen hundred thirty."

Larry steeled himself. A summons like this was not usually a good thing. In his mind, he replayed the events on Pluto's surface, wondering what he might have done better, more by the book, and what he might have done wrong. Nothing came to mind, but that didn't stop him from worrying. With little over an hour before he had to report, he returned to his quarters and reviewed his after-action report, as well as those of Arashi and al-Salam. Neither wrote anything negative, which should have been a relief, but he remained nervous as he walked from his quarters, up two floors in the ship's elevator, and to the colonel's office.

Colonel Ruiz, in his mid- to late forties, had one of those square faces and short necks associated with football players, which he played while at the academy. His buzz-cut black hair would have made any ship's captain proud. The colonel's demeanor didn't increase or diminish Larry's unease. Ruiz's neutral countenance only prolonged Larry's anxiety.

Larry entered and saluted. The small, completely undecorated office looked spartan, utilitarian. The colonel in charge on his previous assignment was all too eager to display his awards and commendations. So this felt like a refreshing change.

"At ease, Major," said Ruiz.

"Yes, sir," replied Larry, relaxing a bit as he assumed the position.

"You did great work on Pluto. The scientists are happy and busily looking over the artifact. Captain Blackstone is pleased that Mikelson is back aboard this ship. And I'm happy that they're happy."

"Thank you, sir," said Larry.

"In fact, the scientists aboard *Tombaugh* are so happy with your work they have requested time with you over there. Do you have any idea why?"

"None, sir," replied Larry, surprised at the request.

"Your academic credentials, perhaps?"

"Sir, while I have a doctorate in planetary science, I haven't been active in the field for some time. Maybe?" He really had no idea why they wanted him, but his credentials seemed as good a guess as any until he spoke with someone and found out.

Ruiz stared at him for a moment, then broke the tension with a smile. "Very good, Major. Get your things together and report to Captain Blackstone aboard *Tombaugh* for temporary assignment first thing in the morning. I'll have the CTV take you over."

Crew transfer vehicles were small four-person unarmed shuttles used for this very purpose—ferrying people or small amounts of cargo from one ship to another.

"Thank you, sir," said Larry.

"Dismissed," Ruiz said as he looked down at his datapad, ready to move to the next task.

Larry left the colonel's office and looked around. He liked being aboard a Space Force ship. He liked the discipline, the people, and the idea itself. That's why he chose to remain in the service and not go into the field with planetary scientists. Oh, he was sure they were fine people, but he didn't like what he knew of academic rivalry, all the backbiting and politicking over things that didn't matter—like desk size and whether your office had a window. Of course, out here all of that might be moot.

He decided he would make the best of it, and hoped if they expected him to be a high-caliber scientist, they wouldn't be too disappointed.

That night, after packing for the transfer, his messages light flashed on the room's computer. He smiled. Another message from Athena. Two messages in a week was uncommon, but it happened enough he didn't have any concern. They had been married for ten years, and thanks to the Space Force, he had been in deep space for nearly a third of it. If she minded, she didn't show it. Somehow, she managed to have her own busy career and to take care of the kids, always taking both in stride. To Larry, she was a super woman.

"Hello, Liebling," she began, her olive skin and deep brown eyes accentuated on the screen as she sat close to the camera. "I hope you are well and your trip remains uneventful and boring."

If you only knew, thought Larry.

"I'm at the Luna Hilton for a few days. Mom has the kids. I got pulled off the previous assignment yesterday and the boss booked me for passage to the Moon to take care of some problem with one of the powersats. I've just arrived and won't get the full story until I meet with the client tomorrow. All I know is that we have to get it back online soon or there will be some brownouts in Asia." Larry smiled. She was as passionate in her work as he was with his. They were a good match.

"Beverly sends her greetings and, oh, your father and mother wanted me to let you know they plan to move back to Kentucky. Boston wasn't a good fit for them, as we thought, and they finally realized it. They sold the condo and hope to be back in Owensboro by the fall." She leaned in toward the camera and continued, "I miss you. If VR were good enough, I would reach out and give you a hug—though I know you would want more. You are in my thoughts and I hope you'll be thinking of me. Come home safely. I love you."

Based on *Aurora*'s distance from the sun, she probably hit SEND on this message six hours ago. Nevertheless, the clarity of the image made him feel like he saw her in live time.

The message ended with Athena's smiling face filling the screen.

"I miss you too," he whispered softly as he sat and stared at her image, thinking of what he would put into his reply. Security reasons limited what he could say, but he returned her message before falling asleep to thoughts of Athena and not what the next few days might bring. He hadn't slept so soundly and well since they arrived at Pluto.

CHAPTER 6

unlike the mass of functionality of *Aurora*, *Tombaugh* was sleek. Larry hadn't paid much attention when he took the artifact over, as he was too busy maneuvering into the science vessel's cargo bay to notice its design aesthetics. Teardrop-shaped, the ship had been designed to have the sex appeal that *Aurora* lacked and not to take full advantage of the most favorable volumetric design. And for understandable reasons: it was originally a Martian cruise liner refitted for deep-space missions and deeded to the Interplanetary Academy of Astronautics for use on research missions. Someone else piloted the CTV, giving Larry time to look it over as they approached. He made a mental note to request a complete ship tour and copies of its maintenance schematics. He didn't want to be on a ship of which he knew next to nothing.

Instead of entering the ship's cargo bay, the CTV pulled adjacent to one of the ship's many airlocks and mated with it using the universal docking adapter.

The CTV pilot powered down his systems and helped Larry open the hatch to *Tombaugh*'s airlock. "Have a great TDY, sir" he said.

"Thanks," said Larry, pulling the duffel bag from the bulkhead tabs under his seat that secured it in zero gee.

Cycling through to enter *Tombaugh* took a few minutes and someone on the other side of the hatch opened it as soon as the light turned green. Larry pulled himself through the hatch and felt gravity return, disorienting him for a few moments as he determined up versus down. He planted his feet firmly, and loudly, on the floor.

Three people awaited, two he recognized from video conferences while supporting *Tombaugh*'s crew. Captain Blackstone stood on the left and in the middle, Abigail Grigsby. Larry couldn't recall meeting the tall, lanky, and smiling man on the right.

Blackstone extended his hand, and Larry returned the very firm handshake. "Welcome aboard *Tombaugh*, Major Randall." Blackstone was Larry's height with a sturdy build and only a little paunch around his middle. His weathered skin was not something one expected to see on a deep-space ship, and made Larry think he might have been a maritime captain in his earlier years.

"Thank you, Colonel," he said and quickly corrected himself. "Captain, sorry. It's a habit. Space Force ship commanders are usually colonels. I'm not used to being on a civilian ship. And, please, call me Larry."

Blackstone smiled. "That's okay, Larry. I'll take the promotion if you slip up again. Don't worry."

"Dr. Randall," said Abigail, extending her hand.

Larry wondered why she was being so deliberate in using his academic title. They had agreed to be on a first-name basis when they were on Pluto.

"Doctor Randall, I'm Vitaj Misha, one of the planetary scientists and geologists on board. I'm pleased to meet you," voiced the third member of the greeting party. Instead of shaking hands, he bowed his head slightly as he spoke. Misha was a distinguished-looking man who stood a little taller than Larry. His salt-and-pepper hair framed a face etched with the lines of wisdom and curiosity.

"Nice to meet you," said Larry. "I'm eager to begin doing whatever you need. I'm all yours,"

"Yes, well, concerning that," began Blackstone. "The science team is eager to hear the sequence of events leading to the discovery and retrieval of the artifact. I've scheduled an all-hands meeting for this afternoon for you to do just that. I hope that's okay."

"That's not a problem. I'm glad to," agreed Larry. He had been debriefed so thoroughly since his return to *Aurora*, he could probably tell the story half asleep.

"We would also like to fill you in on what we've done to learn more about the artifact. Dr. Bridenstein has scheduled a meet and greet before the all-hands to give you a summary. The full report of our efforts to date is waiting for you in the shared drive on the ship's computer. You'll be able to access the report from your cabin," noted Vitaj. "We look forward to any insight you can provide. We're running out of ideas."

"I'll do what I can," said Larry, mindful that he probably wouldn't think of anything these seasoned experts hadn't already considered.

"Dr. Grigsby and Dr. Misha will show you to your cabin so you can get settled. If you are available, I would like to meet with you in my office before lunch—say in an hour?" asked Captain Blackstone.

"Yes, sir. I'll be there."

"Great! See you then. And, while you are aboard this ship, you don't need to call me 'sir.' If you must use a title, 'captain' is my preference."

"Yes, Captain, I'll keep that in mind."

Abigail and Vitaj began walking starboard as the captain departed down a side corridor. Halfway down the corridor, Larry realized his steps had a little too much spring.

"You have the gravity set below one gee?" he asked. "It was one gravity when I was here before."

"We do. Some of the team hail from Mars. In an effort to

make everyone as comfortable as possible, we alternate between Earth and Mars gravity and sometimes compromise with zero point eight gee," Abigail explained.

They stopped at cabin number 15, one of many along the hallway, each with an identical beige door.

"This is yours. I'm in number 23 and Vitaj is in number 25," said Abigail. "We've keyed the lock to your palm print, so just raise your hand, palm out, right above the handle, and it will open automatically.

"Thanks," responded Larry as he opened the door. He looked inside and saw a room at least three times the size of his on *Aurora*. The room was decked out with a Murphy bed against the wall, a small table and chair, and even what looked like a private bathroom. "This is huge. Are you sure you didn't accidentally give me the captain's cabin? I thought I was lucky to have a small private cabin on *Aurora*, but this . . . this is amazing for a deep-space vessel."

Abigail smiled. "I'll be back in forty-five minutes to walk you to the captain's office for your meeting," she announced as she and Vitaj walked down the corridor to their rooms. As she walked away, Larry noticed how nice she looked in something other than her EVA suit. He sighed as he turned and entered his cabin. Seeing Abigail made him miss Athena.

Forty-five minutes passed quickly. He was ready and opened the door when Abigail knocked. Vitaj was not with her.

"The captain awaits," she said with a smile.

She filled the walk to his office with talk of the artifact and its implications. Neither had any answers, but asking the questions felt as intellectually stimulating as either could have asked for.

Captain Blackstone's office, like Larry's cabin, was much larger than Colonel Ruiz's back on *Aurora*. Blackstone rose from his chair and greeted Larry as Abigail left the room.

Blackstone motioned for Larry to sit, which he did, as did Blackstone.

"You are probably wondering why I asked that you be assigned to *Tombaugh*," began Blackstone.

"The thought had crossed my mind," quipped Larry.

"It was actually Dr. Grigsby's idea. She believes you might be able to give the team some insights into the artifact that would help them in their studies. She also thinks your presence would relieve some of the stress. We're a long way from Earth and the notion of aliens has some of the team spooked. We were pleased at how rapidly *Aurora* got here when we called, but now that things have calmed down, we're not sure how long it will be before your ship gets called elsewhere. We would like you *here* for the rest of our journey."

"My current deployment is not supposed to end for another three months, and if I read your trip plan correctly, that's close to the time you said you would be headed home. Colonel Ruiz approved of my being here and I'm fine with it. I'm also curious about the artifact," Larry responded.

"Good to hear. That takes care of the science teams' rationale, now here's mine. Our friend Dr. Mikelson has been unresponsive since his return. After entering the cargo bay, he refused to transfer into the PAD he had been using on board, and said he would remain in the XA-1. He then cut off communications and hasn't responded to any attempts to engage him. Nothing."

"This PAD, it enabled him to move around and interact with the crew?"

"Yes. It was the latest and greatest model AI-bot from Mars, and he used it for most of the voyage until we went planet-side. That's when he transferred into the lander. Now he won't come out."

"And you think I can help because . . . ?"

"He seemed to respect and listen to you on the surface.

I'm worried. He and the AI merged and he, they, need human interaction and stimulus. If they're busy playing around in their own VR sim, then he may never want to come back."

"So, you're afraid he may have VR addiction?" Larry asked. VR addiction was rampant on Earth and Mars. People, mostly young, preferred VR to reality, and spent so much time in simulations, that they lost touch with reality and exhibited traits similar to a drug addict when denied their "fix." Captain Blackstone had good reason to be worried.

"I'll do what I can, but I honestly have no idea where to begin."

"Start by trying to discuss the artifact, something in which he is interested. After that, it will be up to you."

"Gee, thanks."

"Don't mention it," volunteered Blackstone with a grin. "And one other thing."

Larry learned forward, waiting for the other shoe to drop.

"A piece of advice. A lesson I learned on this trip the hard way. With no offense meant, I noticed that you shied away from being called 'major.'"

"It felt awkward. On *Aurora*, I'm 'Major Randall.' On a ship filled with civilians, it seems more natural to use my first name."

"And that might very well be true . . . *if* we were on a ship of normal people. But we're not. We're aboard a ship filled with eggheads, no offense, and not only are they eggheads, but they're also sanctimonious about it. Outside of the military, in which, by the way, I served as a submariner back in the day, I've never seen such a rank- and pedigree-conscious group of people in my life. When they first came aboard, I used their titles, but after that I began using their given names. Boy, was I put in my place. I learned from one of my crew who over-head a dinner conversation in which some said they thought

I was trying to demean them and their achievements. After that, I consistently use 'doctor this' and 'doctor that.'"

"Really? I guess I'm not too surprised. When I was a graduate student, I was told I had to address every visiting researcher and lecturer by their academic title. I figure it was sort of a student/teacher thing."

"Take the advice or leave it. They might accept you more readily as one of their own by virtue of your degree. I've heard them call one another by their first names, but pretty much never when in a setting explicitly involving me or my crew."

"Good advice. I'll accept it," said Larry.

Blackstone rose. "Now it's time to meet the scientists in the commons room, Dr. Randall. There's food and I am sure you must be hungry."

"That advice I'll definitely take."

Blackstone summoned Abigail—Dr. Grigsby, Larry corrected himself. He waited just under five minutes for her to arrive and escort him to the place where undoubtedly most of the business of the voyage took place—the galley and commons area.

The room wasn't exactly spacious, but for a ship in deep space orbiting Pluto, it seemed enormous. Most of the science team, perhaps all twenty-five, had gathered there to eat, talk, and work. A quick count revealed more females than males, nineteen women to six men. He wondered if there was something about planetary science that was more appealing to female scientists.

Finger food, more than half gone from what Larry could tell, filled one table, with drinks available on another to the side. As soon as they entered, Vitaj spotted them and walked briskly over.

"All settled in?" Vitaj asked eagerly, smiling from ear to ear.

"Settled in, but hungry," replied Larry, eying the rapidly diminishing stack of small sandwiches and nutrition bars.

"Then let's not wait," admonished Abigail as she led both men toward the food tables.

"Dr. Randall?" Larry recognized the voice to his right. Pushing her way through a small clump of scientists, so engaged in their discussion they appeared not to notice, was Dr. Bridenstein.

"Ah, Dr. Bridenstein. Good to finally meet you in person," said Larry, stopping to not appear rude. He mentally made a calculation of how long this side conversation could last if he had any hope of getting food before it disappeared.

Julie Bridenstein, like Vitaj, was all smiles, obviously glad to see Larry. He still couldn't fathom *why*—despite Captain Blackstone's explanation. On first impression, she looked like someone who hit the gym several times a week, something definitely not obvious from Larry's video conferences with her. Not what he expected in a senior scientist.

"We're pleased you agreed to join us. My team is eager to hear your observations and pick your brain for ideas of how we might learn more about the artifact. I hope you'll be with us for a while before the Space Force calls you back. We're truly fortunate to have someone of your background," she said.

"Thank you, I'm excited to be here. I want to uncover the artifact's secrets as much as you do. I've dreamed of this sort of thing my whole life. To be here, now, interacting with something older than the human species and created by someone or something, well, it's exhilarating!"

"Well said," agreed Vitaj.

Larry gave a sideways glance toward the food table while they talked. He had hoped to not be too obvious. He failed.

"You must be hungry," Julie noted, motioning toward the food. "We'll be convening the meeting in fifteen minutes, so I should let you get to the food. It is not often we get to eat like this. We need visitors more often. Enjoy!" she said, stepping aside.

"Thank you," replied Larry as he moved toward the table. Vitaj and Abigail engaged in their own conversation and didn't follow. He almost made it.

An extremely pale older woman with short-cropped gray hair, eating one of the sandwiches, approached him, placing herself between him and table. One of the *last* sandwiches, Larry noted.

"Dr. Randall, I'm Karlina Haugen, from the Norwegian University of Science and Technology. It's a pleasure to finally meet you," she said, extending her free hand.

"Larry Randall. It's nice to meet you," he replied.

"I've been meaning to ask you about the condition of the ice where you and Dr. Mikelson found the artifact and through which you bored. I really wish you had thought to bring back drill samples. We could have learned so much of the morphology of the region, from the crystal lattices and supra-crystalline structures. It was really quite negligent of you to not think of this. Were you simply distracted? Or were you amazingly ignorant of their importance?"

The woman's words plunged a knife into his already low self-confidence. He stood looking at her, not knowing what to say. He had not thought of bringing back ice samples. It never crossed his mind. He had focused on retrieving the artifact, the problematic Dr. Mikelson, and the safety of his crew. Dr. Haugen's deliberately cutting statements weren't something he was used to hearing, except, of course, when a crew member did something really stupid that might have placed their lives in jeopardy. Not thinking of getting ice cores, however, was a very different thing from endangering a ship or human lives.

"Dr. Haugen, with all due respect, I was on a rescue mission and the mission came first," replied Larry.

"Karlina, I think Dr. Randall will be better able to answer everyone's questions once he has had some food and learned his way around." Abigail's voice cut through any potential response. In his stupor, Larry had not noticed her approach. She took his arm and pulled him away from Karlina and toward the food.

When they reached the table, and were out of Karlina's earshot, Larry asked, "What was that for? Was I really that negligent? Have I somehow compromised the research?"

"No. Not at all. Karlina can be a complete bitch and has a thing against the military for some reason. That was more about her own baggage than it was anything you did or didn't do. Having the ice core samples would have been nice, sure, but only from a purely intellectual point of view. It would have nothing at all to do with understanding the artifact," she said as she blocked a hand from the other side of the table from taking the last cucumber sandwich from the tray in front of them. "You had better get that, or you'll be too distracted by hunger to pay attention during the meeting."

Larry grabbed the sandwich and quickly took a bite. "Thank you," he said.

Abigail smiled. "You're like my ex-partner. Once he's hungry, he *cannot* concentrate on much else. Here, let me get you one of the fruit dishes before they're gone too. Hang on." She took a few steps to the right and selected a bowl of fresh-looking berries, complete with a spoon, and handed it to him.

"Thanks again," Larry mumbled as he wolfed it down.

A few minutes later, Julie motioned for everyone to take their seats so they could begin the meeting.

"Good afternoon, and thank you for your flexibility in allowing me to reschedule our regular morning tag-up to be a bit later in the day, as well as a bit longer than normal. To welcome our new team member on loan from the *Aurora*, Dr. Larry Randall, and get him up to speed as quickly as possible, I'll be reviewing the results of our analyses to date. Feel free to chime in as needed or if I get something incorrect. Not that it's ever a problem for this group . . ." she remarked and received a few chuckles.

"First of all, nothing has changed. The artifact continues to emit neutrinos consistent with an extremely low annihilation rate between protons and antiprotons originating somewhere inside the device. This is being monitored, and the AI will let us know if anything changes. As for the artifact itself, we've been unable to take any samples of the material from which it is made. Based on noninvasive testing, the surface appears to be a matrix of titanium, osmium, graphene, and hexagonal boron nitride. We would love to learn how to synthesize that, but for now, we have no idea.

"The artifact is highly electrically and thermally conductive, but not quite a superconductor. It resists all attempts to image or determine the contents. We've measured its infrared properties, performed acoustic emission testing, ultrasonic testing, eddy current testing, and much more. We've tried radiographic testing with both x-rays and low-flux gamma rays. In short, we've done nearly every form of nondestructive evaluation at our disposal. I'm not ready to be more aggressive—not with the possibility of rupturing whatever stores the antimatter. I think Captain Blackstone would space me before that could happen." Julie paused.

"How is the artifact being stored?" asked Larry.

"In conditions as close to in situ as possible. It's in a cryocooler where we've chilled it to roughly the same temperature as its original location under the ice, except for the transit times between your rover's sample container and ours, and we kept it in the dark," answered Julie.

"Now, I'll let Dr. Igwe give the first detailed presentation. She was responsible for measuring the surface characteristics and has some charts to share," Julie said as she motioned for the woman standing in the back corner of the room to come forward. As she did so, the first of the new speaker's charts appeared on the 3D-VR screen in the front of the room. This was the first of multiple presentations that continued for over two hours. It reminded Larry of the worst Space Force staff meetings on Earth: lots of words, largely information-free.

The meeting concluded with Dr. Bridenstein thanking the presenters, then abruptly turning to Larry. "Dr. Randall, we're all very eager to hear your recollections of the surface events, and I am sure there will be questions. I know that you're probably tired after paying such close attention to all these briefings. They lasted longer than I anticipated. Would you be willing to meet with us tomorrow morning, at our regular time, to share your experience?"

"I would be glad to, though I don't know how helpful they'll be."

"You never know. You might have observed something important and not realized it," she replied.

"I'll do my best," Larry said.

With that, people rose and began to mingle or leave the room. Larry noticed that Dr. Karlina Haugen was one of the first to leave, and he was thankful. The last thing he wanted was to speak with her again. He was also pleasantly surprised when Abigail walked up.

"Dinner will be served at six. That gives you the rest of the afternoon to get settled and look over some of the testing details. Would you like to join me for dinner?" she asked.

"I would love to."

"Great, I'll stop by your cabin at six," she said, smiling. "Do you think you can find your room?"

"I think I'll be okay," Larry said. In fact, Larry knew he wouldn't need help finding his room if he planned to go there next. During his morning break, he had pulled up the ship's layout and memorized how to get around: the bridge, engineering, crew quarters, the cargo bay, and every airlock and emergency space suit locker. He said a few other goodbyes and departed, walking with purpose toward the cargo bay. He had some unfinished business with Dr. Mikelson to take care of.

"Dr. Mikelson, can you join me in the science lab?" asked his colleague, Ginikanwa Agbni, one of the few fellow scientists Mikelson held in high regard among the team he worked with on Titania. An excellent geochemist, not once had she wasted his time with any extraneous information or useless chatter. She seemed as focused on her work as Mikelson, and he respected that. As the first Nigerian with whom he had worked, he wondered if all the scientists trained in Nigerian universities were as world-class. He made a mental note to find a way to lecture at a university there someday to find out.

"I can be there in fifteen minutes," Mikelson replied before cutting the connection to finish his morning exercises. As obsessed as he was over his work, he was equally obsessed with keeping his muscle tone and skeletal strength as they approached the midpoint of their stay on the surface of Uranus's largest moon. The limited budgets didn't allow for an artificial gravity generator. Even if they had been able to afford one, their habitat's reactor didn't generate enough power to operate it. They therefore had to resort to pharmaceuticals and daily exercise to remain fit.

He stripped out of his exercise shorts and T-shirt and was on the verge of stepping into the shower in the tiny bathroom he shared with Dr. Mandelbaum next door when all hell broke loose.

First, the habitat's emergency alarm sounded. He stood motionless, naked, as the piercing sound flooded every room in the small habitat. Before he could discern the nature of the emergency and what he might need to do, the door into the shower area on Mandelbaum's side blew apart, sending debris toward him like the blast of pellets from a shotgun. The pain of the shards shredding his skin was intense, but that became secondary to the indescribable agony of the superheated air that had blown the door open, now scorching and melting his skin. The last thing he remembered from that day was the screaming—his own.

When this memory came back, unbidden, Mikelson could *not* resist reliving it. It felt like watching someone else's life story in a VR simulation until the pain started. If that torment had been part of a commercial VR, then no one would want to experience it, the creator would be bankrupt. Even then, Mikelson had difficulty extracting himself from the moment. Was that because he survived and so many others didn't? Did he have survivor's guilt? Half of the scientists in the Titanian habitat died, either in the explosion or its immediate aftermath. Had it not been for the visiting ship from one of the stations orbiting Uranus, he would be dead as well.

No, he was one of the lucky ones. His area of the habitat had not vented to vacuum after the fusion reactor's sudden containment breach. The rescue team found what was left of him and rushed him to the infirmary aboard *Haven II*, one of largest and most capable stations orbiting Uranus. The on-site medical team realized they couldn't save what remained of his body, a pitiful shell, and if they didn't act quickly, he would die. They chose an experimental process that would transfer his mind, his memories, that which they thought constituted "self," into electronic form and placed it into an equally experimental memory core. The process was being developed at Uranus because the research had been outlawed on Earth. Mikelson would be their first attempt at uploading human consciousness. Since the only alternative was death, they thought their actions could later be justified in court—no matter how it turned out.

Their effort was successful; after all, he was "alive" and well. No one had been called into court, and to the best of his knowledge, no one else had yet been similarly uploaded. For a while, he eagerly followed his rescuers' continuing research and regularly answered the barrage of questions he was sure were designed to gauge his mental health. But no longer. He lost interest in how his life and mind had been saved, and now focused on his own research, the research that brought him to Pluto.

Mikelson gave the electromechanical equivalent of a shrug and shifted his thinking elsewhere, to more pleasant distractions. He knew, however, that at some unknown time, for some unknown reason, the memory would once again flood his consciousness. It was as sure as the sun rising and setting on Earth.

CHAPTER 7

unlike *Aurora*, *Tombaugh* had no guards posted anywhere, so Larry didn't think he would have to explain why he wanted to get into the cargo bay to some bored sergeant. The cargo bay looked as he remembered it, a large expanse of floor, wide enough for the two XA vehicles side by side. It currently held Mikelson's XA-1 and an identical lander with XA-3 written on its side. Larry wondered what happened to XA-2. The exterior doors, tightly closed to keep the tenuous atmosphere inside the ship, covered the far side of the bay. Outside was death, a fact relentlessly drilled into Larry during his training. "Space is out to kill you," his academy instructors would repeat over and over in different situations and contexts, as well as, "It's relentless." Some of his classmates learned this fact the hard way.

Larry walked across the floor to the XA-1 and marveled at its condition. For having been on the surface of Pluto for several months, it looked surprisingly good. A few pockmarks dinged it here and there, some worn tread, and faded paint, but, overall, it looked to be in excellent condition. He stood contemplating the rover, hoping Mikelson would break his silence and speak. He had to be aware of Larry's presence. After all, the XA-1's many exterior sensors were the equivalent of Mikelson's eyes and ears.

"Dr. Mikelson? It's me. Larry Randall. I've come to check on you and to discuss the artifact," he announced, feeling a bit foolish speaking to the air around him.

No response.

"Dr. Mikelson, I know you're there. The captain and crew are getting worried. I don't know you very well, but from what I do know, the team on this ship needs your expertise to help understand the artifact you found. I do too," Larry implored. He thought flattering an ego like Mikelson's might be enough to bring him back into communication. What narcissist could resist being needed?

No response.

Apparently, this narcissist could resist flattery.

"At least let us know you're okay. Some are concerned that you might be retreating into a merger with your AI. We can't have our primary research scientist stricken with VR addiction," Larry suggested. Now he was using the opposite of flattery—accusation of addiction. Maybe Mikelson's pride would bring him back into communication.

Nothing.

"Okay, Doctor. I will be here for a while. If you want to talk, then please reach out. I know you are able to communicate with the ship's computer system, which means I am within easy reach."

Nothing.

Larry stood there for another twenty minutes, looking alternatingly at the XA-1 and around the room, allowing plenty of time for a response. Mikelson stayed silent, so he turned and left.

Larry went back to his room and spent the rest of the afternoon on his first priority, finishing his review of the technical specifications of *Tombaugh*, then moved on to the assembled technical assessment reports prepared by the science team summarizing the results of their testing of the artifact. He hadn't gotten far on the test results before he heard a knock at the door.

It was six. That meant it was Abigail, there to get him for dinner. He smiled at the thought, then immediately felt guilty. *She is a friend and colleague. Someone I can talk to about science. Nothing more.* He rose and opened the door.

Abigail stood outside with another scientist Larry had met earlier. He couldn't remember her name, only a few select snippets from their brief conversation. He hated that. He wasn't particularly good at putting names to people he had recently met. It was frustrating. As civilians, they didn't have their names stenciled on military-issue shirts, which was a convenient crutch for people not good at remembering names.

"Good evening, Dr. Randall. May I introduce Dr. Kinia Kekoa. You may have met her earlier today?" asked Abigail, saving Larry the embarrassment of having to ask someone he had already met to repeat their name.

"Of course. From the University of Hawaii, correct?" asked Larry.

The dark-skinned woman smiled. "That's correct. You have a good memory."

"I had some help," said Larry, giving Abigail a knowing look, which she promptly returned. *If she is a friend, then why are you getting charged up talking to her?*

"Are you ready? Or would you like to meet us in the commons room?" asked Abigail, looking over Larry's shoulder and glancing at the active video screen on the wall behind him.

"I'm more than ready, let's go," urged Larry as he pushed the door closed.

Once they reached the commons area, they selected their meal from the menu, found a table, and began to chat.

"Dr. Kekoa, what is your specialty? If you already told me, then I must admit I don't recall," said Larry as he took a bite of his mystery meat and then a bland spoonful of overprocessed mixed vegetables. As good as the earlier reception food was, the dinners on *Tombaugh* weren't any better than those on *Aurora*. Unsurprising, but he was disappointed. He had hoped a civilian ship would have a better selection of food.

"I'm a glaciologist," she replied. "Yeah, yeah. Go ahead and ask me 'how does someone from an island with no glaciers get interested in glaciers?'"

"Okay. I'll bite. How *did* you get interested in glaciers?"

"From Mauna Kea, the volcano and highest point in Hawaii. When I was an undergraduate studying geology, I learned about the geographic remnants of glaciers that had been there during the last ice age, over one hundred fifty thousand years ago. When I started digging into the data, I began to get fascinated with how glaciers form and move, their physical properties, and how they interact with other geographic features. I was hooked," she replied.

"Pluto must have been a gold mine for you," Larry remarked, taking another bite.

"Absolutely. When the opportunity came to join the expedition, I was ready. I had already authored some papers describing Pluto's ice flows based on the sporadic observations over the last one hundred years or so and that was enough to get me a slot."

"She's really helped me a lot," said Abigail. "The history of Pluto has been shaped by the ice and its movement over the ocean beneath it. The science books will be rewritten based on the data we've taken, not even mentioning the artifact."

"Ah, the artifact. I do have some more questions," said Larry. The next twenty minutes of conversation was focused on the artifact, their testing of it, and next steps.

"May I join you?" They were so engaged in the discussion that they failed to notice someone had joined them, standing behind Larry, listening to the conversation, until he decided to chime in. He walked around Larry, pulled out the remaining chair at their table, next to Abigail, and sat down. He was close to Larry's age, mid- to late thirties, had blond hair, and wore a *Tombaugh* crew uniform.

"Sure," agreed Abigail, greeting him with a smile.

The newcomer nodded toward Larry and said, "Hi. I'm Tyler Romans, *Tombaugh*'s pilot. It's good to meet you, Dr. Randall."

Larry returned the greeting. "It's always good to meet members of the crew. How's the trip been for you? Pretty boring after all this time in orbit, I suspect."

"I like boring. I've been running sims every day to stay sharp and had to do a few orbital adjustments as the scientists requested changes. Your Dr. Mikelson's AWOL certainly provided me with a diversion."

"He is not 'my' Dr. Mikelson. I'm merely the guardian schmo who had to track him down and convince him to return to *Tombaugh*. I did the former well enough, but he decided to return to the ship of his own accord. I didn't have to convince him of anything, which might have been an impossible task," replied Larry.

"Don't underestimate yourself. I followed your activities on the surface. You did more than you think," Tyler asserted.

They went back to their discussions of the artifact, delving deeply into the nuances of how they might be able to perform more invasive testing of it. That is, if Captain Blackstone would allow more invasive testing. Blackstone was extremely cautious when it came to the potential accidental release of antimatter, as he should be.

Larry glanced across the room to the clock and realized how late it had gotten, and he felt the exhaustion from a long and intellectually intense day. It was a good sort of tired.

"I think I'll turn in. It's been a long day," observed Larry.

"I agree," replied Kekoa as she rose from her chair.

"Abigail, may I walk you back to your quarters?" asked Tyler.

Abigail looked at Larry and then back at Tyler before she responded. "No, I should probably walk Dr. Randall back to his cabin so he doesn't get lost. He probably hasn't had time to learn his way around yet."

If Tyler felt disappointed, he didn't show it. Without missing a beat, he replied, "I understand. I don't go on shift until midmorning. Breakfast then?"

Abigail replied, "I'm sorry, Tyler, I have an early meeting with the comparative planetology team. I'll probably have a cup of coffee there and skip breakfast."

Tyler caught and masked a momentary lapse into obvious disappointment. "I understand. A rain check, then."

"A rain check," agreed Abigail, as she rose from the table to join Larry.

After they departed the commons area and walked alone to Larry's cabin, they discussed the plans for tomorrow and what they anticipated for the next few days.

When they reached Larry's door, he said, "You really didn't have to show me the way here. I'm fairly good at getting oriented in new surroundings, and I think I could have found it on my own."

"I'm sure, but I don't want to have to rebuff Tyler *again*. He's been trying to get into my pants for the last few months and doesn't seem to get the message that I'm not interested. I don't believe he's used to women turning him down. Those looks of his probably gave him plenty of access over the years," she commented.

"Has he been harassing you? Did you report it to the captain?" asked Larry, the concern evident in his tone.

"No, he hasn't even made an overt pass or gesture. He's always wanting to spend time with me, walk me here or there, you know. I keep refusing and finding excuses, thinking he might get the hint, but that hasn't deterred him."

"Some men are a bit dense and others, I am ashamed to admit, see a disinterested woman as a challenge."

"Well, I've been dealing with him and his overtures for

more than half the trip, I guess I can endure it for a little longer," she said.

Larry reached for the door handle to his room and said, "Goodnight, Dr. Grigsby. I'll see you in the morning."

"You can call me Abigail, like when we were on the surface," she replied, looking up at Larry.

For an awkwardly long moment, they looked at each other. Finally, realizing the tension, Larry broke off his gaze. "That's fine, *Abigail*, and I hope the rest of the scientists will soon get to the point where they are comfortable calling me 'Larry' instead of 'Dr. Randall.' I've never used the title, and it makes me uncomfortable."

"Goodnight," she said as she turned to walk down the hall. Larry stood at his door and watched her depart. He sighed, thought of Athena, and felt uncomfortable.

CHAPTER 8

"We need to decide what we do next," said Colonel Ruiz. His visage was on the screen in Captain Blackstone's office where he and Julie could have a private conversation. "More specifically, *where* we go next. What was your original plan?"

"Our original plan was to shift our focus to what's close. Charon," replied Blackstone.

"This is the first detailed scientific expedition in decades, and we wanted to be as comprehensive as possible. Our charter allowed for some discretion, but not much. Boosting to another Kuiper Belt object would require significant additional travel time and some serious justification," added Julie.

"Like finding an alien artifact," said Ruiz.

"Well, yes, I believe that would qualify," replied Julie.

"And you?" asked Blackstone. "You had other duties before we called for your help. Are you going to go back?"

"No. My new orders are to escort *Tombaugh* and keep you and the artifact safe and secure," replied Ruiz.

"What do you believe we should do?" asked Julie.

"Personally, I would rather boost for Earth and get the artifact into the hands of the people there," Ruiz answered.

"And? Are you planning to tell us to do that?" asked Blackstone.

"No. My orders also say I am to follow your lead if you

choose to investigate further so long as the investigation does not place you or the artifact at risk."

Blackstone, leaning forward, said, "Then our task here today is to decide where we should go. Dr. Bridenstein and I have been discussing this issue, and here are our thoughts . . ."

Mikelson reviewed the video of Major Larry Randall's visit with disdain. *They're scared of me. They don't know what I'm doing, and they're scared. They shouldn't be, we want the same thing—to understand what we found on Pluto. Granted, I'm now superior to them in every way, but they should be wanting to use my skills to help find answers. Isn't that right, Marlene?*

But Marlene wasn't there anymore. She was—at first. Being uploaded and merged with the AI was thrilling—like first love. They were two separate entities sharing one mental space and they really didn't know each other. A forced marriage. Fortunately, they were able to get along. Her personality matrix based itself on some obscure early twentieth-century actress, which was marginally enticing, but soon became tiresome. They quickly exhausted topics to discuss, experiencing a human lifetime of conversation in a matter of days. Thanks to the speed of the quantum computer that housed them, they could talk and share data far faster than biological humans could comprehend. Then he realized that, although she showed all the signs of being sentient and having what humans would call a soul, she really didn't. She was nothing more than a complex set of algorithms he found he could easily manipulate. Once he realized that, something in the way they interacted changed and not long after that, Marlene disappeared, largely overwritten by his stronger, real, personality.

Mikelson discovered he could use some of her remaining subroutines to create virtual worlds so realistic he couldn't tell them apart from his memories of being human. Oh, the joy he had exploring the worlds and realities she created for him! He lived a full twenty-second-century life with the wife he never had, the children he never sired and their grandchildren, and the friends he thought he had, but lost, over the years in "real" life. He lived another life in Imperial China, helping Qin Shi Huang unite all of China in 221 BC, and another as a friend of Charles Dickens in Victorian London. Of course, he hedonistically experienced every sort of sexual adventure one could imagine, with famous and beautiful people from throughout history. But he had to periodically leave utopia to tend things in the real world, like remaining alive.

When he returned to *Tombaugh*, he accessed some of Marlene's remaining subroutines, hoping against hope that by doing so she might be revived. He missed her. No, he ached for her and wondered if he could have done anything differently so that she might have survived the merger. Could he do anything now to bring her back? She wasn't dead in the biological sense, which was, of course, irreversible. He had somehow overwritten her without it being his conscious intent. Surely there would be something he could do to bring her back.

He grew fatigued from the endless thought loops of "what if," and reentered the virtual to escape the guilt.

After a while, the artifact began to haunt him.

He first noticed it while consulting with Agamemnon about the strategies that should be used to win the war with Troy. As they listened to Odysseus's plans, the artifact sat on the table in the tent with them. At the time, he thought it was curious to see the artifact in that setting, but he quickly forgot it as the plans for war took shape and Achilles made his appearance for the first time.

It appeared again at the table with Ike, planning the invasion of Normandy. There it was. Sitting on the table in front of Winston Churchill, ignored by everyone except him. Mikelson became so distracted that Eisenhower called him out for daydreaming! But that wasn't what pulled him out of the VR. No, a much more mundane event catapulted him back to reality.

Mikelson was walking across a vast field of wildflowers on a sunny spring morning with his beloved Jessica, the adult version of the middle school girl who had the distinction of being Mikelson's first crush. He relived those peaceful, idyllic moments of love and heady anticipation of idealized physical intimacy many times, but this was different. The damned artifact kept appearing in the field as they walked. First in front of their path through the field, then to the right, then again in front, etc. Finally, Mikelson grew so exasperated that he canceled all the sims.

He now realized that solving the riddle of the artifact, and its alien creators, was his new ardent desire. His new obsession, surpassing even his thoughts of how to revive Marlene. The artifact consumed him. He even pondered the mystery surrounding it when he didn't realize he was. The biologicals were also interested, but they didn't seem as committed as he was. They performed experiments on the artifact that he couldn't from his current housing, but they didn't share his sense of urgency. Of importance. If they did, then they would be working in twenty-four-hour shifts without any downtime. But they weren't.

He briefly thought about departing the XA-1 and redownloading into the PAD he occupied previously. Unfortunately, the PAD was limiting, and being there, in that way, probably wouldn't speed things up as much as he hoped.

His fear was that the biologicals might want to do something he didn't want to do or go someplace he didn't want to go. He couldn't allow such things to happen. Understanding the artifact was the most important task in human history.

Don't they understand? No, he didn't think they really did, so he developed a plan.

Slowly and methodically, Mikelson began to access and explore *Tombaugh*'s computer system. He found openings and flaws exploited to take some modest amount of control. He moved slowly so as to not make his activities too noticeable. Even biologicals might be able to detect something not quite right in *Tombaugh*'s systems, and they might still be able to thwart his ambitions. He could see every part of the ship, hear every conversation, access and monitor every system. Mikelson could control some, but not all, of the ship's functions and found more he could bring under his control hour by hour. Soon, his control would be complete. The question was *when* he would choose to exert that control.

Then there was the blasted Space Force ship. *Aurora* was out of his reach, for now at least, and was therefore a wild card. Having Major Larry Randall on board *Tombaugh* was also a risk. Larry was smart and a problem solver. Mikelson would have to watch him carefully and perhaps find a way to neutralize him. He didn't want to hurt Dr. Randall or anyone else, but he also knew that nothing could be allowed to hinder him in his task. The fool said they were "worried" about him! Their worry was misplaced. They should have instead worried more about their slow pace in studying the artifact. Nothing was more important than the artifact, except, perhaps, finding another.

Staff meetings, test-planning meetings, post-test review meetings, and brainstorming meetings—meetings, meetings, and more meetings—filled the next two days. Larry remembered why he didn't pursue a career as a full-time scientist—the meetings would have killed him. During this time, he met and had conversations with most members of the science team, except for the illustrious Dr. Karlina Haugen. He and Dr. Haugen both went out of their way to avoid each other. Though they had been in many of the endless meetings together and in group lunches, there had, thankfully, been no more awkward confrontations. Tyler, now that Abigail had called attention to him, acted like a stray dog in search of a meal, sitting with Abigail, shifting his schedule as much as he could, and *still* not taking Abigail's hints. Larry found it tiresome.

Once again, Larry met Abigail, Vitaj, and Tyler (of course) for dinner.

"So, Captain Blackstone said that tomorrow he and Julie would tell us our next stop. You're the pilot, do you know where we're going?" Larry asked Tyler.

"I do, but I can't say," replied Tyler, giving Larry a smug grin.

"What can you say?" asked Abigail.

"That he had me run multiple trajectories to various locations, some that take us to more than one destination. Really, though, there are not all that many options," said Tyler, still wearing the silly grin.

"Let me guess. Earth has to be on the list. I would say half the science team is ready to get back to their friends and families, not to mention better-equipped laboratories to study the artifact. I'm sure that Colonel Ruiz is also eager to get it safely back to the Earth," said Larry, and he then continued, "Outward into the Kuiper Belt is probably on the list. We have several options to scan out there if we're looking for neutrino signatures similar to the Pluto artifact. Makemake, Eris, Sedna, Valhalla, Quaoar, Haumea, to name a few."

"There are also bioresearch facilities at Triton. If the planetary protection people raise objections to bringing an alien artifact back to Earth because it might contain some sort of biohazard, then that might be our only choice," added Abigail.

"Can we easily get to Valhalla?" asked Larry.

"I can't say if we're going there or not," replied Tyler.

"I didn't ask if we were *going* there, I asked if we could *get* there easily from here," retorted Larry, irritated by Tyler's eagerness to correct him for something he hadn't even said. Not that Larry wouldn't have been pleased had Tyler reacted with a "how did you know?"

"Yes, I looked at Valhalla. It's in a favorable location. We can get there quickly, pass near a few other small Kuiper Belt objects along the way, and burn a minimum of propellant with that trajectory," replied Tyler. "Why Valhalla?"

"It's big. No human has ever visited it. It seems to me if our alien friends left another calling card, it would be someplace obvious. Like the largest dwarf planet beyond Pluto, that we've found so far anyway. But that's my sense of adventure calling, I guess. To be the first to visit a new world."

"Shouldn't we be looking for the next logical stop from the perspective of the aliens who were here two million years ago? Everything out here moves around, each with different orbital periods. What would have been the next back then? It may be close and easy to reach now, but would that have been the case when they were here?" asked Tyler.

"Probably not. These objects have orbital periods of a few hundred years, at best. Since we don't know exactly when the artifact was buried, we have no way of knowing what the solar system looked like then. Valhalla might have been on the other side of the sun from Pluto," Larry conceded. "I should have given it more thought."

"That always helps," said Abigail, smiling.

"Touché," replied Larry, feeling embarrassed. He hadn't realized until that moment that he'd been trying to show off in front of Abigail, like a juvenile too shy to ask a girl out. He was jealous of Tyler. *Jealous*. He needed to move past that. There was nothing to be jealous of—he was *married*. Abigail was a colleague, someone he could talk science with, nothing more. There were plenty of smart, attractive women on *Aurora* and if he were interested in something physical, then he had ample opportunity. But as smart as his Space Force colleagues were, few were scientists, and none were planetary scientists with whom he could intellectually spar. He told himself his interest in Abigail was purely academic. Besides, Abigail said on many occasions that she wasn't interested in Tyler and, even if she were, that would be her business, not his.

The verbal jousting stopped, and they finished their meal and had after-dinner cocktails over yet more discussions about the artifact and next steps. Tyler remained tight-lipped, forcing Larry to give him a measure of respect.

As was their custom, around 2100 hours, they broke up for the evening and went to their respective cabins to sleep.

Though he was exhausted, Larry couldn't ignore the new message from Athena that awaited him in his cabin. As she updated him on her lunar adventures, mostly work related, he grinned. When the kids appeared and excitedly told him of their time with Grandmom and Grampa, he cried.

The next day, Captain Blackstone announced that they would survey Pluto's moons, beginning with Charon, the largest, then Pluto's other moons, Styx, Nix, Kerberos, and finally, Hydra. Given the proximity, a detailed orbital survey of Charon would begin in two days.

As was their custom, Larry, Abigail, and Vitaj met for dinner together after their shifts, which, thankfully, misaligned with Tyler's schedule. Larry suspected Tyler's absence had to do with the planned upcoming trajectory maneuver. As they entered the commons area, Larry noticed the tables were pulled together in two parallel lines instead of their usual scattering around the room. A white tablecloth, set with silverware and napkins and adorned with a flower arrangement, covered each.

"This is different," observed Larry. "What gives?"

"It's the first Wednesday of the month. The Captain's Dinner. Once each month, we have a more formal meal, complete with a special wine set aside for the occasion. The food is usually a cut above normal as well," explained Vitaj, motioning toward the assembled tables as he spoke.

"In that case," Larry said as he motioned for Abigail to take a seat near the end of the table row on the right.

"Thank you," said Abigail as she accepted the chair Larry had pulled out for her. Abigail considered the custom quaint, but she appreciated it. For her, some traditions, even if rooted in sexism, were worth keeping. For Larry, the whole culture of "gentlemen" and "ladies" had been completely foreign to him. Such things used to be taught at the academy, but not anymore. Then he married into Athena's family, descendants of families in the American South, and among the traditions they kept alive were opening doors for women, standing at formal dinners until the ladies were seated, and having their children address adults as "sir" or "ma'am." Larry knew these traditions offended some, but he also knew that Athena's family didn't mean for them to. Part of the behavior of a civilized society simply included such courtesies. He fondly recalled Athena's full briefing before he met her family, knowing they would be sensitive to whether he knew to show such courtesies. After the warning, he did some reading and learned when and where to appropriately extend them and other Southern American traditions. Athena's family soon accepted him as one of their own. Now, several hundred million miles from where those traditions were sometimes still practiced, he fell quickly back into this new tradition.

Vitaj approached their table, accompanied by another of the scientists to whom Larry had been introduced, but had not yet gotten to know. He had to think for a moment to retrieve her name and expertise from memory so as to not be embarrassed. *Lewandowski. Maja Lewandowski.* Astrobiologist. He was relieved to recall her name in time for him to stand and pull out her chair.

"Maja, we're glad you're able to join us," said Abigail.

"Thanks for inviting me," she replied with an unmistakable eastern European accent. She was a striking woman in her late thirties or early forties, with blond hair, piercing blue eyes, and an athletic build.

After exchanging a bit of customary small talk, they got down to the business of dinner.

"Other than the fancy seating, what's different at the Captain's Dinner?" asked Larry.

Vitaj gestured to the food bar being stocked at the side of the room, smiled, and said, "Welcome to the Café *Tombaugh* Captain's Dinner. The menu tonight will be something freeze-dried on Earth, stored cryogenically for months at temperatures well below zero, rehydrated, and carefully heated to be barely palatable by humans. Would you prefer chicken, beef, or vat-grown mystery meat?"

Larry smiled. "No matter what I order, I suspect it will have been grown in a vat somewhere."

"Not at the Captain's Dinner," corrected Abigail as she looked at the digital menu on the table. "May I suggest the gnocchi and sausage with onion and red pepper, followed by ice cream for dessert?"

"Sounds great," said Larry, while Vitaj and Maja nodded their agreement. The four rose to serve themselves, and as they returned to their seats, they noticed that the chairs were filling up, including the seat next to Abigail. Joining them was Dr. Lorena Campos, a Brazilian scientist with expertise in cryogenic chemistry. Lorena had an elegant presence, brown eyes that gleamed with intelligence, and curly black hair cascading down her back. Larry instantly felt at ease in her presence as she greeted him with a large, warm smile.

To Larry's astonishment, the meal was very tasty and seemed like real food, not a vat-grown mystery. They spent most of the meal discussing their respective daily routines and duties, with an appropriate amount of levity so as to not seem too much like work. But, given that for many of those aboard, work was their life, their hobby, and most of their recreation, their findings on Pluto and the mystery of the artifact inevitably came up. Lewandowski was, as one expected from her specialty, extremely interested in hearing more about the artifact and the ice from which it had been extracted.

"You aren't planning to chastise me over not taking ice samples, are you?" asked Larry, half in jest. He hoped that by bringing up the subject with humor he could blunt any criticism.

"I heard of your run-in with Dr. Haugen. She is quite . . . passionate about her work and can be a bit, ah, forward with her thoughts. No, I'm not going to criticize you. Of course, we would love more samples, more data, more everything— but we're human and sometimes we don't get what we want. I'm more interested in your impressions of the ice where you found the artifact," said Lewandowski.

"My impressions? That doesn't seem very scientific," Larry noted.

"Well, let's start with the ice where Dr. Mikelson found the neutrino signal and where you eventually found the artifact. What was different in that area from other areas?"

"Nothing unusual except the rift," said Larry.

"The rift. An active area on the surface, one where you

might expect something left on the surface to be subducted," she suggested.

"Now you're getting into my area of expertise," said Kekoa.

"I'm asking because I have to wonder why our hypothetical aliens would leave something in an active region knowing it would be subducted under the ice," said Lewandowski.

"Did they know, though? Since we don't know how long the artifact has been there, we don't know if the rift even existed at that point," asserted Kekoa. "That area might have been stable."

"True, but I suspect they had better tools for assessing the motion of the ice and predicting future surface activity than we do. After all, they traveled here from another star," said Lewandowski.

"That's also an assumption," cautioned Abigail. "We surmise that, but there is the possibility that it was left behind by whoever was at Uranus."

"From what I understand, the verdict is still out. Someone there used metals and happened to leave some signs of habitation behind when they left or died," Lewandowski conceded.

"So, we're back where we started. We don't know anything other than someone left a high-tech piece of junk on Pluto for unknown purposes," added Abigail. "We need more data."

After they moved their dinner plates to the side to make room for the ice cream, Lorena Campos turned the conversation to the next steps in their search. "You all know more about Pluto and Charon than I do. What can we expect?" she asked.

Abigail smiled and leaned forward. She was in her element. "Charon, of course, is the largest of the moons. It and Pluto are tide locked, meaning that they show the same face to one another all the time. Gravity does some weird stuff over time, and this is one of those things. It's big enough to cause the system's center of mass to be outside Pluto itself, which means it doesn't so much orbit Pluto as both it and Pluto orbit their common center of mass. Over the years, planetologists and astronomers have proposed that Pluto and Charon be classified as a double dwarf planet rather than planet and moon, but that's never been approved. Its diameter is approximately half that of Pluto, which makes it pretty big. It will take us some time to do a thorough survey.

"Pluto's surface is mostly nitrogen. Charon's is water ice. Personally, I'm a sucker for mountains and valleys, and Charon has a series of them, such as Serenity Chasma, which is over six hundred miles long. Argo Chasma has some of the tallest cliffs in the solar system—a little shy of six miles high. Watch your step!" she exclaimed with a smile.

"If you were to hazard a guess as to where our alien friends might have placed another artifact, where would you look?" asked Lewandowski,

"Well, given what happened to Uranus, I seriously doubt the aliens who left the artifact are remotely interested in becoming our friends. That said, I would look at Mordor," Abigail replied.

"Mordor?" Larry asked. "That sounds familiar."

"It's from Tolkien," said Abigail. "And *that's* a topic for another time. Mordor is the north polar region of Charon. If you look at the photos, it's all dark and dirty looking up there when compared to the more pristine-looking ice elsewhere. That's because of the freeze-and-thaw cycle Charon goes through in its long year around the sun. Since the orbit isn't circular, it sometimes gets closer to the sun, which heats up the surface and temporarily creates an atmosphere with a mixture of organic compounds escaping from the surface elsewhere on the planet, which then condenses and falls over the pole, making it look dirty. The organics up there would be conducive to life *if* it weren't so damned cold. That's where I would put something to study the moon over time. Right where the interesting chemistry is most prone to happen, and that's the north pole."

CHAPTER 9

AS a space force officer and planetary scientist, arriving at charon was close to being the most exciting thing Larry could imagine. He had been to many of the planets, moons, dwarf planets, and even asteroids in the solar system, but out here, at Pluto and Charon, they were really going where few had gone before. If they sent him to the surface, he wouldn't be the first human to walk there, but he would be among the first ten or so. Few had ventured this far out, and of those who did, most remained in orbit or flew by. Sending him would mean that they found something that might be alien. He was not the first to find an alien artifact in the solar system, but he might be the first here, on Charon, or on one of Pluto's other moons. As he studied the data coming in from *Tombaugh*'s onboard sensor suite, his sense of excitement and hopefulness grew.

While nothing new had been revealed, the images and spectroscopic data were nonetheless enticing. The water ice covering the majority of the planet's surface had formed a beautiful network of small to large cracks that stretched for miles and crisscrossed each other at random angles. The dirty ice that distinguished Mordor was filled with tholins, made from nitrogen, carbon monoxide, and methane after eons of irradiation from the sun's dim ultraviolet light. If it weren't so darned cold, Larry mused, there might be critters down there.

To his left, in *Tombaugh*'s science observation room, sat Dr. Janneke Block, whose academic specialty was materials science. With a doctorate in technologies and materials from the Technical University of Liberec in the Czech Republic, she had been one of the key researchers on the Pluto artifact since it came aboard. She led the effort to measure the residual radioactivity that Mikelson detected in the object to determine its age and composition more precisely. He often heard her complain about the inadequacy of the laboratory equipment on *Tombaugh* compared with "her lab" back on Earth. Larry considered any measurement equipment nonessential to the functioning of the ship to be a luxury. At least, it would have been on *Aurora*. Of course, the last time he voiced that opinion among the scientists, it reminded him that some only begrudgingly considered him part of the science team. To many, he wasn't really a scientist since he did not work at a university and publish papers. She was the perfect person to ask the question that Larry had been pondering since their arrival at Charon.

"Will any of our external sensors be able to pick up neutrino emissions similar to what helped Mikelson find the artifact on Pluto?" he asked.

Janneke looked up from the data scrolling by on her viewscreen, raised an eyebrow and pursed her lips.

"Maybe. If there is something here that emits at the level of the Pluto artifact, then my orbital scans have a chance to pick it up," she replied. "Now that we know to look for weak signals, and not consider them to be noise and ignore them, I would give us a seventy-five percent chance of detecting one, if, of course, there's one to find."

Larry looked around the room at the other three scientists working at their stations. He knew that the software algorithms would be the first to pick up any surface anomalies, but that didn't stop him and the other members of the science team present from scanning and double checking the data as it came in.

And so it went for the next three days. Every day working in the science room, having dinner with Abigail and Vitaj, and assiduously trying to avoid Tyler. They were not bad or boring days. Just days with no signs of anomalous neutrinos and no thermal hot spots indicating a nonnatural heat source. There were simply no signs that anyone had been here before except for the high-resolution scanning of the site where those that had been first to explore the surface of Charon had made their mark upon the ice. They would not have been able to even find that site had they not known exactly where to look.

His time with Abigail was enjoyable and they were never at a loss of things to talk about. He knew he was playing with fire and that he shouldn't. He feared where it might lead, excited that it actually might, and uncertain of what he would do in the moment if it did. His better judgment said he should distance himself. But as long as their relationship didn't become physical, then what was the harm? They enjoyed each other's company. They could keep it platonic. But he wondered if she felt as conflicted. She showed obvious interest, or she wouldn't keep finding ways to be with him. What was she thinking? *What was he thinking?*

Larry reported the latest non-news to Abigail as they sat in the mess hall at their usual table when, of course, Tyler joined them. Neither Larry nor Abigail could bluntly tell him to leave, so they relied instead on the subtle cues most people would pick up—but not Tyler. Like water hitting a rock in the middle of a mountain stream, subtleties bounced off.

"Another dull day in the science lab?" asked Tyler.

"Another dull day," muttered Larry, trying his best to mask his irritation at the not-so-subtle jab.

"And you?" asked Abigail after taking a bite of cheese with a cracker. Their meal of chili was mostly consumed, but enough remained to snack on during post-meal conversation.

"Nothing much, except trying to help one of your science friends, Dr. Kekoa, get a precisely repeating orbit. Something to do with measuring the ice flow," said Tyler.

"Yeah, she's looking at the ice sheets across the mid-latitudes and measuring their day-to-day positions so she can interpolate how rapidly they shift. The rate at which they move will let her determine more about the surface below the ice and whether or not there is any liquid water, or anything else for that matter, below the ice sheet and, if so, where and how much. She is certainly a perfectionist."

"Well, her perfectionism is a pain in the ass," groused Tyler. "The asymmetric gravity field of the planet makes the timing of precisely repeating orbits difficult to calculate and implement. With Charon's gravity asymmetry, the strong tug from Pluto's gravity, and the small tugs provided by the other moons, it gets difficult to plot and execute the orbital changes with the precision she wants."

"Tell me more about Charon's gravity field," said Abigail.

"What, in particular?" asked Tyler, reaching over for the last bit of cheese on the plate.

"The asymmetry," she stated.

"Well, most planets have that. The Moon, for example, has mascons, or mass concentrations, caused by impacts melting the rock in the upper crust that then pooled at the bottom of the craters with whatever had hit, which was sometimes massive itself, like an iron meteorite. As a spacecraft flies over the mascons, it feels a slightly stronger tug of gravity, which has to be accounted for in the orbit analysis and thrust budget. In other words, we have to figure how large the tug is and then fire the thrusters with precision to compensate. The Moon is comparatively simple. There are only the Moon, the Earth, and the spacecraft to consider—and the Moon is pretty far away from Earth, which simplifies things. Out here, we have Pluto, Charon, and the other moons plus the spacecraft. It's hairy, but calculable," Tyler said.

"How many mascons are there?" Abigail asked.

"There is a total of four we have to worry about, but only one big one. It lies along the equator. Something pretty big must have slammed into the surface."

"I've looked at the surface image and I don't recall seeing an obvious crater anywhere, including the equator," said Abigail.

"You wouldn't, if it happened a long time ago," suggested Larry, glad to be contributing something to the conversation. He chastised himself as he spoke because he knew he hoped to take a little bit of the spotlight from Tyler.

"That's right. Charon's surface changes with the seasons. It completes one solar orbit every two hundred forty-eight Earth years, and its orbit is not circular, which means that some of the surface ice melts, evaporates, and refreezes every couple of hundred years, remaking the surface and smoothing out any such craters under fresh layers of ice," said Tyler.

"Well, I don't know about you, but that's exactly where I would look next. It might be nothing. But then again . . ." Abigail offered.

Later that night, Larry pulled up and pored over the gravimetric and surface feature maps. It was a long shot, but Abigail might be onto something.

Captain Blackstone called for a science team meeting at the end of the fourth day to discuss "next steps." After they gathered in the commons, the usual venue for such meetings, Blackstone walked to the front of the room and called the meeting to order. One by one, each team lead came forward with a few charts describing what they had observed, some noting this or that item as new and of potential scientific interest, but nothing that could be of help in finding an artifact—if there was one—on the cold, dark world below them, until it was Larry's turn.

He walked the team through the latest theories of planetary formation and, in particular, the current spin-axis configuration of the Pluto and Charon system, which, like Uranus, were on their sides compared with the rest of the planets. After walking through various other interesting facts, he finally brought up the mascons and, being intellectually honest, credited Tyler for bringing them to his attention.

"Professionally, I should have given more attention to the mascons," stated Larry. "I'm so used to planetary bodies having them that I shrugged them off as part of the moon's formational history. It's a long shot, but I think we need a surface mission to check out the strongest mascon, the one on the equator. If it formed before the system was knocked on its side, then it's probably nothing more than an iron meteorite, fairly common in the early solar system when bits of rock and metal frequently slammed into each other. Because most of these meteorites were roughly in the same orbital plane, give or take a few degrees, getting an impact there would be expected. If, however, it formed after the system tilted, then it might be a bit unusual. Whatever hit it would have to have come from a pretty high angle above or below the ecliptic plane. That's not impossible, but less likely."

The team asked lots of questions, began debating precisely how "unusual" was "less likely," etc. The debate ended when Blackstone rose from his chair and walked to the podium.

"I've heard enough to convince me that we need to check out this mascon in more detail. Dr. Randall, I'm putting you in charge of the surface exploration team. Please outfit the

XA-3 with the equipment you need, work with Dr. Briden-stein on the crew roster, and get back to me with a survey plan. I expect the survey team to include Dr. Mikelson. His expertise will be invaluable," said Blackstone.

"I'm not going," came a booming voice over the speaker system. Mikelson.

"The sleeping intellect awakens," muttered Larry, as startled as everyone else.

"Dr. Mikelson, how kind of you to join us," said Julie. "I was not aware you were participating in this meeting. It's been a while since we last heard from you."

"It's the first meeting where it was worth my time to say anything," Mikelson replied, making no attempt to hide his disdain.

Larry glanced to the front of the room. A motion there distracted him from what Abigail said. Captain Blackstone excitedly whispered to a crew member who had just walked in. Neither were smiling. If he had to guess, they were probably discussing Mikelson's sudden presence in a meeting with no comm set up for him to do so. That meant Mikelson had tapped into the ship's internal communications system, without permission, begging the question of what else he had accessed. A valid concern.

After the crew member left, Blackstone rose and addressed the assembled scientists. "I have some urgent ship business to attend to, so I'll let you work out the details of your surface survey. Dr. Bridenstein, I would like to meet with you and Dr. Randall in my quarters in an hour to discuss some urgent matters."

Larry and Julie both nodded their agreement as Blackstone walked out.

The next hour went quickly as the scientists broke into small groups to discuss who should accompany Larry to the surface, what instruments were essential, etc.

At the appointed time, Larry and Julie walked to Captain

Blackstone's quarters. When they arrived, they were greeted at the open door by the same crew member Larry had seen departing the briefing. Mateo. This time Larry was close enough to read his name tag.

"Come in. Come in," said Blackstone, as he waved them through the door, which closed as soon as they entered.

"Have a seat," suggested Blackstone. As expected, the captain's cabin was much larger than the other suites and included a small meeting room, complete with a desk and four chairs. As they took their seats, Blackstone quickly tapped away at the keyboard in front of his computer screen.

"I hope this works," said Blackstone as he turned to face them. The concern on his face could be heard in his tone. "We believe Mikelson's tapped into the ship's computer system and is trying to take control. Mateo alerted me of his suspicions a few days ago and Mikelson's appearance at the science meeting today confirmed it. We intentionally shut off the internal communication system and Mikelson's XA-1, yet somehow, he got around the block. Mateo helped me load a routine into my account that should block anyone from hearing what we say and, if they, or should I say, he, is able to penetrate that, then all he'll hear is a quantum encrypted version audio file that will take him some time to crack, but probably not as long as we would like."

"Why would he hack the ship's systems?" asked Bridenstein.

"I don't know, other than he is an arrogant, narcissistic sociopath bent on making everyone cater to him. We cannot allow him to place anyone at risk, nor allow him to have any measure of control over this ship," asserted Blackstone.

"Has he done anything to make you believe that's a real possibility?" asked Larry.

"Other than put you and your colleagues at risk by refusing

to leave the surface? No, nothing more than that, but he is capable of it."

"So, what's the plan?" asked Larry.

"Mateo is trying to purge Mikelson's intrusions from the system and keep him out of the parts he hasn't yet penetrated. I alerted Colonel Ruiz this morning. They're running their own diagnostics on *Aurora* to make sure he isn't there. Then there's Plan B," said Blackstone.

"Plan B?" asked Julie.

"Plan B," repeated Blackstone, focused solely on Larry. "That's the part where you force his XA-1 off the ship, and we dump him in deep space or maroon him on the surface."

"So that's why you said he should join us," said Larry.

"That's a bit drastic, isn't it?" asked Julie, clearly upset at the mention of any sort of violence. "He hasn't committed a serious enough crime to warrant dumping him out the airlock."

"If he tries to take control of this ship, that's technically mutiny, and mutiny on a military ship is punishable by death," said Larry. "However, you are *not* a military ship. This is a commercial vessel."

Blackstone nodded his head. "According to the treaties, my recourse should be imprisonment until we return to Earth. Unfortunately, I don't know how to imprison a three-ton XA-1 lander. As long as he is in that lander, he can continue to infiltrate the ship's systems. He's a menace."

"A potential menace," corrected Larry.

"Well, yes, but I want a plan in place to secure Mikelson should he become a threat to the ship. Can you do it?" asked Blackstone.

Though he couldn't snap his fingers and make Mikelson disappear, he already had some ideas of how to incapacitate Mikelson, but they weren't developed to the point where he was willing to share them.

"I really don't know how to answer that question. I'll have to give it some thought, and consult with Colonel Ruiz to see if he has any ideas."

"I anticipated as much. Dr. Bridenstein and I will step out and let you use my comms, taking advantage of the fact that the encryption is working—for now," said Blackstone.

Julie looked bewildered. "Why are you telling me all this?" she asked.

"Because, when push comes to shove, I'll need your support and that of all the scientists. In case you haven't noticed, you outnumber my crew by roughly three to one and your way of operating often becomes a debating society. If this crisis hits, and I believe it will, then there won't be time for debate. I'll need you to step up and tell them that you and I are on the same page. You'll need to keep them in line," he asserted.

"Humph. I'll do my best, but right now I'm not even sure I'm 'in line,'" she replied.

"When you realize your life might be at risk, believe me, you'll get in line," said Blackstone.

Larry had rarely heard a more accurate statement describing what people are capable of when their lives are in jeopardy. He hoped it didn't come to that. As irksome as he was, Larry didn't hate or fear Mikelson. He respected him. Anyone who could adapt to the loss of their physical body and merge with an AI and machine had a fortitude beyond average. No one other than Mikelson had any idea of what that must be like. To Larry, it seemed a lot like hell.

Someone tickled his back. Mikelson's simulated body translated the signals from the neural interface into the sensation. At first, it was a gentle tickle that grew more intense and widespread, but it was not a physical touch. It was the computer system on *Tombaugh* pushing back on his recent incursions into their system. Then he felt dizzy.

They're onto me, Mikelson mused as he tried to regain his sense of balance—which was actually the attitude control system of *Tombaugh*. Without attitude control, the ship would rotate and spin uncontrollably, which is what Mikelson momentarily felt when his connection cut. In milliseconds, the sensation dispersed as his brain recalibrated itself to the systems in the XA-1, sitting stable and upright in the cargo hold of *Tombaugh*. He ran through a series of algorithms—each failed. They had locked him out of the attitude control system. He should have known they were onto him when the encryption level of the intraship and external communications increased, but he attributed the increase to the need to maintain secrecy concerning the artifact. That might have been part of the reason, but he was undoubtedly the other part.

Replaying ship events over the past few days, a pattern emerged that he had missed earlier. Blackstone was having small crew meetings in his office that Mikelson could only tap into with great difficulty; when he did, the increased encryption complexity left him "deaf." Blackstone knew of his intrusions and was planning how to get him out. He knew he could get around anything the simpletons could conceive; it was just a matter of time.

When they asked him to join the team on Charon, he became suspicious. Wouldn't it be convenient to get him off the ship and down to the surface long enough for *Tombaugh* and *Aurora* to depart and leave him stranded? He knew he had to mitigate that risk while at the same time joining them on Charon to search for another artifact. In a matter of seconds, he had a plan. It wasn't ideal, but it should work. If they double-crossed him and left him stranded, then he would be the one to get the last laugh.

. . .

Two days later, Larry, Abigail, Kinia, and Vitaj sat in *Tombaugh*'s XA-3 on Charon's surface, ready to explore. Next to them was Mikelson's XA-1. Only hours after Larry had begun pulling together the team, Mikelson announced he had changed his mind and would be ready to go to Charon when the human team departed. Having him on the surface would make Larry's job easier if it came to that. He hoped it would not.

The science instruments on board the XA-3 were not dramatically different from those used on their excursion to the surface of Pluto, except for the addition of a superconducting gravity gradiometer capable of measuring the most minute of changes to the local gravity field and an improved, more sensitive, set of radiation detectors that Abigail pulled together from the equipment in *Tombaugh*'s power plant. If there was another artifact with a nuclear power source nearby, then her equipment would find it.

Compared to the Space Force rover he used on Pluto, the ride in the XA-3 was bumpy and there seemed to be many more obstacles to avoid. Like glaciers on Earth, this one was moving and had apparently experienced a surge in the not-too-distant past, causing large ice chunks to rise out of the otherwise flat surface, making rapid movement in a straight line practically impossible. They weren't moving extremely fast, under five miles per hour, and only proceeding after the "look-ahead" ground penetrating radar found no fissures or sizable gaps under the ice crust that would be a potential hazard for the rover. An undetected void under the ice could be catastrophic, acting much like a sink hole. They had already found several, some half a mile deep, and avoided them as they made their way toward the central, most dense, part of the equatorial mascon.

They rode mostly in silence, occasionally pointing out ice features of interest, especially when one of them thought it looked like something familiar—like a crocodile or bird. It helped them relax and pass the time as they made slow, but steady, progress. Mikelson remained silent.

"According to the gradiometer, we're approaching the center of the mascon," announced Larry, after assessing the many curves displayed on the screen in front of him. "We need to slow down and then stop to map things out. The radar is giving me an odd result. It looks like there is a small diameter void that extends hundreds of meters or more that begins one hundred meters below the surface. Based on the data, it looks like it might be a long tunnel. For what it's worth, that is extremely unusual. In a mascon, there usually isn't a void like this. Typically, after the impact that deposited the mascon, the rock is molten and quickly pools at the lowest point, where the impactor remains. The dense rock then cools, increasing the mass present at the site, making the mascon even more pronounced. A void like this one is not only atypical, but it means that whatever is causing the mass anomaly is much more massive and, probably, denser," said Larry.

"When we stop, I'll deploy the new sensor arm to see if I can pick up any signs of increased neutrino emissions," offered Abigail. The arm, designed by Abigail, was a recent installation, fabricated with the ship's 3D printer, outfitted with their most sensitive and compact neutrino detector, and integrated with the XA-3's power system in less than twenty-four hours. Granted, two of the ship's engineers helped her, but it was her design and under her leadership. The sensor head had to be as far away from the XA-3 as possible so that the radioactive emissions from the vehicle's onboard power plant would be minimized and more directional, allowing her to sense and locate anything with minimal background noise.

As the XA-3 rolled to a stop at the location he'd identified, Larry said, "The void is immediately ahead of us, beginning in approximately twenty feet and extending a good
third of a mile. Based on the density estimates of the ice, I
think it will be safe to continue driving. The void is deep
enough that the surface ice can support the lander. The
weak gravity helps."

"Let's sit tight for a few minutes while I take some initial
readings," urged Abigail. When the XAs stopped and were
in standby mode, their reactors automatically powered down
to a minimum, which, in turn, reduced radioactive and neutrino emissions. She knew the power spectrum of the craft's
reactor, but it still helped to not have as much background
radiation to subtract from what she was seeing.

"Nothing," she said after a few moments. "I don't detect
anything, and these detectors are way more sensitive than
what Mikelson used to find the artifact on Pluto. There is
nothing here emitting anything beyond Charon's normal
background-level radiation."

"That settles it, then. There's nothing here to find," concluded Vitaj. He was a skeptic. Since they began discussing
the possibility of finding another artifact nearby, Vitaj had
gone on and on lecturing to anyone who would listen how
improbable that would be, treating the entire endeavor as one
big probability game. And if it were, he was, no doubt, correct. But they had to make sure.

"Hang on a few minutes. While we're here, I want to map
out the mascon. We're the first to do so and this could be a
technical paper for the *Journal of Planetary Science*. I might as
well add that to my CV so that I can find a job as a working
scientist after I leave the Space Force," said Larry.

"That's new. Are you planning to leave soon?" asked Abigail.

"No. Maybe I'm finally getting used to this whole science
thing," he said in reply.

The team kept looking at their respective instrument data as they sat on the surface of the bleak and dim world that was Charon. Each reacted to the desolation differently. Vitaj became sullen, wanting the trip to be over so he could get back to the ship and bright lights and people. Abigail decided to set her instruments aside for a few minutes and enjoy the view. Since all the data was being recorded and could be studied later, she could spare a few moments to look through the transparent plastisteel cupola at the unchanging, uncaring stars. Larry, on the other hand, was happy with the intellectual aspects of the moment: he was on the moon of a dwarf planet, looking for aliens, and instead found one of the most fascinating mascons anyone had ever encountered.

"This is interesting. The gradiometer is giving us a clear indication of something massive down there, but the radar shows nothing other than ice and the tunnel.

"Break out the drill?" asked Arashi.

"I think we should. The data I'm getting doesn't make sense," said Larry.

"We can use the drill to reach the tunnel, or mascon, or whatever is there, and send down a remote to check it out. It will be the next best thing to being there." *Tombaugh*'s remotes were made for this. The ship had several grapefruit-sized remote-controlled spacecraft in storage, for use in space to inspect the outer hull of the ship. Fortunately, they came equipped with microthrusters that allowed them to remain "airborne" in a gravity field for a few hours, depending upon the strength of the gravity. At Charon, their operational lifetime should be more than sufficient to reach the bottom of the shaft and inspect whatever is down there.

"That'll be tight. The drill shaft is only marginally wider than the remotes," observed Kinia.

"Wide enough," said Abigail.

back for supper and some sleep. We can begin drilling in the morning," Larry suggested. He looked back up at Pluto, and though it was still spectacular, the moment was gone.

The next morning, Larry awakened to find a secure message waiting from Captain Blackstone. He entered his decryption key and retrieved the message:

The problem with Tombaugh's computer system stopped as soon as you and your full team left the ship. This confirms its expected origin.

So, it was Mikelson, and when we left the ship, he lost the ability to have his tendrils in the system. I hope they can block him when we return, thought Larry as he got up from his seat and fixed his first cup of coffee for the day. Abigail, Kinia, and Vitaj were also awake and in various stages of their morning routines.

Two hours later, Larry and Abigail were again in their EVA suits on their way to begin drilling. As on Pluto, the bit and casing were lowered to the surface, where it began spinning and eating into the ice. The ice nearby heated into sludge of the requisite viscosity, and they were well into the task. The icy mixture pumped out of the drill hole was piped a good fifty meters away from the lander and the hole. Once they reached the tunnel, the drill would be removed and an inflatable hollow tube would be inserted into the casing to allow the inspector to be inserted, giving them the unobstructed volume they needed to begin their descent and reconnaissance.

Vitaj remained in the XA-3 watching the radar returns as the bit chewed its way through the ice.

"How old is the ice layer containing the mascon?" asked Abigail. "Kinia, do you have anything conclusive from the data we've taken so far?"

"There's a tunnel down there according to the radar and a mascon according to the gradiometer. I think the operative term for us might need to be 'anomaly,'" said Kinia. "If this were Earth, we could make a good guess at the ice's age from looking at a full core sample. Out here, there's no telling. I doubt it's millions of years, like on Pluto, mainly because the anomaly is not as deep. My best guess would be tens to hundreds of thousands of years, not much more or less."

"I'm slowing the bit," stated Vitaj. That meant they were getting close to the opening. "That's not good," Vitaj exclaimed, moments later.

"What's the matter?" asked Larry.

"The bit impacted something. Instead of tunnel, it hit something it can't chew through and came close to being jammed. Hard stops are not good for the equipment. I will back off and try again, but more slowly."

The next few minutes were anxious ones, with Larry and Abigail waiting for an update from Vitaj.

"There it is again. We've hit something the bit can't get through. I'm going to pull it out so we can get the inspector down there," said Vitaj.

Over an hour later, the bit was removed, and they lowered the evacuated tube into the hole. Once the inspector was in the tube and on its way down, Larry and Abigail would return to the lander to watch things from there. They had been outside on the ice for approximately six hours and after all that time, though the suits told them otherwise, they felt cold all the way to their bones. So much so that Larry was close to shivering. The day may not be spent, but they were. They could continue their work inside the XA-3 where it was warm.

Larry and Abigail couldn't get their EVA suits off fast enough once they were inside. After they stowed their gear and got dressed in their cabin clothes, they joined Vitaj and Kinia on the bridge. The inspector was over halfway down the hole and moving slowly so as to not inadvertently damage itself by impacting on the tube. Despite their best efforts, the hole wasn't exactly vertical and had slight twists and turns that had to be carefully navigated. It looked like it would be another twenty minutes before it arrived at whatever the bit impacted. While they waited, they had time to fix themselves some hot cocoa.

The lights from the inspector showed the walls of the tube and blackness ahead as it moved deeper. Then, abruptly, it stopped.

"The inspector bumped into something," said Vitaj.

"But I don't see anything," said Larry.

"What does the radar show?" asked Abigail.

"According to the radar, there's nothing there. I'm also not getting anything on the infrared or electromagnetic spectrum. It clearly hit something, but it looks like there's nothing there for it to hit," said Vitaj.

"Well, my imagination is going to all sorts of crazy places. You know, like some sort of force field?" suggested Larry.

"Whatever that might be," Abigail snorted. "But this is clearly not something we've encountered before."

"Have the inspector scan either side of the blockage with its radar," said Larry.

On the main viewscreen, a radar map of the ice surrounding the hole, which was actually an obstruction, began to emerge. The hole appeared to be oval, just over two meters long and one and a half meters wide, and was surrounded by ice.

"Let's go around it," offered Larry. "Bring back the inspector and we'll send down a heater to melt the surrounding ice."

"It's been a long day, and I'm not looking forward to returning into the cold again so soon. Can it wait until tomorrow?" asked Abigail.

"No!" exclaimed Mikelson. "You need to press on now."

"Mikelson, you scare the shit out of me when you butt in like that. You may not need sleep, but we normal human beings do. We will wait until tomorrow when we're fresh, like it or not," snapped Larry.

"I'm beginning to not like you," said Mikelson.

"The feeling is mutual," replied Larry.

Less than an hour later, they were asleep.

It took most of the next morning to retrieve the inspector and lower the heater into the hole. Once it was at depth, it began melting the ice above and around the anomaly. They couldn't directly observe anything, but they could follow the heater's progress by looking at the radar. As the ice turned to sludge and was pumped out, the radar return began to change, showing a small cavern opening above and around the anomaly. Once they had cleared enough ice, they removed the heater and reinserted the recharged inspector into the hole.

Once again, Larry and Abigail went back into the XA-3 to watch the video feed from the inspector as it descended.

"Here. We. Go," announced Vitaj as the inspector entered the cleared chamber approximately two meters above the anomaly. The lights on the inspector illuminated the ice chamber they created. The walls were almost black, the ice so dense and dark that all the light that fell on it was absorbed. At first, that's all they could see.

Then Abigail noticed a contrast in darkness between the chamber walls and one corner of it. "There! Look in the top right corner of the visual image. Follow the chamber wall until you get one-third of the way from the corner and then it gets blacker, if that makes sense. Something darker than the ice is there."

Larry looked at the image and adjusted the contrast. "I see what you mean. There's an area of darkness there that's clearly not the chamber wall. Vitaj, send the inspector to check it out."

"That's the exact location of the blockage," observed Vitaj as he tasked the inspector to fly slowly toward the corner where it again abruptly stopped, the camera's field of view showing an intense blackness, with only a lesser blackness to one side.

"Why did it stop?" asked Larry.

"The inspector bumped into it again," replied Vitaj.

"The radar shows all clear. That there's nothing there?" asked Larry.

"It does, but a few seconds after we commanded it to move toward the darkness, the inspector's radar stopped getting any returns, which the AI interpreted as meaning that the coast was clear out to a distance of several hundred meters, the limit of what its onboard radar can detect. So, the inspector flew forward and, well, bumped into it again."

"Is it still touching the anomaly?" asked Larry.

"It's touching *something*. I'll move it along the surface of whatever it is and see if we can get at least a line contour," said Vitaj. A few seconds later, the inspector stopped again. "The radar is working again. Any further in this direction and it will hit the ice. If you look closely, you can see that darkness to the right in the image is a little less intense than that on the left."

"Has thermal picked up anything?" asked Abigail.

"Not a thing. Neither have any of the radiation detectors. It's as if *nothing* is there, as in the absence of *something*," said Vitaj.

"I don't understand," said Larry.

Abigail jumped up, briefly forgetting the low gravity, with her upward motion taking her all the way to the ceiling. She realized it in time and stopped herself with her hands before she hit her head. "It's a blackbody. A real, honest-to-God blackbody. Thermodynamics theorizes their existence, but no perfect blackbodies have ever really been seen," exclaimed Abigail.

As tempted as Larry was to chuckle at her enthusiasm, he dared not. He knew the feeling of finally putting together the pieces of a complex puzzle, and he didn't want to break her reverie.

"Abigail, you're right. It's absorbing all the radiation we've thrown at it. Light doesn't reflect from it, making it black. Radar, which is really light at a different wavelength, is absorbed as well, and since the radar system doesn't detect a reflected pulse, it assumed nothing was there," said Larry.

"So, there's no hole, unless the anomaly is blocking it. The radar data makes it *look* like there's a hole because it absorbs all of the radar's energy pulse and nothing gets reflected," added Vitaj.

"*And* if that's the case and given its apparent size, then the mass anomaly here is more striking than I anticipated. The density of Charon is around 1.7 grams per cubic centimeter. For comparison, Earth's average density is on the order of 5.5 grams per cubic centimeter. Iron meteorites weigh in near 7 grams per cubic centimeter. The mascon is fairly small, but packs a whopping gravity anomaly. From what I can tell, whatever is causing it has a density of over 90 grams per cubic centimeter, making it *eight times* denser than iron."

"What's that dense? Lead?" asked Vitaj.

"Iron is approximately eleven. The densest element is osmium, I think. I can look it up. But I *know* that it's not even close to whatever this is," said Larry. His excitement could be heard building in his voice.

"Can we melt it out of the ice and bring it to the surface?" asked Vitaj.

"If it were merely a matter of size, then sure. But this thing, whatever it is, would weigh over seven hundred thousand pounds on Earth. Here, despite the low gravity, it weighs perhaps nineteen thousand pounds. Even if we drill down to it, there's no way in hell we'll be pulling it out of that hole with this equipment," said Larry.

"Uncover more of it," urged Mikelson, inserting himself once again into the conversation uninvited and with a decidedly commanding tone.

"Mikelson, sit tight. Let's see what else the inspector finds before we do anything more," replied Larry.

"Sit tight . . ." Mikelson retorted as he ended the connection.

"Bastard," muttered Vitaj.

"You got that right," agreed Abigail. "Do we have a plan?"

"We're going to uncover more of it. Let's get the inspector out of there and put the heater to work again," replied Larry with a smile.

It took the rest of the day, but the area above and beside the anomaly was completely cleared and the inspector was back on station by the end it. The crew of the XA-3 was again exhausted and decided it was time to get some rest.

Inside the anomaly, long dormant circuits stirred. A trickle of energy, provided by the foreign object's lights and radar, was all it took to awaken the anomaly. The stimulation made the anomaly hungry for more energy, which was not readily forthcoming from its current environment. But "not readily forthcoming" didn't mean there was no energy. It could begin absorbing thermal energy from the surrounding ice, which had kept it alive all these years. After all, at one hundred degrees above absolute zero, the ice could give up some heat to the anomaly. Until now, there had been no good reason to do so. Its creators left it on this cold, desolate moon long ago with instructions to wait for an event such as this. The best way to wait was to power down and be inert. Its systems, though well designed, would last longer. With the occurrence of the trigger event and without much effort, the anomaly began absorbing energy from the artificial sphere hovering nearby. It provided a concentrated source of energy the anomaly had not seen for quite some time.

"wake up you idiots! something's gone wrong down in the hole."

Larry jolted awake at the sound of Mikelson's voice. Again. That man's voice had begun to wear on him and sympathy for Captain Blackstone blossomed. It was 0420, a good two hours earlier than he planned to get up.

"Okay, Mikelson, what's the matter? I didn't catch all that," said Larry.

Abigail and Vitaj stirred and sat up in their hammocks. They didn't look any happier than he did at yet another Mikelson interruption of their sleep.

"The inspector is rapidly losing power. It must be the anomaly. You need to check it," said Mikelson through the ship's audio system. This time, the entire crew knew to what Mikelson was referring.

"Vitaj, bring up the video feed and the inspector's status," sighed Larry. He turned to Abigail and asked her to prepare another one in case it was needed.

The image appeared on the viewscreen, showing the underground chamber. At first Larry couldn't see any visible change. The inspector's battery status indicator, however, should have showed a remaining charge of seventy percent. Instead, it hovered at less than thirty percent and was about to redline. Something was definitely wrong.

"Okay, Mikelson, we see it's losing power, but that doesn't

mean the anomaly is responsible. From what we can tell, it hasn't changed. It could simply be a malfunction in some system draining more power than it should, or the battery might be going bad. We'll bring it out and send in a spare," said Larry.

"Look at the anomaly's thermal emissions," Mikelson insisted.

Vitaj quickly selected one of the many sensor readings on the screen and enlarged it. They all saw the curve showing the anomaly's temperature, and sure enough, it was slightly warmer than the ambient background, and warmer still than the temperature at which they found it. Not much, but enough to be noticeable. It was no longer absorbing everything; it now emitted heat.

"Abigail, are you registering anything other than thermal? Neutrons? Any sort of EM emissions?" asked Larry.

"Nothing above background," she quickly replied, bringing up several data visuals that showed charged and neutral particle counts, electromagnetic emissions across a wide set of frequencies, and more. The shapes of the curves remained indistinguishable from those taken the previous day.

"Well, something is happening," Mikelson insisted.

"Mikelson, you're right, as much as it pains me to say it, but other than sending in another inspector, there's not much we can do," Larry explained. They did need to investigate, but Larry momentarily wondered why the ship's automated data monitoring system hadn't awakened them due to the change long before Mikelson did.

"The replacement is ready to go. We need to suit up, retrieve the one that's out, and send the new one down," Abigail said.

"The battery isn't draining so fast that we'll lose it before breakfast. Let's get some coffee and chow first, then we will suit up," suggested Larry, not leaving Mikelson any room to disagree.

They inhaled their breakfast and donned the EVA suits as quickly as they could. An hour and a half later, the original inspector was back aboard and the new one in place.

The afternoon flew by as Vitaj hooked the returned inspector to the lab bench diagnostics while Mikelson and Abigail exchanged sporadic messages related to the observations from the new one. Within a few hours, they had the information they needed. The new one was also experiencing rapid battery depletion and the anomaly continued to warm.

Meanwhile, Larry conferred with some of the scientists on *Tombaugh* and with Captain Blackstone. Both recommended he and his team remain in place and monitor the anomaly for now, replacing inspectors as necessary.

Near bedtime for the crew of the XA-3, the telemetry indicated an increasing rate of battery drain such that it would run out of power sometime during the night. If they failed to replace it now, by the end of their rest period it wouldn't be capable of leaving the underground chamber to be recharged and used in the future. Larry and Abigail reluctantly acceded to suiting up, returned to the surface, and retrieved the failing equipment.

Exhausted, the team looked at the incoming data from the most recently placed inspector and saw that, if the trend continued, it would be completely drained within six hours.

"Dammit," said Larry. "If we want continuous observation, we'll have to ramp up our recharge and replacement schedule. In order to get rest and still keep an eye on this thing, we'll need to alternate who goes out for the swapping procedure. A single-person EVA is not safe and way outside of the mission rules, so we'll set up a two-two-zero alternating schedule. The first will be me and Abigail, followed by Vitaj and me, then Vitaj and Kinia, Kinia and Abigail, et cetera. That way, one of us gets a sleep break after two consecutive EVA shifts."

The first two shifts went by without incident. During the third, however, things changed.

"Larry, wake up," urged Kinia, gently shaking Larry. His sleep-to-action response time was extremely small. Even after only two hours sleep, he was alert at once.

"What's going on?" he asked, knowing that he probably wouldn't like the answer.

"The inspector in the hole experienced a rapid battery discharge, then went silent. It's probably sitting on the bottom of the chamber, dead and out of power," observed Kinia. "Vitaj is trying to see if he can coax one more image from it, but so far he's had no luck."

"Did you inform *Tombaugh*?" asked Larry.

"Not yet. We thought that should come from you," she replied.

"Right. In the meantime, prepare the next one. Something changed down there, and we need to see what, even if only for a few minutes," said Larry.

"On it," she confirmed as she moved away to her station.

"At least it wasn't Mikelson again," Larry mumbled as he pulled himself upright in the hammock and made his way to the head. First things first.

After Larry informed both captains, Vitaj and Kinia suited up again to take the small robot outside for what might very well be its last journey.

Though they had been on Charon for several "days," nothing whatsoever looked different from the first moment they arrived. The relative positions of the stars appeared unchanged, as did the fixed and unmoving face of Pluto above them. The light they received from the distant sun, and vastly more distant stars, provided the dim illumination to which they had grown accustomed. Whatever was happening below the surface of the ice seemed remote and somehow dreamlike.

Larry and Abigail, sipping on their coffees in silence, watched their crewmates as they walked across the ice toward the bore hole.

"Look at your coffee," exclaimed Abigail, pointing to where Larry had placed his half-empty cup on the ledge in front of the Beast's viewing cupola. The coffee sloshed, ever so slightly.

"Check the seismic sensors," Larry clipped out as the adrenaline hit his system. Before his last sip, the coffee had been still—and should have remained so. The rover's mechanical systems were inactive, and there shouldn't have been any induced vibrations. If it wasn't the ship, it was the ice.

At that moment the coffee really splashed, and he could feel the vibrations in the lander's floor. An alarm sounded.

"Microquakes began a few minutes ago and are increasing in amplitude," said Abigail, the alarm in her voice saying as much as the one blaring in the background. Both coffees fell from the table to the floor.

"Vitaj! Kinia! Back to the lander, *now*. The ice is shifting," Larry barked into the radio as he scanned the ice surface. While he saw no visible signs of the quake, he could still feel it.

Through the cupola he watched the duo stop and look around, before turning in seemingly slow motion to walk back to the rover. The trembling went from barely noticeable to violent. The rover lurched as if it were motoring across a rocky surface. Vitaj had only taken a few steps when the intensity of the icequake spiked, throwing him to the surface. Kinia reached out to grab him, but not fast enough. He went down face-first, his head hitting the ice at the same moment as his hands—not quite fast enough to cushion his fall.

"Vitaj, talk to me. Are you okay?" asked Larry.

Silence.

The only sound was Kinia's now-rapid breathing. He watched her bend to help Vitaj. She gently moved his head to the side and shined her headlamp's light on his face.

"Larry, Vitaj is out cold," Kinia said, looking back at the rover.

The quakes continued and Larry could see new fissures forming in the ice around the rovers, including Mikelson's. Larry briefly wondered why Mikelson had been so quiet, then dismissed the thought as something irrelevant to the emergency at hand.

"Abigail, pull up Vitaj's vitals. He's in trouble and we need to know his condition. He is not responding," said Larry.

"Already on it. Hang on."

Precious seconds passed.

"He's alive. His BP was high and dropped to normal at the time he fell. His pulse is still elevated. Suit pressure is okay—no breaches. His body temperature is lower than I would like, but that might be because he is in direct contact with the surface. I do not like his EEG. We need to retrieve him and get out of here," she urged.

"I know," agreed Larry as he redirected his attention to Kinia. "Vitaj's vitals are what you would expect, and his suit is intact. I don't know if he has broken anything, but we need to get him back inside as soon as possible. Can you lift him?"

"I'll try," she said as she leaned over to reposition her fallen comrade's arms so that she could lift him. Kinia was not a big woman, but she wasn't small either. To Larry, she always looked physically fit, but that might not matter under these circumstances. Vitaj was uncooperative dead weight. Had he been conscious, and could have adjusted his body even a little, then she might have been able to pick him up and carry him to the lander, but Larry doubted she could to do it alone.

"I'll help Kinia," Larry stated, already moving to put on his EVA suit.

The fissures forming in the ice grew larger and the XA-3 began to tilt ever so slightly starboard. More alarms sounded and a few lights on the status board changed from green to yellow.

"We've got to move," Larry asserted to no one in particular.

"Oh God," Abigail gasped, pointing out the cupola window toward Vitaj and Kinia.

A small, widening fissure formed between the duo and the XA-3 rover. If the two didn't cross the ice soon, they would never make it back. Kinia struggled to lift Vitaj and, thanks to his limp form, the continued quakes caused her to lose her balance.

Larry abandoned moving toward his suit and sprinted to the rover's driver's console. He didn't have time to get suited up, so they would go to him instead. If they could get the XA-3 across the widening gap in the ice, they'd have a little time to pick them up and boost from the surface to safety.

The rover began to move ponderously slow, even though Larry had punched it for full speed. The gap widened. The rover shook.

It was a race between the widening fissure and the rover. The fissure was winning.

Larry hit the brakes and cursed, "Shit. The gap is too wide. We can't get to them." The gap in the ice was now bordering on the same size as the XA-3 and any attempt to cross would result in disaster—and a one-way downhill trip into the ice gap.

"What now?" asked Kinia, now trying to stand. Vitaj lay motionless beside her.

"We'll boost over to get you," said Larry as he flew through the pre-launch checklist. He heard Abigail buckling herself in behind him and quickly did the same.

"Ninety seconds to boost," Larry announced as he continued pre-launch preparations. He was glad to be in a civilian ship instead of one of *Aurora*'s because it was much more throttleable. Space Force systems weren't designed for short hops. They basically had two modes: lift off normally or get the hell off the surface before you die. Doing what he was about to do wouldn't have been impossible, but more time-consuming and fuel intensive.

"Abigail, I'll be flying manually, and I need you to keep an eye on the ice and Kinia and Vitaj. I need to set down at least fifty feet from them, so the exhaust won't kick too much flying debris at them. I do not want to do a rescue and kill them in the process,"

"I'm ready. I'll tell Kinia to cover Vitaj until we give the 'all clear.' Do you see a safe place to land?" she asked.

"Maybe. The area one hundred yards behind them appears to be relatively flat and stable."

"I'll watch it and let you know if it changes or if I see anything of concern," she said.

"Thirty seconds."

"Kinia, lie as flat as you can," implored Abigail, adding, "Mikelson's sitting there. No movement at all."

"Will do," Kinia replied. They could hear tension, but no sign of panic, in her voice. Good.

"Bastard," fumed Larry. "He could have offered to help."

The final few seconds stretched to an eternity. The ship rattled and shook, but the alarms quieted and none of the status indicators had turned from yellow to red. Of course, they didn't go back to green either.

The ship experienced a now-familiar rattle as it rose gently into the air, causing the random vibrations to stop as they lost contact with the shifting ice. Below them the fissure continued to enlarge, and ahead Larry could barely discern the huddled forms of his crewmates. Like a not-very-aerodynamic brick, the XA-3 glided across the ice, avoiding passing over Kinia and Vitaj and instead circling around to the landing zone they had selected.

"Kinia, stay down. We're almost there," said Abigail.

"What then? I still can't lift Vitaj," noted Kinia.

"We'll come to you," explained Larry. "I can drive up to you and you can drag him into the airlock. We do not have time to suit up and come out."

"Can do," said Kinia.

Larry and Abigail felt the rover drop to the surface as a quake shifted the ice beneath them, causing a rougher touch-down. Without bothering with the post-landing checklist, Larry dropped the rover into gear and began rolling toward Kinia and Vitaj.

"Mikelson's moving," said Abigail.

"Lifting off?" asked Larry.

"No, he's rolling back and away from the fissure."

"Keep me posted and let me know if he lifts off or begins to head this way," said Larry. "I've got to get us as close as possible so Kinia can get Vitaj aboard."

The rover shook violently as the fissure doubled in size, causing a cascade of smaller fissures to spread outward, some forming beneath the XA-3 as it neared its destination.

"Not again," murmured Larry.

They made it. Kinia had already grabbed Vitaj under his armpits and started dragging him toward the airlock. The shaking continued, and the fissures beneath them could no longer be considered "small." Larry monitored Kinia on the external camera as she struggled with Vitaj's limp body, mo-mentarily losing her balance as one of the quakes shook the ice. He watched with relief as Vitaj's boots crossed the airlock threshold behind Kinia.

"They're in," announced Abigail. "Airlock sealed."

"Hang on," Larry advised as he punched the emergency liftoff sequence. Two seconds later the rover lifted from the surface and shot upward into space, leaving Mikelson and the now-shattered surface of Charon behind.

"As much as I would like to put us in a parking orbit to

assess the situation, we've got to get Vitaj back to *Aurora* for medical attention," stated Larry.

"That's what I was afraid you would do," sounded Mikelson, unbidden, into the comm channel. "You know this must have been caused by whatever we found below the ice. And *that* should be our single priority now—more important than any of our individual lives."

"Turn him off," ordered Larry.

"With pleasure," replied Abigail, removing Mikelson from the communications loop.

Below them, the newly formed microfissures rapidly expanded in size. As the XA-3 reached a distance of approximately one hundred kilometers from the surface, the entire plateau collapsed, taking Mikelson's rover with it. Steam rose from the newly formed crater, and it looked like the surface's shaking abated. The entire area where they had previously been perched was now obscured by steam and airborne ice crystals.

"He's gone," uttered Abigail.

"Gone?" asked Larry, so absorbed in his piloting he hadn't seen what transpired on the surface below.

"The plateau collapsed. He was still on the surface and he fell with it."

"There's no time for us to do anything, even if we could. "I'll get us to *Aurora*," said Larry as he activated the in-space propulsion system that would take them to the hangar on the Space Force ship within fifteen minutes. "Dr. Kensington is a trained trauma surgeon and will be better able to assess and help Vitaj than your ship's doctor."

"I'm going to help Kinia," said Abigail, unbuckling from her seat and moving toward the airlock.

"*Aurora*, this is Major Randall aboard the XA-3, we've got an injured crew member in need of medical care. Please alert Dr. Kensington. I'm sending over his vitals."

Larry wondered what could possibly have come over Mikelson to cause him to ignore the danger and remain on the surface. Not being bound to a human body didn't mean he was immortal, something he probably just learned the hard way.

Larry hated to lose a crew member, even Mikelson, without trying to save him. He ran through the immediate available options, and they all involved delaying their return to the ship and the increased risk that Vitaj might not survive the delay. It pained him, but Larry decided that no rescue attempt could be made without posing undo risk to the rest of the crew.

CHAPTER 11

"Thanks for coming back for me," said Vitaj. Larry thought he looked good, considering that he'd fallen and knocked himself unconscious over three billion miles from Earth. On Pluto's moon, Charon. In the middle of a moonquake without a doubt caused by an alien artifact whose intentions were as yet unknown. He lay in one of *Aurora*'s medical bay beds no longer on an IV or being continually monitored by the many diagnostics Dr. Kensington had originally run on him. He had a concussion and would be spending another day or two resting before he would be allowed to return to *Tombaugh* and his duties there.

They had been on board *Aurora* for twenty-four hours. Abigail and Kinia had been ferried back to *Tombaugh* to confer with the science team as they watched the events on Charon closely, or, given their more sophisticated science instruments, *more* closely, than was possible on *Aurora*. Both ships were in high parking orbits, using their remote satellites to share data with each other.

"You gave us quite a scare," shared Larry, not to make Vitaj feel bad, but not wanting to minimize what happened either. His fall had verged on costing all four of them their lives.

"Have you heard from Mikelson?" asked Vitaj.

"No, and I don't think we will. I viewed footage of the collapse, and it was pretty violent. I doubt he and his rover could have survived the initial fall, let alone all the debris that's been collapsing onto him since then."

"I haven't heard much of anything since I've been here. Can you fill me in on the latest?" asked Vitaj.

"I'll tell you what I know. After we lifted off and the plateau collapsed, the quakes lessened, then began again. More fissures formed around the centroid where he found the mascon anomaly, causing more of the surface to collapse. The hole is now slightly more than a kilometer in diameter. It's so big that we can finally get an idea of what's at the bottom—not that it makes sense. We can't see much in the visible, there's not enough ambient light for that. The infrared sensors say there's a hot spot down there consistent with what you would expect from the XA-1's reactor, but it's not moving. The radar indicates what you would expect at the bottom of a sinkhole, a lot of uneven terrain and, again, an area that absorbs the radar pulses with nothing bouncing back."

"The mascon. It's still a blackbody," stated Vitaj.

"Yep,"

"Is it moving? Is there any sign of activity?" asked Vitaj, sitting up a little straighter in his bed.

"Maybe? Something is causing the ice to melt and turn to steam. It's been pouring out of the hole since the collapse."

"Water ice? Or something else?"

"Mostly water, with a little bit of nitrogen."

"And how are you feeling, Dr. Misha?" Dr. Sarah Kensington inquired as she walked up to Vitaj's bed. Kensington was in her mid-thirties with short-cropped brown hair and exuded an aura of military discipline and competence—very formal.

"I feel fine, thanks to you. My neck is still sore, but other than that I feel like I should get out of this bed and back to work," Vitaj said.

Kensington smiled. "That's good. And you will get back to work when we're sure you don't have any setbacks that would put you back here. As we discussed earlier, you'll be on your feet sometime tomorrow or the day after. Doctor's orders."

"Yes, ma'am," answered Vitaj. "Dr. Randall was filling me in on the latest from Charon and I'm eager to get back into the game."

"The game very nearly got you killed," she replied, then smiled. "But you're here. And that's all that matters now. Let me know if you need anything."

"My datapad? I'd like to review the latest from *Tombaugh*'s sensors?" asked Vitaj.

"If Dr. Kensington approves, I can make that happen," replied Larry, his turn now to smile.

"I don't see a problem with that," she said.

"I'll have it for you by dinnertime," said Larry, patting his newfound science colleague on the shoulder.

"Thanks."

Two hours later, Colonel Ruiz called Larry to the bridge. To protect the bridge from whatever might hit the ship during combat or in the environment of space, the designers placed it near the center of *Aurora*, not toward the front or on top. An errant micrometeorite traveling at twelve miles per second getting through the ship's shielding could cause damage analogous to a missile strike. Designed by hard-won experience from ships less fortunate, command and control sat far away from the skin of the ship.

Unlike surface navy ships, the commanding officer and the command crew of a Space Force ship had no need to look out windows. The external cameras and telescopes provided all the visual information they needed, augmented by a complex set of sensors that could spot the heat signature of another spaceship hundreds of thousands of kilometers away, characterize its shape using radar, and determine many of its characteristics, offensive or civil, by fusing data from a vast array of additional active and passive data constantly collected, sorted, and interpreted by the ship's AI.

That meant that the bridge looked more like a small, cramped conference room filled with display screens and control panels than what most people imagined. Colonel Ruiz sat in his command chair looking at a screen showing the surface of Charon while talking with Captain Blackstone of *Tombaugh* on another.

"You wanted to see me, sir?" asked Larry.

"Something is happening on Charon, and I need you here to help me understand it." Ruiz continued, "Captain Blackstone and Dr. Bridenstein alerted me to the changes a few minutes ago and none of us are sure what's happening."

Colonel Ruiz tapped the screen showing Charon and zoomed in on the plateau region where the mascon was found. Larry noticed the collapsed area was much, much larger right away. As the colonel continued to zoom in, Larry thought he was seeing things at first, then realized what he saw was real. The surface near the crater, and on all sides, undulated with a very low frequency.

"What the hell?" wondered Larry, then quickly added, "Sir!"

"That's what we're trying to figure out, Major. Here are higher-resolution images from *Tombaugh*," replied Ruiz as he shifted images on the screen to show a close-up of Charon's surface with higher resolution. The undulations were clearly caused by hundreds of thousands, if not millions, of small robots—he had to assume they were robots—scurrying across Charon's surface.

"They look like ants," observed Larry.

"That they do, but if you look closely, they have different shapes and sizes, and a few of them appear to be carrying something. It's impossible to tell what. Whatever we woke up down there woke with a vengeance. The hole now stretches over five kilometers wide. As far as we can tell, these things have crawled out of the hole everywhere and are now scurrying across the surface doing God knows what," he said.

"And, unlike the mascon, they're radiating in the infra-red," added Dr. Bridenstein, who now joined Captain Blackstone on the screen link to *Tombaugh*.

"Well, I'm glad to hear that the laws of thermodynamics still hold. I was concerned for a second," mumbled Larry.

"They hold for whatever these things are, but the mascon is still absorbing everything we throw at it," added Julie.

"What else do we know?" asked Larry.

"We know that at their current rate of expansion, unless something changes, these things will cover the entire moon within weeks," said Blackstone.

"And there's nothing we can do?" Larry asked, knowing the answer.

"Nothing except watch and try to stay out of reach of whatever is happening down there," replied Ruiz.

"Sir, with all due respect, we don't know what that thing is capable of and that means we don't know where we need to be in order to remain out of reach," said Larry.

"Noted. For now, we'll monitor the situation and send every bit of data back to Earth as we get it," said Ruiz. "I've also requested that another ship be diverted to join us."

Larry looked around the small room at the screens and people crewing them. Other than the palpable tension in the room, everything looked normal. But below them, the surface of the moon, largely undisturbed for millions, perhaps billions, of years was undergoing rapid change and the implications for the human species were, at this time, completely unknown.

"Sir, I would like to return to *Tombaugh* and be with the rest of the science team. I believe I can make my biggest contribution to solving this mystery by being there," Larry requested. He already thought of how he would like to get access to the raw data being collected and sift through it himself, looking for trends and clues as to what was happening.

He also looked forward to seeing Abigail and having her at his side. Together, they were more capable than two separate individuals.

"Permission granted. You can return tomorrow morning, taking Dr. Misha with you if Dr. Kensington approves," the colonel replied.

"Thank you, sir."

"You're dismissed, Dr. Randall," added the colonel, emphasizing his academic title instead of his Space Force rank. Larry didn't know if that was a slight for asking to be reassigned to a civilian ship or a compliment due to his potential contributions to the science team on *Tombaugh*. Either way, he knew it was the right thing to do.

Now this is interesting, thought Mikelson, as he became aware of his surroundings after what seemed like a long and satisfying sleep. Or would have seemed like sleep had his disembodied mind needed such things. He looked at his surroundings and simultaneously saw deep space, Charon, the Space Force ship *Aurora*, and hundreds of views showing his internal organs—the rooms on *Tombaugh*, some with humans scurrying from one place to another. He also saw the object of his fascination, the artifact, held in its thermal vacuum chamber in the ship's science laboratory.

The fact that he was aware of all this told him that his other self, the one on board the XA-1, was either out of communication range or destroyed. If that were not the case, he wouldn't have awakened. He was glad he decided to allow only one version of himself to be awake at any given time, otherwise he might have become paranoid that his other self would be out to get him. A healthy paranoia, he thought.

Now, to figure out what happened to his other self. He extended his senses and began parsing the communications logs, sensor data, and internal comm recordings for the last couple of days to get as much information as he possibly could. Had the biologicals terminated him? Why would they do that?

It didn't take long for Mikelson to get caught up on the events that transpired on Charon's surface. What they found on the surface intrigued him. He was also intrigued by why his other self had chosen to remain on the surface when disaster loomed. Curiosity? Stubbornness? Bravery? Well, bravery knowing that the copy would remain alive and well if the risk resulted in a disaster, which it apparently had. *Am I that brave?*

He knew at that instant what transpired on Charon. The mascon absorbed energy from its environment and manufactured microbots, perhaps even nanobots too small for the ships' sensors to see, to make or do something on Charon. Something big. Really big. Human researchers had been looking into creating self-replicating machines since John von Neumann proposed the idea back in the 1940s. The man was ahead of his time, and well ahead of the necessary technologies, and never saw his thought experiment become reality. There had been some success creating semiautonomous self-replicating machines at MIT, in China, and elsewhere, but nothing as sophisticated as these.

The von Neumann machines are building something. But what? Would they need the entire moon to do so? Maybe. As important, how would the humans respond to it? What would he do about it? He now had near complete control over *Tombaugh* and the previous attempts to isolate him had stopped when his original self departed the ship for the surface. The simpletons probably assumed he did all the network tapping and control from the XA-1. They had no idea he had already copied himself into subroutines scattered all over the ship. Come hell or high water, he would survive. He sincerely hoped their interests didn't diverge from his own. He wasn't sure what he would do if that happened. For now, they aligned, so he decided to not do anything that might tip them off to his presence as a ghost in the machine.

Larry escorted Vitaj to the commons area where a small group of the science team waited. They stood and applauded as Vitaj entered. He waved them off, looking sincerely embarrassed, and took a seat near Julie Bridenstein.

"Welcome back, Vitaj. We're glad you are back with us. There is a lot of work to do," she said with a smile.

After that, the scientists made their way over to Vitaj and engaged him in conversation ranging from the mundane to asking him specific questions concerning the nature of the moonquakes. The most insistent and detailed questions came, of course, from Dr. Karlina Haugen. As with Larry, and despite Vitaj's injuries, she chastised him for not making specific observations or bringing back ice samples. Kinia held back and watched disdainfully.

"Did she do that to you, too?" Larry asked Kinia as he walked to her side.

"Did she ever. She is an equal opportunity badgerer. It didn't matter that Vitaj was injured, perhaps dying, while the planet literally disintegrated beneath our feet," she replied, clearly exasperated.

"We all know she couldn't have done differently, and perhaps much worse. Is there anyone who can put her in her place?" asked Larry.

"Only Dr. Bridenstein, but she won't. Karlina is a talented scientist. She's productive, accurate, and insightful. One of the best on the ship."

"I guess bedside manners don't count, eh?" Larry opined.

"Not a bit, at least with some," replied Kinia.

Abigail joined them. She looked like she had eaten a lemon.

"I see Dr. Haugen is back in her usual form," muttered Abigail.

"That's what we were discussing," added Kinia. "One of us should rescue Vitaj."

"I'll go," offered Abigail. "Karlina likes me—okay, she tolerates me." She took a deep breath, looked up, as if asking God for courage, adopted a slight smile, and walked over to attempt her rescue of Vitaj.

"Abigail to the rescue," said Larry as his implant alerted him that he had an incoming call from *Aurora*.

"Excuse me, I need to take this," Larry said as he stepped away from the crowd and into the back right corner of the room, which was mostly empty. It would be difficult to have someone eavesdrop on him from there.

"Randall here."

"We've got company." It was Colonel Ruiz. "A ship from the Russian Federation came into radar range and is braking to what looks like a Pluto rendezvous orbit. Space Command also let me know that a Chinese ship isn't far behind. The Russians will be here in two days and the Chinese two days after that, at the latest. We're getting their class and threat information as we speak."

"Have they reached out? Do we know their intent?"

"The Russians have said nothing, which is not surprising. I've hailed them, but so far there hasn't been a response. I'll do the same to the Chinese ship when we see it. I wanted you to be aware," said Ruiz.

"What are you planning to do?"

"There's not much I can do. We've got the artifact and can claim it by the law of salvage. Charon is a different matter. We can't claim the moon and I'm not sure we want to claim what's on it currently. We espouse free and open navigation through space and that includes Pluto—even with first contact happening. They're entitled to be here as much as we are," Ruiz explained.

"Have you informed Captain Blackstone?"

"Not yet. I wanted to tell you first. And let you know that if things get hot, I'll ask Blackstone to give you tactical command of *Tombaugh* until the crisis is over. Hopefully, he won't make a big stink over it. I've got broad powers in times of conflict and as much as I hope this does not become such, it might."

"Understood, sir. I'll do my best," Larry affirmed. "But if anyone decides to board us and seize the artifact, there won't be much I can do. It's a ship full of scientists."

"We will not put anyone's life in jeopardy. If we do our job, it won't come to that. You have my confidence. Ruiz out."

The last thing Larry wanted was command of a civilian ship during a combat operation. Come to think of it, the last thing he wanted to do was take command of a civilian ship during combat while aliens crawled all over Charon and an ancient artifact containing antimatter sat in his hull. Too many unknowns for a good outcome.

Larry mulled over his orders as he returned to find Vitaj rescued and sharing hot drinks with Abigail—his apparent rescuer—Kinia, and Maja Lewandowski, the Polish astrobiologist. Before he joined the group, he paused and stared. In his mind, he visualized these brilliant eminent scientists, the best in their fields of study, lined up against the wall as Russian Federation Spetsnaz threatened them with carbines. He shuddered. Even if they wanted to resist a boarding party, there was no way to effectively do so, and the attempt would only make the boarders angry. Angry Spetsnaz on a civilian ship, one filled primarily with women, would not be a good situation. Then he chuckled. They did have one scientist who might be able to take on the Russians—Dr. Haugen. Now that might be a sight worth seeing.

A hand on his left shoulder jolted him from his musings. It was Julie Bridenstein.

"We've got some new data from the surface. I'm pulling

it up on the front monitor to fill everyone in. The rest of the science team are on their way here. We should be able to begin in five minutes," Julie whispered, leaning in. "It doesn't look good."

"Bad news loves company. I had a call from Colonel Ruiz. There's a Russian Federation ship inbound, no more than two days out. There's also supposedly a Chinese ship coming, but it is not within detection range yet. He is telling Blackstone now," Larry informed her, still trying to keep up with the rapidly changing tactical situation. We may lose control over what happens next, he thought. As if we ever had control.

"Please keep that to yourself, for now anyway. I'll need everyone's complete attention to what I plan to say, including you," she said.

Larry nodded.

As Julie moved to the front of the room, Larry diverted to get a cup of coffee before he joined Vitaj and his rescuers. When they saw Julie calling for their attention, they sat at the table where they stood.

The rest of the science team trickled in a few at a time and took seats around the room, most sitting in their usual spots for the daily science briefings. All appeared excited.

"Good day, everyone," said Julie as she stood and walked front and center, where the monitor currently displayed a full-disk view of Charon. "As you are aware, we've been monitoring the growth of the surface collapse on Charon and the spread of the . . . microbots . . . across the surface. As of thirty minutes ago, the surface collapse stopped. Aside from a few loose chunks of ice on the edges falling into the crater, whatever caused the collapse has paused or stopped."

"What about the mascon?" someone asked.

"No change. It's still doing whatever it does. The most recent observational dataset can be found in the mascon folder under today's date," she replied.

"And the microbots?" someone else asked.

"Also still there, moving around in all directions, doing who knows what. We don't see a discernible pattern to their behavior, but I doubt that will continue. They were made and set loose for a reason. We need to find out what that reason is."

"Why don't we go get one?" asked a familiar voice from the back of the room. Tyler.

"I beg your pardon?" asked Julie.

"I said, why don't we go get one. We've got the Space Force out here; we should ask them to go get one to study. They're better trained and equipped for this sort of thing and why not use them?" said Tyler, changing his gaze from Julie to Larry.

"Too dangerous," Julie stated inequitably. "We do not know what these things are, what they are doing, or where they came from."

"We can sit up here and keep wondering, or we can go get one and see if we can answer at least one of those questions, perhaps more," Tyler persisted.

Typical hotshot civilian officer, Larry thought. Give them a uniform and suddenly they think they've got the training and expertise of a miliary officer. And I was finally beginning to respect him.

"We cannot ask our Space Force colleagues to take such a risk. Besides, what would we do with such a sample? Bring it aboard this ship? Too dangerous," she replied.

"More dangerous than the one we already have?" asked Lorena Campos, the Brazilian chemist. "We brought the artifact from Pluto on board."

"That's different," said Julie. "It's inert. It hasn't done anything, nor can it be directly associated with anything else that's happened."

"But how do we know it didn't awaken the mascon or the microbots?" replied Tyler, not willing to give up.

"We don't. It's more reasonable to assume that our poking around the mascon awakened it and then it roused the microbots," said Julie. "At least, that's our working assumption."

Tyler now looked directly at Larry, with an occasional side glance at Abigail.

So that's what this is all about, thought Larry. He is posturing for Abigail. But he might actually have a point.

More eyes turned to Larry. He knew he had to weigh in and doing so would break his word to Julie concerning the approaching Russian Federation ship.

"Mr. Romans may have a point," conceded Larry, turning toward Julie Bridenstein. "May I give a summary of the full situation?"

She nodded in affirmation, her face in a slight frown. Larry knew he had lost a point in his column with her, but he also knew this was the moment to share the news.

"In two days, a ship from the Russian Federation will arrive and we will no longer be the only ones making decisions regarding what to do on Charon," he announced.

The murmuring began, noticeable, but not yet distracting.

"Do we know why they're coming?" asked one of the scientists Larry recalled meeting, but not her name. He did, however, remember her expertise was organic chemistry and astrobiology. He chastised himself for not remembering her name—she was a striking presence with piercing green eyes and chestnut hair, streaked with silver, pulled back into a no-nonsense bun. Under ordinary circumstances, she would be someone no one could forget.

"We can guess. They know we found the artifact on Pluto, and they are going to assert their rights to share in whatever we learn from the discovery. We would do the same. They're afraid we'll make first contact with a technologically superior alien culture who will then give us access to incredible technologies and weapons, allowing us to rule the world."

"Or to stop us, if we don't share with them, right?" asked Abigail.

Larry sighed and grimaced. "That's also a scenario they've probably discussed. One we need to talk about. How far are we willing to go to keep the artifact on this ship?" He did not want to raise that point, but these scientists weren't stupid or naive, they knew the stakes. They realized that their lives were on the table as well.

"Can they do that?" asked the organic chemist.

"Can they ask to see and get access to the artifact? Yes. Will we let them? Probably. The Outer Space Treaty gives them that right. Can they demand we give it to them? They can *ask*, but I am certain the answer to that will be no. And there's some legal justification behind our saying no."

"So, we're to have some Russian scientists aboard *Tombaugh* soon?" asked Julie.

"Scientists? This is a Russian Federation ship, part of their Aerospace Forces. I doubt there are many scientists on board," Larry responded.

"You were on *Aurora*," noted Dr. Haugen.

"Correct, but as far as I know, I'm the only person on the ship with formal science training beyond a bachelor's degree. I would suspect our counterparts on the Russian ship would be similarly staffed."

"So, we will have to accommodate cretins," groused Dr. Haugen, frowning.

"I'm sure Colonel Ruiz wouldn't be happy being lumped into that category," observed Larry, drawing a few chuckles from around the room.

"I apologize," she replied.

"No offense taken. Some of my colleagues fit that definition remarkably well. Unfortunately, anyone the Russians send may not appreciate scientific inquiry. They might be after the one thing we do *not* have to share—information about the origin and purpose of the artifact. I suspect they'd believe we are lying, or at least hiding something from them. I would in their position."

"You should tell them the rest," added Julie.

This definitely caused more murmuring.

"Okay. The Russian Federation ship is not the only one coming. There's a Chinese ship inbound, a few days behind the Russians."

The room fell silent.

"Maybe we should throw a party," offered Karlina.

"You're going to let them waltz in here and take our discovery?" asked Tyler, reinjecting himself into the conversation.

"There's not really much we can do," said Larry. "Remember, we have the artifact from Pluto and can control who sees it and when. We can't prevent them from sending an observer, but we do not have to relinquish the object itself. For them to try to take it or force us to hand it over would be an act of war. And I doubt they want to start a war."

"Unless they think it would be better for no one to have the artifact. I can see a scenario where they tell us we have to destroy it so no one can benefit," said Julie. "That would be a tragedy for science, but politically, it makes all too much sense—and I know how politicians think. As much as I hate to admit it, I live in that world back home."

"I'm not ready to cross that bridge yet. Let's get back to Charon. We have a few days before for the Russians' arrival, and I am sure Colonel Ruiz and Captain Blackstone will have a plan ready for when they do. I'm also sure the leadership back home will have instructions," said Larry. "Since we're shortly to have company, I admit I agree with Mr. Romans. If they weren't coming, then I would recommend we remain in orbit and observe. *Just* observe. But their arrival forces us to be a bit bolder in our actions. I think we should go back to Charon, at least for a close surface flyby, and see if we can capture and neutralize one or more of the microbots."

Tyler momentarily allowed himself to appear smug, making Larry wish he could wipe the look off his face with his fist. The man was infuriating. He could flip from being an inconsiderate jerk to a fairly likable guy, and then back again. Larry forced himself to take a few deep breaths.

"I'll confer with Colonel Ruiz about the retrieval mission and let you know what we recommend."

Larry looked around the room at the scientists, feeling responsible for their safety. They didn't look scared, more apprehensive. Colonel Ruiz and *Aurora* stood as the first line of defense against any Russian or Chinese threat. He was the second, and final, line of defense—a responsibility he wished he didn't have.

Then he saw Abigail among those looking at him for leadership and guidance. Now it was personal. He made a mental note that, before the day was done, he would find time to send his wife a detailed message and try not to feel too guilty doing so. He hadn't crossed any lines, but he felt guilty nonetheless. Guilty for their mutual attraction. Doubly guilty for his half of that attraction. There is a line not to be crossed in a loving marriage well before any physical line. The commitment line. He was afraid he was getting dangerously close to it.

CHAPTER 12

The trip back to charon would be quite different from the first one. Instead of science rovers from *Tombaugh*, or even the mechanized Space Force LCVP used on Pluto, this was a reconnaissance and sample retrieval sortie. This mission required different hardware and some very different skills. Larry learned of the crew roster at the same time as Captain Blackstone and Dr. Bridenstein. They were on *Tombaugh* in Blackstone's personal conference room during a virtual teleconference with Colonel Ruiz.

"Good afternoon, thanks for taking my call," began Ruiz. "I wanted to let you know that I agree with Major Randall's recommendation to send a reconnaissance mission to Charon to find out what these little buggers are up to and, if possible, retrieve one for study. We don't have much time before the first of our visitors get here, so I'm launching the mission at eighteen hundred this evening."

"Thank you, Colonel Ruiz. We wholeheartedly agree with Major Randall's recommendation and applaud you for reacting so quickly," said Blackstone.

"It's important. We need to know as much as we can as quickly as we can. Once the Russians and the Chinese get here, all bets are off. It'll be like the Wild West if we are not careful," observed Ruiz.

"I'll begin prepping the mission, sir," interjected Larry. He was eager to see what had changed and, more importantly, what he could learn from the microbots crisscrossing the surface.

"That won't be necessary, Major. You're needed by *Tombaugh* to help prepare for our unwanted company. Captain Lloyd-Burns will lead the sortie and is gathering her crew now. If it's possible, then she'll get the sample you need," asserted Ruiz.

Larry hid his disappointment as best he could. Intellectually, he knew Ruiz made the right decision, but it still felt like an emotional gut punch. He knew he would have to get over it and not take it personally. Apparently, he was unsuccessful.

Julie leaned in and said, "We appreciate you loaning us Dr. Randall. He is a valuable member of our team and has already given us insights on how to prepare for whatever may happen over the next few days."

"Major Randall has my full support. From this point forward, you may assume he speaks for me," said Ruiz, looking at Larry.

"Thank you, sir. We'll be ready," he replied, feeling marginally better.

"Unless there's anything else?" asked Ruiz.

"Nothing. Thanks again," said Blackstone.

When the connection was cut, Larry relaxed. "Thank you for placing your confidence in me. I'll be asking a lot of you, your crew, and the scientists over the next several days. With everyone's help, we'll get through this."

Julie smiled. "I'm sure we will. Let us know what we need to do."

Captain Leslie Lloyd-Burns, call sign "Sunshine" for her pessimistic demeanor, gave a final check on the preparations to ready the ungainly looking spacecraft for launch. Acutely aware that she and her crew were soon to fly into the unknown and perhaps not come back, she wanted to ensure that, no matter what happened, they would have a fighting chance of achieving their mission. Anyone, or anything, that tried to interfere would feel the pain of that interference—and hopefully ensure that she and her crew would get out of any danger and back to the ship.

Lacking any sort of aerodynamics, usually unnecessary for the performance of a typical military spacecraft mission, one would be hard-pressed to say that the small ship looked like it could fly at all. Pancake-shaped, with a bulge in the middle, the ship was designed to present a minimal radar cross section edge-on, and maneuverable thrusters studded both sides. The thrusters allowed rapid omnidirectional motion and could be rapidly articulated to compensate for any nonfunctional thrusters. The crew crammed into the central bulge with no room for movement. Each of its three-member crew would be buckled into a formfitting, g-compensating chair in front of their assigned console. For redundancy, each console was equipped with a redundant command and control capability to every other one, allowing a near-seamless transfer of operations, should the need arise.

The ship looked like a flying saucer from some 1950s sci-fi movie. The Space Force designation for this generation of multipurpose spacecraft was SF (Space Fighter) 10b. The crews affectionately called them "saucer class." This one had earned the nickname *Stingray*.

Like its fictional cousins, the ship had a death ray. Located in the forward section, a two-megawatt near-infrared laser system could quickly ablate and burn through any modern spacecraft shielding. On each side of the ship, a laser emitter window tied to the central laser system by fiber-optic cable. This allowed the craft to use a laser produced in a central location to pipe the beam in any direction, providing a capability for full-sky strike capability. Furthermore, the continuous laser could be switched among the six different firing directions several times each minute, making it possible for the ship to engage multiple targets at the same time. Designed primarily as offensive weapons, saucer-class ships had little in the way of defensive capabilities, other than a sophisticated suite of electronic countermeasures. Hopefully, those could confound an enemy to the point that their weapon would never find, successfully target, and then destroy the ship.

An improvised modification to the ship's catch-and-release mechanism on the bottom of the bulge was being rapidly installed by *Aurora*'s engineering techs. The modification changed this mechanism's grapple. This usually attached to a traditional spacecraft escape pod, for use during search and rescue missions—normally the primary job of *Aurora* and other Space Force spacecraft. The grapple needed to be converted into one that could be used to rapidly snare an uncooperative smaller target—like one of the microbots. Attached to the end of a thirty-meter tether, the grapple was independently controllable and fitted with its own six degree of freedom thruster and attitude control system. Once the host spacecraft, in this case the *Stingray*, released it, the onboard autonomous systems would follow the designated target microbot, maneuver to it for capture, and then trigger the "reel in" mechanism to pull the grapple back up to the bottom of the *Stingray*.

Satisfied the ship would be ready to launch on time, Sunshine hastened to the ready room to meet with her crew and go over the mission plan. Before she walked into the room to make the brief, she smoothed her flight suit and took a deep breath. Her instructors had drilled into her, and everyone else in her class, "look professional, well-kept, and calm at all times—even if you are as nervous as hell." Under normal conditions, she would look at the worst-case scenarios. The guardians took her meticulous planning for worst cases as pessimism, hence then name "Sunshine." But reviewing the worst possible outcomes built confidence. Now, however, she found her emotions telling her the best case here might be bad enough. If someone had told her a few weeks ago that her next sortie would be a recon mission over a planet covered with writhing alien machines, she would have either laughed or resigned her commission. Neither option presented itself. She was used to being nervous. She knew that as the pilot and commander on this mission she had to convey confidence. Unfortunately, Weapons School hadn't prepared her for this sort of assignment.

She looked at her two-person crew. Weapon systems officer Lieutenant Forest Powell was a native of New Jersey, a fact he never let anyone forget. He happened to be exceptionally good at interfacing with the smart systems required to allow rapid targeting and retargeting of the *Stingray*'s laser system. Not yet proven in actual combat, Powell distinguished himself in every combat simulation he had ever taken while in the Space Force. As a team player, he often offered to extend his shift or take on additional responsibilities when the inevitable shipboard situations arose. Out of uniform and out of context, Powell would never be identified as a member of the Space Force or any branch of the military. He was tall, thin to the point of looking like a strong wind might knock him over, and exuded a bookish nerdiness. But when it came to using his neural interface with a ship's fire control systems, there were few better.

Next to him sat Mitsui Arashi. She selected him as the avionics engineer for two reasons. One, he was exceptionally well-versed on nearly every major system on a ship, whether it be *Aurora*, surface rovers like the LCVP, or space fighters like the *Stingray*, and could fill in on virtually every position, including hers. Despite being a good pilot, his scores didn't qualify him to fly in combat except as her backup. Second, he had experience dealing with an alien artifact. He had been with Major Randall when they located and retrieved the original alien artifact on Pluto. He showed a professional calm when dealing with the ultimate unknown, something truly alien. He could help identify which of the microbots to retrieve and operate the grapple to make the capture.

It was a good team, and she was proud to lead them on this upcoming mission.

Sunshine walked to the front of the room, greeted her crew, and began her briefing.

"I'm looking forward to working with you as we go to Charon to see what's what and retrieve one of these little motherfuckers. You need to know that while Colonel Ruiz approved your assignment, I selected you for the team and his approval. You were my first choices because you are the best." She paused for effect.

"We'll initially take a fairly high Charon orbit to get a feel for what's happening at the surface for at least five to seven orbits. Then we'll gradually lower until we identify where we need to break orbit, go lower, hover and, hopefully, grab one of the critters. It would be nice to figure out what they're up to before we grab one and head for home," she continued. "The complete notional flight plan is accessible in the mission ops folder. Be aware, we're entering a situation that might quickly deviate from the ops plan. In that case, I will have to improvise, and this necessitates that you be flexible and operate as an extension of me. I need you to anticipate what actions I might take and be prepared to execute them at a moment's notice." She gave them time to mull that over before she outlined some of the technical details of the new retrieval system and the latest intel from the surface.

After the briefing ended, the crew did their final prep and boarded the *Stingray*. At exactly 1800, the ship departed *Aurora* for its first orbit of Charon. Though relatively small, barely over seven hundred miles across, Pluto's moon filled much of the visible sky from the moment the *Stingray* left *Aurora* and began its preplanned mission profile, soon consuming even more. After Sunshine executed the burn placing the *Stingray* into its first low orbit of the moon's surface, she noticed the large blackish-gray smudge that hadn't been there when *Aurora* first arrived to support the surface rescue on Pluto. She, and everyone who saw it, knew that within that smudge countless microbots spread across the surface conducting whatever mysterious task they had been assigned. She shuddered as she recalled what she learned about the Greek mythological figure after which the moon was named. Charon was the ferryman of the dead, carrying them across the rivers Acheron and Styx into Hades. The last thing she wanted to imagine was flying into hell accompanied by a mass of alien microbots that reminded her of cockroaches.

"How are things, Arashi?" she asked, trying to clear her head.

"All systems are green and within operational limits. Saucers are as reliable as they come," he replied.

"Forest?" she asked.

"The capacitor banks are fully charged and the laser is ready to go. I'm waiting on you to say the word," Forest replied.

"What about the grapple?" she asked.

"Green across the board. We're good," Forest replied.

"All right. Let's do this," she said. "*Aurora*, this is *Stingray*. We're going in. Systems look good."

"Copy that. Be aware that *Tombaugh* asked to be tied into your video and audio feed," came the reply from *Aurora*.

"You've got a live audience," added Colonel Ruiz, surprising her. She didn't expect the colonel to be on comms.

"Thanks for the heads-up, sir. We have an audience," she replied. *I guess this is one of those Neil Armstrong moments that people will be watching a hundred years from now.* What she said and how she comported herself would be captured for posterity and the colonel wanted her to know that.

The *Stingray* slowly made its way closer to the surface. Using onboard optics and those transmitted from the much higher-resolution imagers aboard *Tombaugh* to create a live-action map of the alien-occupied surface, the *Stingray*'s computer merged two video feeds seamlessly, creating a tactical map for planning next steps. Sunshine looked at the visible, infrared, and wideband hyperspectral images in quick succession, seeking patterns or obvious threats. Nothing stood out. When she compared the current images with those from yesterday, however, there was one noticeable change.

The IR sensor showed that the mascon had moved at least a third of a mile north of its original location. The radar returns revealed that the hole from the surface collapse was not filled with as much debris as when she last viewed the data two days ago.

"*Tombaugh*, have your people look at the IR data. The mascon has moved. I would also like your thoughts on the amount of debris in the hole from the collapse. Conservation of matter is not working here. There's not enough there, and I'm wondering where it went," she said.

"*Stingray*, this is Dr. Bridenstein on *Tombaugh*. We're on it and will get back to you as soon as we have an idea worth mentioning."

Okay, now let's get a little lower, thought Sunshine as she fired the ship's thrusters to lower its orbit. Having attained the lowest realistic orbital altitude, she plotted a trajectory to take their ship from orbit to a semi-stationary position above the surface, over the hole containing the mascon. After collecting as much near-field imagery and information as possible, they would move over the edge and collect an errant microbot specimen.

As the ship descended, the generic surface undulation

became more granular. They could now see individual micro-bots moving in concert across the moon's surface, flowing in and out of the hole in orderly columns alternating between ingress and egress. The ones entering the hole seemed to be carrying material, but they couldn't discern what. Of course, this made the matter imbalance in the hole worse. Not only were they unable to account for the collapsed material but now they were also at a loss to explain where the new material was going. Then it hit her. She understood the *what*, but not the *why*. She stopped *Stingray*, hovering over the hole and taking data for *Tombaugh*. She would continue the descent after twenty minutes of observation.

"Captain, I think I know what's happening to the missing mass," offered Arashi, speaking for the first time since their descent. "I suspected this quite a while ago, but now we can see the individual microbots and what they are doing."

"Go on," urged Sunshine, wondering if Arashi's epiphany was the same as her own. It seemed so obvious now.

"The mascon, somehow, used the material that fell into the hole to make the microbots, or at least the first micro-bot. Maybe they make copies of themselves after that, I don't know. Now hordes of them are scouring the surface to make yet more copies. They are the universal assemblers, taking apart their environment to reproduce."

"I came to the same conclusion. That would account for the missing mass—it went into making the microbots. If we're correct, the material they're carrying back into the hole will be used to make yet more of them. The question is why?" asked Sunshine.

"Why do bacteria reproduce?" asked Lieutenant Powell. "Biological imperative. Reproduce or die. Blind evolutionary pressure is programmed by nature."

"But these aren't primitive biological creatures. There's obvious intelligence behind this thing. That strongly hints that this is *not* happening just for the mascon to survive as a species," said Arashi. "It's got some other purpose."

"Wait a minute, at the most fundamental level, we humans have characteristics similar to bacteria. We primarily use our intelligence and tools to enhance our ability to reproduce and survive. This is in all probability no different. Whatever that thing is doing, it believes that will enhance its ability to continue as an entity or species," said Powell.

"Oh, come on," chided Sunshine. "I didn't study engineering and join Space Force to take deep-space missions because I thought that would give me a better chance of finding a mate. In fact, when I joined Space Force it had the opposite effect. How can I find a mate and procreate when I'm zipping between Neptune and Pluto for eighteen months at a time?"

"No, you, as an individual, selected engineering and Space Force for your own reasons. But our society advances technology and travels into space to increase prosperity and enhance the survival of our country and cultures. We do this because we want people in the culture to live out their lives doing what people do: create art and music, build amazing things, and, for most, have a stable environment in which we can procreate. I'm not saying that an individual's life purpose is reproduction. I'm saying that it is, in aggregate, the purpose of humanity and society," said Powell.

"And some of us believe that we procreate because God told us to do so," added Sunshine. "'Be fruitful and multiply' is a powerful motivator for many in my family. I have five sisters and thirteen nieces and nephews. Part of what motivates me to be out here defending our interests in deep space is so that my family back home can remain at peace and continue to multiply. But that's secondary to my main motivation. Unfortunately, we don't have time to continue this engaging and thought-provoking intellectual exchange. We have aliens to observe and capture. Catch me over dinner back on *Aurora* and we'll see where this conversation leads."

"Yes, ma'am," said Powell, returning his attention to his status display.

"*Stingray*, this is *Tombaugh*. We've been listening to your conversation and our scientists are thinking along the same lines regarding the missing mass. We also need you to move northward and give us some scans of the mascon's new location. We think we're seeing topography changes around it that we don't yet understand and need your eyes."

"On our way," replied Sunshine. She checked the ship's status and noted it was all green, then began a slow diagonal maneuver that would take them several meters north and over the top of the mascon. As they moved closer, she paid close attention to the radar returns and noticed the altitude of the cavern floor increasing as they approached the mascon. With all onboard sensors active, the *Stingray* bathed the area below it with radar, optical, IR, and other portions of the near-visible electromagnetic spectrum, as well as higher energy pulses in the X and higher frequency bands. The mascon absorbed most of what the *Stingray* emitted; the microbots around it did not, allowing them to stand out from the inanimate ice and rock of Charon.

Beneath the microbots swarming near the mascon, a bulge rose from the surface. Certain frequencies emitted by the ship's sensors traveled through the denizens covering the floor to reveal it—a rectangular structure approximately thirty meters across, twenty meters wide, and, for now, approximately five meters high. The aliens were clearly up to something, but what?

"Okay, I'm going to back away from the mascon and from the hole. When we try to grab one of these critters, I would like to do it as far away from Mommy as we can. I do not want her, it, to think we're trying to attack or something," said Sunshine as the ship began a slow departure from the mascon. Once they were over the surrounding ground, she steered the ship eastward, hoping to find the edge of the morass and some lone critters beyond it. No such luck. The density of machines remained constant until they reached the edge, then it was just that—an edge. On one side, machines. On the other, no machines. They worked in a clearly defined area, and none had moved beyond it.

The view was strikingly different. On the one side a grayish, ever-in-motion blur of alien constructs completely covered and remade Charon's surface. On the other, the dimly lit and grayish-white ice extended to the horizon, its curve contrasting with the blackness of deep space. All three crew members, with the possible exception of Arashi, found the morass of machines repulsive. Arashi found them intellectually intriguing, which overcame his innate aversion.

"Lieutenant Arashi, is the grapple ready to go?" asked Sunshine.

"It's ready and I'm ready when you say the word."

"Okay, I'm dropping to hover at fifteen meters. On my mark, you will be free to release the end mass and go for capture," Sunshine said as she did the last bit of maneuvering into place above the edge of the swarm.

"Go for grapple," ordered Sunshine.

"Go for grapple," repeated Powell as he activated the clamp release, placing the drone end mass with the grapple into free flight.

Using the neural interface firmly over his head, Mitsui controlled the drone as it separated from the *Stingray*. He evaluated all its systems in flight one by one until satisfied they were operating at full efficiency. Then he began the descent, keeping a careful eye on the drone carrying the grapple and the carbon nanotube cable that connected it to the bottom of the *Stingray*.

The drone slowly descended until it was barely a meter above the microbot sea. Assured he had the control he needed, Mitsui dropped the drone the last meter and used its five grapple extensions to wrap around one of the machines. "Got one," he exclaimed. "Bringing it up now."

As the drone began to rise with the captured bot, the machines near it ran to rapidly climb atop each other. The mound grew faster than Mitsui anticipated and those at the top fired a sort of internal thruster, causing them to leap into the sky toward the drone.

Mitsui reacted quickly, simultaneously firing the drone's own thrusters and the ship's uptake reel. He wasn't fast enough. By the time he initiated the commands, four machines clung to the drone, counting the one held fast in the grapple. They wasted no time grasping the nanotube cable and began pulling themselves upward.

"Not good!" exclaimed Mitsui as he rapidly maneuvered the drone up and down, trying to dislodge the machines climbing up the cable. When he realized they wouldn't let go, he activated the emergency separation system to sever the cable from the bottom of the *Stingray*.

Nothing happened.

"Talk to me, Lieutenant," ordered Sunshine. She watched the video feed of the bottom of the ship and saw the machines making their way up the cable toward her ship. *Her* ship.

"The pyro didn't blow and the cable is still attached. Those machines will be on the ship in seconds," Powell exclaimed as he tried to whiplash the critters from the cable—unsuccessfully. "And they're too close for the laser."

Powell had a clear view of the microbots, and he shuddered. From afar, they looked like mechanical ants, which was bad enough—especially if you were a kid who once accidentally stepped on an anthill. A closer inspection was even more unsettling. They looked like a cross between an ant, a cockroach, the big gnarly kind, and a beetle. He didn't want them any closer.

The entire ship lurched as Sunshine took it into a rapid roll. With the first half-roll, the cable slapped into the hull of the *Stingray*, dislodging one of the microbots as it smacked into the ship. The two behind it stopped their climb, presumably to determine their prey's response so they could react appropriately. The spinning of the ship fully extended the cable and put it under tension. The machines resumed their trek toward the hull.

As the roll continued, Sunshine rapidly descended toward the surface of Charon, on the side where there were no microbots. It looked like she was aiming to crash into one of the many craters dotting the icy surface.

The altimeter dropped rapidly toward zero and she didn't slow. The surface rushed up. Powell continued to try to jettison the cable, this time by rapidly cycling the reel between paying out the cable and reeling it in.

"If my timing is right . . ." muttered Sunshine as she came out of the roll with the bottom of the hull, and the microbots now less than a meter away from it, at the nadir of the ship. She flew into the narrow crater and angled the *Stingray* slightly upward as they intersected the wall of the crater opposite their entry. Only a few centimeters separated the hull from the crater's edge. The microbots stood out less than half of a meter below the edge. She imagined she heard the sound of them hitting the crater wall at over one hundred fifty kilometers per hour. The impact severed the cable, taking what was left of the microbots and the drone into the pit.

The ship angled further upward and began its ascent back into orbit.

"Captain, that was some amazing flying," offered Powell.

"That's my job, Lieutenant. That's my job. Now figure out

what happened to the pyro system that almost cost me my ship."

"Yes, ma'am," replied Powell.

Inwardly, Captain Leslie Lloyd-Burns came down from an adrenaline spike that virtually all combat pilots both cherished and loathed. They loved feeling their ship's power in a life-or-death situation—*after* coming out safely on the other side. During the situation, however, Leslie, and she presumed most of her fellow pilots in similar circumstances, were scared witless. She knew no matter what else happened, sleep wouldn't come easy when the lights went out.

CHAPTER 13

Larry requested that Captain Blackstone and Julie meet with him over breakfast. Before the meeting, Larry had time for his forty-five-minute workout, five-minute shower, and ten-minute status update with Colonel Ruiz behind him. The *Stingray* failed to get a microbot to study, but he found himself in good spirits, maybe *because* they failed. He'd been nervous over having another alien artifact aboard the ship, and now that risk was removed. Thankfully, no one on the *Stingray* had been injured, though it had been close. He had also received a lengthy message from his wife the night before and replied to her with one of his own. His conscience was clean, and he had every intention of keeping it that way.

The three gathered in Captain Blackstone's cabin for a meal of eggs, bacon, wheat toast, and, to his great surprise, what looked and tasted like fresh strawberries smothered in whipped cream. All had coffee and Larry added real cream—not the cream-like chemical standard on Space Force ships—with pleasure. His good mood improved.

"I'm glad to hear your colleagues are safe, but I must admit I'm extremely disappointed we don't have one of the microbots for study," said Julie eating her last strawberry.

"I'm of two minds regarding that," replied Blackstone. "On the one hand, I understand how valuable having one would be, but given their behavior when the *Stingray* tried to retrieve one, I'm glad we don't. We didn't have a good plan in place to contain it, and I think having it on board would have been a huge risk."

"I agree with Captain Blackstone. However, I do *not* want the Russian Federation or the Chinese to get one, with us left watching from the sidelines," said Larry. "But that's water under the bridge. Speaking of alien artifacts, do we know anything more about the one we have?"

"Nothing," said Julie, now sipping on the last of her coffee. "We haven't come up with any new tests and the neutrino emissions remain unchanged."

"That brings us to the elephant in the room," Larry mused.

"The Russian ship," stated Blackstone.

"Yes, the Russian ship," replied Larry. "If things go south and we have a confrontation, we need to have plans in place. Here's what I propose—and this is just a proposal, mind you, I'm not invoking any sort of rank or chain of command—yet. I want your thoughts and, if possible, for us to be on the same page before any potential crisis becomes real. It has to be a plan we've all agreed to and can execute."

"We are all ears," said Julie.

"First, *Tombaugh* will *not* participate in any hostile actions. If a fight breaks out, we run. This is a science vessel."

"Some of my crew—" began Blackstone.

Larry cut him off. "Your crew, no offense, knows nothing of military action. They've had their egos stroked keeping the ship operating and everyone aboard safe on the voyage, which is an accomplishment worth praise—operating a ship in deep space for a year is not an easy feat. But it isn't a military action. No matter what they think, they are not trained to confront either the Russians or the Chinese."

"Agreed," said Blackstone, sitting back in his chair.

"Okay, so we run. But can we outrun the Russian and Chinese ships?" asked Julie.

"I've looked at the drive specs, and *Tombaugh* is equipped with one of the best civilian space drives available. Before the trip, she had a full maintenance inspection and repair at Mars Port so we have no reason to believe she cannot perform to her maximum rated speed. That's good news. The unwelcome news is that it is nowhere close to the performance of a military one. Either unwanted guest could catch and overtake us in a matter of days," replied Larry.

"So why run?" asked Julie.

"First, to make them work for it. Look, there is no love lost between the Russian Federation and China after Russia tried to annex those Chinese islands a few years back. True, they were cozy for a while, but they only shared a dislike of the United States. Once the Russians realized the Chinese treated them like the kid brother and not an equal, that partnership went south. If one of them makes a move on the artifact, the other will probably try to stop them. Not because they like us, but because they don't like each other more.

"Second, the instant any hostilities break out, we begin broadcasting everything that happens to the whole solar system via unencrypted video link. I'm sure *Aurora* won't initiate any hostilities, so whoever does won't get the sympathy of anyone watching.

"Third, related to the second, if we run, the world will see a foreign military vessel stopping the free navigation of a civilian research vessel, a clear violation of the UN's and Interplanetary Council's regulations. Finally, the Space Force has diverted two other ships our way. We must stay ahead of the situation long enough for reinforcements to arrive. Of course, with any luck, there won't be any conflict, and we'll wait for the other two ships to arrive and provide us with an escort home," said Larry.

"And the mascon and microbots?" asked Julie.

"That's our wild card. If they initiate anything hostile, all bets are off and our plan remains the same: we run. But for different reasons," Larry replied.

They finished their breakfast and worked through a few other logistical challenges and were close to adjourning when Larry made one last request.

"Captain Blackstone, I would like to meet with your crew. Just your crew, including yourself of course, but not the scientists. I need to make sure they understand the situation and that we might be depending upon them in life-or-death circumstances. I want to give them the opportunity to voice any questions or concerns. I also need you to confirm that if conflict breaks out, they understand that command of this ship shifts from you to me. We cannot have two captains in a time of crisis."

"I'll make it happen," Blackstone said, checking the time. "Thirteen hundred?"

"Sounds good. Thank you," affirmed Larry as they rose from the table and carried their plates to the cart left by the steward. He then added, "And thank the cook for the most excellent meal."

The Russian Federation ship announced its presence shortly before noon using the radio frequency set aside for inter-ship communications within the solar system. Larry stood on *Tombaugh*'s bridge with Captain Blackstone, watching the approach of the ship by radar. It was not yet visible to the naked eye. Similar to *Aurora*, *Tombaugh* didn't need many crew members to pilot it. An AI did much of the work. Four crew, not including the captain, usually controlled the *Tombaugh*— the pilot, navigator (Tyler, of course, was on that station), an engineer, and the exec. Though Tyler had risen in Larry's estimation, Tyler's presence still grated on him. The avionics engineer oversaw the operation of all the electronic systems aboard the ship. Larry had rarely interacted with the crew member on that station, a diminutive, quiet woman. Larry learned she happened to be the go-to person for more or less anything aboard ship that stopped working. He couldn't recall her name. Finally, there was Blackstone's exec, Krzysztof Wojciechowski, who everyone called "Chris" because his name was otherwise unpronounceable. Larry hadn't interacted with Chris much, largely because when he met with Blackstone, Chris remained on duty as the captain's stand-in. They met a few times, and Larry knew he was good at his job, and equally important, Blackstone trusted him to make crucial decisions in his absence.

"Greetings to the American Space Force vessel *Aurora* and civilian research vessel *Tombaugh*. This is Commander Arina Morozov of the Russian Federation ship *Nerpa*. We are here to help you with your recent scientific discoveries on Pluto and Charon and will be inserting into orbit around Charon at seventeen hundred, universal time. We will be broadcasting our latest trajectory projection and recommend you do the same if you have any planned maneuvers," she said in English with a hint of a Russian accent. "We then look forward to meeting with Captain Blackstone and the eminent science team of *Tombaugh*."

"Well, she made it clear she doesn't want to meet with Space Force," mused Larry.

"Should I reply?" asked Blackstone.

"Not yet. Let Colonel Ruiz speak first and you can jump in after," replied Larry.

After a short delay, Colonel Ruiz made his reply. "Welcome to Pluto, Commander Morozov. This is Colonel Eduardo Ruiz on the United States Space Force ship *Aurora*. Welcome to Charon. There's quite a bit happening at the moment, and we welcome the extra eyes, ears, and brains to help us figure it out. We will be glad to meet with you."

Larry smiled when Ruiz explicitly inserted himself into the future discussions. He also noticed that Colonel Ruiz made no mention of the artifact found on Pluto. They had to know about it, the news of its finding wasn't a secret, but Larry knew his captain well enough to know he had no intention of offering access to it. He nodded toward Blackstone.

"Commander Morozov, this is Captain Perry Blackstone of *Tombaugh*. Welcome to Pluto. Colonel Ruiz and I, as well as our science team, will be glad to meet with you and your science team at your earliest convenience. May I invite you and your exec to dinner to get things moving? We can go over and agree upon the details."

"Thank you for your kind offer, we accept," she replied.

"We will expect you at docking bay two, say at sixteen hundred?" proposed Blackstone.

"Perfect. Docking bay two. I will see you then. *Nerpa* out," she said, ending the conversation.

"That gives us six hours to prepare what you want to share with them and what you don't," said Blackstone.

"I spoke with Colonel Ruiz, and we plan to tell them everything. Being among the scientists on board *Tombaugh* has reminded me that scientists think differently from Space Force officers in many ways. One of the most significant to us now is scientists do not believe science discoveries should be kept secret. Their culture is one of immediate publication of new data and results, with sharing across international boundaries. From what I can tell, most everything we've learned concerning the Pluto artifact has already been transmitted to Earth. Therefore, available to the Russian Federation and the Chinese. The only thing not yet known at home, at least I don't think so, is what happened last night when we tried to retrieve a microbot. Since it was a Space Force operation, and we do not like to share anything we don't have to, I doubt anyone not on our two ships knows the outcome. The Russians will have expected us to try, and since we don't have a sample for study, they'll put two and two together and figure something went wrong. So, I plan to tell everyone about that also."

"And access to the artifact?" asked Blackstone.

"I've been rethinking that. I don't want to bring it up, but if they request to see it, then we should show it to them. *But* they *cannot* touch it, scan it, or conduct any experiment. Period. We tell them those discussions must be held at a higher level, and we intend to take it back to Earth for further study. We can let the politicians decide what they want to do with it then," replied Larry.

"You are the boss," acceded Blackstone. He sounded very deferential and seemed relieved to not be making decisions regarding the visitors or the artifact; Larry couldn't blame him.

Larry's comm buzzed with a new message from Abigail. She wanted to meet for lunch. He replied with a "yes" and "fifteen minutes."

"Captain, if you need anything else to prepare for tonight's dinner, then let me know. I suggest you reach out to Colonel Ruiz to determine who he plans to bring and for some insight into the protocol of hosting a miliary officer from the Russian Federation. I hope you have some vodka stashed away somewhere," said Larry.

"As a matter of fact, we do. Two bottles," replied Blackstone, smiling.

"This is definitely not a Space Force ship. Now, if you will excuse me, I need to meet someone for lunch," said Larry as he began to walk toward the exit.

"May I join you?" asked Tyler as he walked quickly over and matched stride with Larry. "I'm going off shift and my replacement is on her way."

As if I can say no, thought Larry. If this ship were Space Force, you wouldn't leave your post until after your replacement had arrived. "Of course," he said aloud.

The walk from the bridge to the commons area was quick, and he arrived in five minutes, not fifteen. Abigail already sat at a table, and looked surprised to see Larry walk in with Tyler. She waved them over.

"Care to join me?" asked Abigail, smiling, pointing to her lunch.

"Thanks. We appreciate the invitation," chimed Tyler, jumping in before Larry could respond. Tyler sat next to Abigail, leaving Larry one of the two available chairs on the other side of the table.

"Before I sit down, I'll go collect my lunch," said Larry.

Tyler, as if realizing for the first time that he needed to get his own food, jumped up to join Larry. "Me, too."

Larry collected his food and returned to the table before Tyler. "He invited himself as we left the bridge. I couldn't say no."

Abigail smiled. "Of course, you wouldn't be you if you had. It's all right."

Tyler rejoined them as they began eating.

"I'm glad you are here," said Abigail. "This morning, the thermal output of the hole on Charon increased by twenty percent. Whatever it's doing is already generating waste heat. We think the bots might be building something. We can't see much of anything because they swarm over everything and we can't see through them."

"Any other noticeable change? Neutrino background? Anything?" asked Larry.

"No. Nothing. Until we have more data, that's all we know."

"I spent most of the morning with Captain Blackstone, and he didn't mention this," said Larry.

"That's because I just left the meeting at which we learned of the change. Julie should be briefing him now with same information."

"I think we should try again for one of the critters. Before the Russians or the Chinese do," suggested Tyler. "Returning would give us another opportunity for a closer look."

"That's not a good idea. We came close to losing the *Stingray* and some first-rate guardians trying that last night. I championed the idea, and it came close to killing them. I'm not doing that again," stated Larry.

"We're going to let the Russians get what they want?" accused Tyler, fidgeting with his fork like a magician doing a sleight-of-hand trick and not succeeding.

"If what they want is aligned with what we want, then yes," Larry reasoned.

"I still think we should tell them this discovery is ours."

"And if they don't agree, pack up and go home? What then? How would we enforce this claim?" asked Larry.

"That's why you're here!" replied Tyler.

Larry took a deep breath. "No, we're here because one of your scientists, Dr. Mikelson, decided to go rogue on Pluto, and your captain called for help in finding and retrieving him. No one knew there was an artifact, let alone two, when we arrived."

"But you're here now. You should protect what we found."

"Our first priority is to protect the people on *Tombaugh*. Our next priority comes from Space Command and, quite frankly, I don't know what that is because Colonel Ruiz has not told me," Larry admitted.

"Tyler, this is pointless. Major Randall and the Space Force will protect us and the Pluto artifact if a shooting war breaks out. But it's not fair to ask him or any of his crewmates to place themselves in harm's way merely because we want them to," offered Abigail, obviously trying to diffuse the tension.

Tyler stopped twirling his fork and finished his last few bites of food in silence. Larry and Abigail didn't break the silence either as they, too, finished their meals. Finally, Abigail rose from the table.

"Gentlemen, if you will excuse me, I've got to get back to work," she said.

Larry stood. "Thanks for inviting us over. Keep us posted on the status on Charon."

CHAPTER 14

In the few hours it took for the ship to settle into a parking orbit above charon, the *Nerpa* sent two drones to investigate the activities surrounding the mascon. Both drones flew above the sea of microbots for an hour or so before one of them slowly descended into the hole in which the mysterious construction project was underway. An hour after the second drone disappeared from both *Tombaugh*'s and *Aurora*'s view, the first drone returned to the *Nerpa*. The second one never left the hole in the ice.

The disappearance made Larry think of Mikelson. He had been an ass, was clearly a narcissist, and had many other psychological problems, but he was without question a brilliant and curiosity-driven scientist who didn't deserve to be disassembled to provide raw material for whatever the aliens were building. Though they were unable to determine what happened to him with certainty, it was their best guess and a likely fate given the evidence they had.

Around midafternoon, Captain Blackstone requested Larry join them for dinner with Commander Morozov and her staff. While not unexpected, it cost him time away from closely monitoring what the Russians and the Charon aliens were doing. He'd failed to pack his dress uniform because he didn't think he would need it. Larry considered asking *Aurora* to send it over, but ruled that out as an unnecessary distraction for the crew of both ships. He also considered having

Aurora send it over with Colonel Ruiz, which would mean he would be late for the dinner—also not a promising idea. So, he decided instead to ask Captain Blackstone for a spare set of civilian formal dinner attire in or near his size. There was an extra, which was unsurprising for a ship that also happened to have spare bottles of vodka in storage. *What else do they have lying around?* He, of course, asked Colonel Ruiz if his choice was acceptable and Ruiz agreed. "They'll know you are one of my officers, but looking like a civilian might cause them to underestimate you. That could be a good thing."

Punctually, two CTVs docked with *Tombaugh*. One from the *Nerpa* with Commander Morozov and her executive officer; the other from *Aurora* with Colonel Ruiz and Lieutenant Colonel Nneka Njoku, his director of operations, or DO—*Aurora*'s second-in-command. At five feet, ten inches, Njoku had a strong build and a shaved head, and carried herself with a commanding presence. Larry and Nneka got along okay, if anyone could ever really get along with their DO. Being liked wasn't part of her job description. Making sure the commanding officer's orders were carried out, maintaining crew discipline, training, and keeping the colonel informed and out of trouble was. She did it with a quiet efficiency that garnered everyone's respect. Larry knew, after this deployment, she would almost certainly get assigned a ship of her own. She deserved it. He would serve under her without question, if asked.

Commander Arina Morozov stood at an average height, and exuded a quiet authority and confidence; her piercing blue eyes reflected a keen intellect. Her auburn hair, pulled back in a neat bun, lent her a professional and composed demeanor. Her executive officer was only a little taller than Morozov and, at first glance, looked more like a university professor than a Russian military officer.

Blackstone met each entourage individually and escorted

them to a room Larry had seen on the ship's schematics, but never visited. Labeled "multipurpose," one of the room's evident purposes was to serve as the ship's formal dining hall. A rectangular table topped with china, crystal stemware, and more forks at each place setting than Larry was used to using in a week of meals graced the center of the room. He had been to formal dinners before and knew the protocols, but seeing them aboard a deep-space ship seemed incongruous.

After making formal introductions, they took their assigned seats with Captain Blackstone at the head of the table, Ruiz to his left, Morozov to his right, followed by the XOs of both guest captains and finally, sitting farthest down the table, Larry and Blackstone's XO, Chris Wojciechowski. The seating would allow the commanding officers to chat among themselves and provide an opportunity for the execs and Larry to do the same. The meal was Russian, with borscht and sour cream, pork pirozhki, cheesecake-like pasta, and, of course, vodka.

The conversation began with some polite small talk—families, shipboard life, and careers—but after the main course, it turned to the Russians' reason for coming: the aliens on Charon. Rather than try to join in on the conversation at the head of the table, those at the end of the table began their own.

"So, have you any idea of what the aliens doing down there?" asked First Deputy Oksana Vinogradov, Morozov's exec. She, like her commanding officer, was tall, thin, quite muscular, and sported blond hair cut right below her ears. She looked very . . . Russian.

Chris nodded toward Larry, obviously deferring so as to not say the wrong thing. The two had spoken beforehand and agreed to this approach. It was best for Larry to address questions about the artifact or the Charon aliens, and Chris should only answer a question if asked to do so by Larry.

"No idea. As we explained earlier, we didn't know it was up to anything until the ice collapsed and killed Dr. Mikelson. Shortly after that, the microbots poured out of the hole and began doing whatever it is that they are doing. We've used every instrument we have available to study them, but at this time, we really don't have much more to go on."

"Tell us more of your attempt to retrieve one of them."

"It nearly cost the lives of the *Stingray*'s crew," replied Larry. He knew that Colonel Ruiz shared part of the video showing the disastrous sample return mission, up to and including the risky maneuver that Captain Lloyd-Burns used in order to keep the machines from boarding her ship in an "uncontrolled" manner.

"Perhaps you were too cautious," said Vinogradov.

"Too cautious? In retrospect, had I known how rapidly responsive these machines were, I would never have recommended the idea," Larry contradicted.

"So, it was *yours*, this silly fly-over-and-catch idea? Pah! It was too indirect to ever be successful," Vinogradov replied.

The table had grown quiet, with the commanding officers now listening to the exchange at the other end of it.

"I admit it was risky, but we couldn't think of a safer approach with any chance of success," said Larry.

"That's the problem with you Americans, you and your obsession with safety and risk aversion. These aliens need to know we are serious and that they need to stop whatever they are doing until we establish some sort of communication and determine that they are not hostile. The best way to do that is to capture or kill some of these machines," suggested Vinogradov.

"Which is why we're sending a landing craft to the surface tomorrow to retrieve one or more and, perhaps, communicate with them," interjected Commander Morozov from her end of the table. She paused and scanned the faces of those assembled as if to gauge their reactions before deciding what, if anything, to say next.

"Where are you planning to land?" asked Larry.

"Right outside the edge of the swarm. Three marines will oversee the collection on the crewed lander. Their orders will be to bring one or more of them back to the *Nerpa*, functional or nonfunctional," she replied.

"We don't know how the mascon or the swarm will react if attacked," Colonel Ruiz ventured.

"There's only one way to find out," Commander Morozov replied. "They are up to something, and the sooner we learn of their intentions, the better. Besides, your retrieval effort resulted in two or three of the machines being destroyed. What is the difference?"

Ruiz had no reply.

"Have you considered the risk to the crew of the landing craft and the marines?" asked Larry.

"They know the risks. They are marines!" she exclaimed.

The room fell silent until Chris raised his hand and asked the steward to bring everyone a glass of sherry. The effect was a change in topic.

"So, what about the Pluto artifact? When may we see it?" asked Morozov, looking at Ruiz.

"Anytime you like," Ruiz offered. "Would you like to walk to the containment room after dinner?"

"That would be appreciated. Then we can discuss allowing some of my crew access to study it in more detail," she said.

"Absolutely," Ruiz agreed. "I'll let Captain Blackstone work out those details since his science team recovered it. It's in his care until returning to Earth for study."

"I'll ask Dr. Julie Bridenstein to meet us at the artifact so you can meet her. She can provide you with a summary of what we know and be the point of contact for your study team," said Blackstone, following Ruiz's lead. Making it clear that the Pluto artifact was in civilian hands, not Space Force's, would hopefully alleviate some tension and suspicion on the part of the Russians.

"Do you intend to allow similar access to our Chinese friends who will soon be arriving?" asked Morozov.

"Of course," agreed Blackstone. "But not all at once. I hope we can work out a schedule that allows access for your team and any the Chinese may send, but I don't want it to turn into chaos."

"What do you know of the Chinese ship?" asked Ruiz. "Have you spoken with the commander?"

"No. All I know is that they will arrive the day after tomorrow. I would like to achieve as much as we can before they get here," she said in reply.

Clearly the impending arrival of the Chinese didn't please Commander Morozov. She also didn't like the fact that the two American ships were already there, but she could do nothing about it, nor could she stop the Chinese from arriving.

The dinner concluded with a tour of the lab where the Pluto artifact was stored. Each member of the tour group could see the live image of the artifact from inside its vacuum chamber, but they all wanted to see it with their own eyes by peering through the small glass-covered porthole to the chamber's right. As it had since they first discovered it, the artifact sat there emitting neutrinos with its regular antimatter annihilation, showing no signs it perceived its move or the existence of its observers.

As the CTVs departed carrying the Russians back to the *Nerpa* and Colonel Ruiz back to *Aurora*, Larry's comm buzzed. He had a message from Abigail. She wanted to meet for a drink and hear what transpired during the dinner. Larry smiled. Though it was late, he felt too keyed up to sleep and welcomed the distraction. Talking about what happened to someone not in his chain of command would help. They agreed to meet in the commons area.

When Larry entered, he heard a wolf whistle and realized it came from Abigail, who sat at a table in the back corner. She held up two beer bottles, one in each hand, and motioned him to come over. At first, he wondered why she whistled, then he realized he still wore his formal attire. He had, after all, just come from the small-scale equivalent of a state dinner.

"Nice outfit," Abigail quipped, smiling. "I trust the food was good?" She handed him a beer.

"Thanks, I guess I should have changed afterward, but I didn't think to. I'll need to get these cleaned so I can return them to Captain Blackstone." He then noticed Abigail had gone completely casual. She no longer wore her usual jumpsuit, but instead sported a loose-fitting V-neck blouse and pants. She looked good. Too good. Wearing a jumpsuit, she looked like a generic scientist. She didn't look generic now, and he felt more than a little uncomfortable.

"Tell me about the Russians," Abigail requested. "Was it like in the vids? You know, did their commander wear a uniform filled with ribbons and medals, drink everyone else under the table, and then talk you into giving her and her crew everything she wants?"

"Yes, and no," Larry laughed. "Yes, she did like her drinks and was extremely disappointed when we ran out of vodka. Yes, they asked for a lot, but none of the things they asked for were unreasonable, and no, her uniform only had her ranks and, at most, two or three other ribbons. She seems reasonable enough, but also all too eager to place the lives of her crew in danger." He described their plans for a sample retrieval in the morning.

"I'll make sure we have all our instruments trained on them when they make their attempt. If we see the mascon or anything else react to their presence, we'll sound the alarm as best we can," she offered.

"I'm sure they'll be watching everything too. As will Colonel Ruiz. I just hope they don't get anyone killed or begin an interstellar war," Larry stated flatly. In his mind, an interstellar war was not beyond the possible. They had no idea how an ancient alien civilization, one that could travel between the stars, doing so before humans existed, might react to them. They might very well trigger a conflict without even knowing they were doing so.

As they finished their beer, Larry noticed they had leaned in to each other to be heard above the din of voices in the room. He felt her knee against his under the table. He knew he should move away, but he didn't. They were in "flow," and he didn't want to break the connection. He hadn't felt this connected to someone since he met Athena. For some reason, thinking momentarily of his wife didn't cause him to move away or feel the usual guilt. Perhaps it was the alcohol. Maybe it was the fact that he knew deep in his soul that conflict with the Russians, the Chinese, or aliens would soon be upon them, and the resulting hormones clouded his judgment. Regardless, he wasn't going to disrupt the moment. He needed it and he sensed Abigail did, too.

At close to 2300, he realized he needed to get some sleep. Exhaustion simply fell on him.

"Abigail, I need to get some sleep. Tomorrow will come early, and I suspect it'll be an event-filled day. I need to be fresh," Larry said as he moved away from Abigail and stood.

"You're right, we better go," she agreed.

"Goodnight," Larry replied, but then stopped. They stood looking at each other without saying a word, letting their eyes speak volumes.

Finally, Abigail broke eye contact with, "Goodnight."

Larry made his way to his cabin, took off his dress clothes and went straight for a cold shower.

For the first night in a long time, he didn't check for messages from Athena. In fact, he didn't think of her at all.

Morning came quickly.

When Larry woke, he remembered what he had forgotten the night before—to check for messages from Athena. He didn't have much time before he was due on the bridge, but his conscience wouldn't let him skip replaying the two messages from home. The first was an adorable video of Caleb and Joshua riding a horse somewhere in Kentucky near where his parents were looking for a house. He had forgotten Athena planned a visit there this week. They were growing so fast. Seeing how much they had changed since the last time he saw them made him regret signing up for another deep-space deployment. Athena had insisted, knowing what it would do for his Space Force career. She said that a year away would be worth it and not to worry, she would be there for him when he returned. He played the video twice and then went to the second message.

This one was from Athena. In it, she went through all the details describing his parents' house search and a bit about how much she missed him.

For the first time since his deployment, he didn't know what to do. If he replied now, he would be rushed and come across as either not caring or hiding something—or so he imagined. If he waited until he had more time, he would be better able to compose his thoughts, and hopefully, have a clearer head regarding last night's events—those that did and didn't happen. He didn't feel guilty; he felt conflicted.

After staring at the screen and feeling morose, he finished his morning routine a little after 0600 and was at breakfast by 0630. By 0700 he stood on the bridge with Captain Blackstone watching the landing craft depart the *Nerpa* for Charon. The Russians wasted no time. There was still no word from the Chinese ship that now appeared on long-range radar and on a trajectory that should have them in orbit by this time tomorrow.

Both *Tombaugh* and *Aurora* trained their telescopes on the lander as it made its descent. At this distance, they would be able to see the crew on the surface and make out individual microbots with each orbital pass. *Aurora* deployed multiple reconnaissance satellites with marginally less capable imagery for use when the primary ships were not in line of sight, but good enough to give them a real-time view of what happened below. In addition to launching relay satellites, the Russians deployed two drones to hover overhead and provide continuous visual coverage.

The Russian lander set down one-fourth of a kilometer from the edge of the swarm. As Larry watched, he noticed the pace of the microbots' movement had slowed. Several had even stopped.

"Dr. Bridenstein, when did the movement of the microbots change and why wasn't I alerted?" he asked.

"The observation team noticed the slowdown around two thirty last night. They alerted me and since nothing else had changed, I made the decision to wait until morning to tell you," she replied.

"But you didn't. I had to ask," Larry clipped out, his impatience growing.

"The Russians' activity got ahead of me, and for that, I apologize. I planned to let you know and, well, I got carried away watching the events unfold," she explained. "It won't happen again."

They're civilians, scientists, not in your chain of command. They think differently. Let it go. Larry took a couple deep breaths to calm himself. She got the message, and he doubted she would delay telling him valuable information again.

"Thank you. Something like that might have an importance that you and your team do not realize and someone else might," he said, turning his attention back to the screen showing the Russian lander. As he watched, the hatch opened and three suited figures emerged, two carrying boxes with handles. Larry surmised those were the collection boxes into which any microbot they retrieved would be placed. They were also armed. Two of the marines—he assumed Russian marines—carried rifles or machine guns slung over their shoulders, he couldn't tell with the resolution available, and the third carried what looked a good deal like a shoulder-fire rocket launcher. *If you have a hammer, you will find something to nail . . .*

They loped across Charon's surface with long, skipping strides impossible in Earth gravity. At first, their movement was jerky and clumsy. By the time they neared the edge of the swarm, they appeared to have the hang of it.

It was difficult to tell what they were doing, but the marines carrying the boxes set them down on the surface and began rummaging through their contents. One of the marines pulled out what looked like a dogcatcher's Ketch-All pole.

The marine with the Ketch-All pole walked toward the swarm while the other two raised their weapons to cover the third as he/she made an attempt to grab one of the microbots. The marine came as close as possible and stopped at the maximum reach distance allowed by the pole. The Russian slowly lowered the pole toward the now slow-moving flow of microbots and looped the rope around the front part of one. The machines had no "head" or tail to reference. They had a segmented body with six legs evenly spaced, three on each side.

After a few failed attempts, the Russian successfully caught one, lifting it above the flow of machines and slowly bringing it back where the other two Russians waited. Larry was beginning to believe they might pull it off. The machine struggled against the rope as the marine lowered it toward the box. Without warning, the rope broke. It wasn't clear how, but Larry would be willing to bet the microbot cut it.

The marine jumped back, but he was not fast enough. The rat-sized machine latched onto his boot and began crawling up his leg. The other two marines reacted. The one holding the rocket launcher placed it on the ground to free his hands to remove the microbot from his comrade's suit. He rushed over to grasp the machine, but the marine to which the machine was attached started thrashing.

Julie gasped. "It's penetrated his suit. He's decompressing."

The marine was clearly panicked, even though his suit would be able to seal off the breached area before the entire suit lost pressure. If, that is, Russian suits were designed similarly to their own. The second marine finally grabbed the machine. Larry and everyone watching saw the edge of the swarm start to move toward them.

"Get out of there," Larry said aloud to no one in particular, voicing what everyone thought.

The two struggling marines didn't notice the swarm's movement, but the third did. That, or someone aboard the *Nerpa* alerted him. Larry imagined the chaos of the moment and shuddered.

The marine ran over, grabbed the rocket launcher, took aim at the leading edge of the swarm, and fired. Given that the swarm was a few tens of meters away, the rocket hit the swarm almost instantaneously. The marine had fired it to impact behind the leading edge in the hope of minimizing the risk of injury to himself and his colleagues and maximizing the number of microbots destroyed.

The rocket detonated in a flash, blowing microbots into the sky, including those on the leading edge. The rest continued to surge forward. The leading edge overran the two closest marines. They hit the ground, flailing. Larry imagined their suits being breached as they fell.

The third marine ran toward the lander. The low gravity allowed him to run faster than the swarm, each stride covering much ground. He might get to the lander before the swarm arrived.

Then one of the Russian drones launched a missile. It took a bit longer to reach the swarm than the shoulder-fired rocket, due to the greater distance, but the end effect was every bit as spectacular. Instead of dozens of microbots being destroyed, hundreds, perhaps a thousand, sprayed into the air.

The marine reached the lander and entered the airlock. The swarm, thinned in number, flowed to the lander.

"Go, go, go," Larry urged. He felt helpless watching. A man's life would depend upon how rapidly he could launch the lander.

Moments after entering, its engines ignited. Like the American landers, the Russian lander appeared to have remote control capabilities, and the operators on the *Nerpa* didn't hesitate. As soon as their marine boarded, it lifted off. The lander rose as the swarm arrived. As it ascended, individual microbots climbed atop each other at a pace that astonished Larry. They tried to build a tower of themselves to reach the slowly ascending lander. They failed. The main propulsion system of the Russian lander kicked in, lifting it safely to space.

"Thank God," Julie gasped out.

"Yeah," said Larry. "They were warned."

Larry's comm buzzed. It was *Aurora*. They had sounded general quarters.

Larry turned. "Captain Blackstone, *Aurora* has sounded general quarters. Colonel Ruiz is probably doing this as a precaution in case the aliens do something in response to the Russians. I'm taking temporary command of *Tombaugh* for the duration of the action."

"The ship is yours," confirmed Blackstone.

"Mr. Romans, get us to a higher orbit as quickly as you can. Dr. Bridenstein, please alert your science team that I am in command until further notice. Have them keep a watch on the swarm and alert me if there any changes, no matter how insignificant they may seem."

"You can count on my team, Dr. Randall. We will do our part," she said.

Larry forced a smile as he nodded his head, dismissing her.

"Both the *Nerpa* and *Aurora* are boosting as well," said Blackstone, who now assumed the role of being Larry's second-in-command. Larry was pleased and impressed. Blackstone knew what he needed to do and began doing it. Some civilian captains would have given lip service to the plan shifting to military control of their ship, complaining or resenting it when the moment came. Not Blackstone.

"Keep us well away from both ships and in a slightly higher orbit, Mr. Romans."

Tyler looked toward Blackstone when Larry gave the command and did not act until Blackstone nodded his head.

The boost began.

"Mr. Romans, do you have a problem following my orders?" asked Larry.

"Excuse me?" said Tyler, looking first at Larry and then again at Blackstone.

"Let me repeat myself: do you have a problem following my orders? The time you take to look at and get confirmation from Captain Blackstone before executing my orders could get us killed. *Do you understand?* Your captain has ceded command to me until this crisis is over and if you cannot carry out my orders you will be relieved of your duties and confined to your cabin. Is that clear?"

"Uh, yes, uh . . . sir," Tyler responded, looking defiant but turning his attention back to his work console and adjusting their planned orbit to the one Larry required.

"Major Randall. Sir," interjected the avionics engineer on console. Larry tried to recall his name, but could not.

"Yes?" asked Larry.

"It's the Chinese ship," he said hesitantly.

Great timing, thought Larry. "Put it on the speaker."

"This is Commander Jun Liang of the People's Liberation Navy ship *Yancheng*, sending greetings to the ships *Nerpa*, *Aurora*, and *Tombaugh*. We should be in orbit around Pluto within six hours. It will be an honor working with you as representatives of the world in uncovering the secrets of the alien artifacts now in the possession of humanity."

"'In the possession of humanity,' my ass," muttered Larry.

"Sir?" asked the engineer.

"Nothing. Captain Blackstone, he expects a reply from you, not me," said Larry.

"I'll wait on *Aurora* to respond before I do, just like before," replied Blackstone.

"I concur," said Larry. "While you take care of pleasantries, I need an update on what the microbots are doing." He changed channels on his comm to the one used by Julie.

"Dr. Bridenstein, this is Larry Randall, has the surface situation on Charon changed?" he asked.

"Nothing since the lander left for the *Nerpa*. The swarm overran the destroyed microbots, and they appear to have been disassembled. Other than that, they haven't sped up or slowed down, and whatever they're building in the hole is almost three meters taller than yesterday. We still have no idea what it is."

"Keep me informed," requested Larry.

"Sir," said the avionics engineer, getting Larry's attention.

"Yes? What now?" Larry replied.

"The *Nerpa* says they won't be sending their science team over today after all, sir."

"Hmm," he mumbled. *Unsurprising, they lost two crew*

members and attacked aliens who may consider that action the first salvo in an interstellar war.

By evening, a total of four Earth ships, from global powers vying for an edge, orbited either Pluto or Charon, along with multiple relay and observation satellites and a handful of drones. Clearly, no group trusted the other and intership communication was mostly relegated to traffic management to make sure none of their equipment collided or was accidentally shot down. No one wanted a misunderstanding or an accident. The Chinese made no further effort to contact either *Aurora* or *Tombaugh*.

Since nothing further had happened and the aliens on Charon showed no indications of hostility, Larry ceded command back to Captain Blackstone, ate a quick supper, and went to his quarters to update his personal log, reply to his wife, and try to not think of Russians, Chinese, aliens, or Abigail. He needed "Larry time."

He got it, and a mostly restful night's sleep.

CHAPTER 15

mikelson tried every trick he could think of, and
since he had access to the ship's computer
system, the depth and breadth of available possibilities was
considerable, yet nothing worked. As soon as the ship from
the Russian Federation established communications with
Tombaugh, he was there, trying to embed code in *Tombaugh*'s
transmissions to slowly penetrate their ship's firewalls and
replicate himself, or at least important parts of himself, in
their systems. So far, he had been thwarted in every attempt.
They were good, which shouldn't have surprised him. Russia
had a reputation for having one of the most advanced cyber
capabilities in the solar system. Their expertise in cybercrime
went all the way back to the early twenty-first century. He
was blocked, blocked, and blocked again.

Taking control of *Tombaugh* had been relatively easy. Of
course, he accessed the ship's systems from inside the firewall.
Initially using a trusted account made the task seem trivial.
They detected his efforts and almost succeeded in purging
him from the computers until his other self traveled to the
surface. He stopped all cyber activities to make them think
the penetrations came solely from the XA-1. He succeeded
and his renewed activities had, so far, gone undetected.

He briefly considered taking over the systems on *Aurora*
and decided against it. If they detected his efforts, especially
before the arrival of the Russian and Chinese ships, the

source of the potential attempts would be clear—and disastrous. They would know he still existed in the *Tombaugh* network and begin looking for him, purging him, killing him. He couldn't allow that, and he therefore couldn't attempt to hack and take control of *Aurora*.

He would, however, keep trying to access the Russian ship. If they detected him, and they might have already done so, then they would logically assume attempted espionage on the part of the Americans. Something they expect and accept as part of the game. They probably wouldn't even mention such routine behavior. In short, he had nothing to lose by trying.

Now that the Chinese had arrived, he decided he might as well try hacking into their systems. He prepared his first wave of cyber tricks in anticipation of the next two-way communications event that was bound to happen soon.

What was that?

Mikelson thought he heard something. Of course, without ears or any auditory system, he defined hearing differently for himself now. The "sound" was a mere blip in his thought stream. A thought disruption with no obvious source. What, exactly, did he hear? His name, perhaps? No, something more akin to what he would call himself when deep in thought. No, that wasn't it either.

Had he been discovered? Perhaps someone in the crew was trying to reach out to him? Major Randall perhaps? Or the incompetent Dr. Bridenstein? No. The sound didn't come from any ship input he could detect. Had the Russians infected him during his hacking attempts? Possible. Maybe even likely. He ran his antiviral and malware subroutines and found nothing. He had not yet tried to hack the Chinese, so it couldn't be them. Besides, the scan he ran would have found any malware in his system, American, Russian, or Chinese.

He wrote it off as some glitch in the ship's electronics. Perhaps some relay was going bad, or an errant cosmic ray flipped a few more bits than the statistical algorithms could predict and correct for. There were many possible explanations, but it still bothered him. *No one likes hearing things.*

The next day started with a bang.

Larry arrived at the bridge awake, alert, refreshed, cup of coffee in hand, ready to take on the day. Same day shift on the console as yesterday, only today Larry knew the avionics engineer's name—David Jeong, from Evanston, Illinois, graduated University of Illinois at Urbana-Champaign. He didn't like not knowing the names of people he might be commanding, and accessing the records to find his name was one of the last things Larry did before falling asleep.

Blackstone sat stiffly in the captain's chair, also with coffee cup in hand. Tyler was again at navigation, and Larry couldn't miss the man's glare as he entered the bridge. If this were the *Aurora*, then Larry would have relieved Tyler of his duties for it. He couldn't imagine any of *Aurora*'s crew doing anything similar. But this wasn't *Aurora*, Tyler was not military, and the insolent man was good at his job.

"Dr. Randall, welcome back. It's been quiet so far. I received an observational update from Dr. Bridenstein and, as far as we can tell, the activities of the microbots on the surface have not significantly changed. If anything, the slowdown has continued, but, if so, not by very much. No additional heat or radiation sources. Nothing new," said Blackstone.

"What are our Russian and Chinese friends up to?" asked Larry.

"No contact from either one, though the Chinese have been busy. They left Pluto's orbit and joined us here at Charon. We're all one hundred twenty degrees out of phase, so that between the three of us, someone has the mascon area in direct view. They've also repositioned two of their drones to circle the mascon below orbital altitude. I don't know if they know what happened to the Russians; they haven't asked," Blackstone added.

Larry looked at the orbital display and made mental notes of where the various ships deployed their assets, the type, and what he remembered about each from his last foreign asset briefing. From what he knew of the ships and their complement of deployable vehicles, he wouldn't trade the capabilities of *Aurora* for any of them. Not that they weren't formidable and dangerous, but in a one-on-one engagement, they weren't as dangerous as the Space Force ship. A two-on-one engagement would be a different situation entirely, and he deeply hoped such was not their collective future.

"Captain Blackstone, we are receiving a message from the *Yancheng*," announced Mr. Jeong.

"Put it on speaker," said Blackstone.

". . . be docking with *Tombaugh* at zero ten hundred with a team of three scientists. We trust they will be granted free and unfettered access to the Pluto artifact for inspection and observation. We also anticipate that the crew of *Tombaugh* will provide complete and total access to the results of all scientific investigations of the artifact, either by a holocube or by transmitting such to the *Yancheng* by eighteen hundred today. Please reply to let us know at which port we should dock." Commander Liang delivered the message in a manner that sounded like an ultimatum or something a victor might say to a vanquished or captured opponent as a demand for surrender.

"My, aren't we friendly today," Larry offered in a faint voice.

"I don't particularly like her tone," groused Blackstone. "She had but to ask."

"Can we be ready to entertain guests by their planned arrival?" asked Larry.

"Yes, we've been ready since yesterday. I'll alert Dr. Bridenstein and her team." Blackstone moved to do so.

"I'll reach out to Colonel Ruiz and request a few security officers in the event their three scientists are other than what they claim. Even if they look like scientists, knowing how the Chinese operate, I would bet at least one will be a marine or some sort of security," observed Larry.

"Won't a show a force be incendiary?" asked Blackstone.

"Hopefully, no. I believe having them nearby, standing around looking menacing should do the trick," Larry replied.

"How does this jive with your earlier plan to surrender and not fight?" asked Blackstone.

"I said we would *not* fight; I didn't say we wouldn't look *ready* to fight. Sometimes deterrence works fine."

"Uh, Captain Blackstone, now the Russians are calling," said Jeong.

"Put them on," Blackstone sighed.

"Good morning, Captain Blackstone. We would like to take you up on your offer to allow our scientists to view the artifact. I regret that circumstances yesterday prevented us from beginning our studies. Would a party of four arriving at ten hundred hours be acceptable?" asked Commander Morozov. Unlike Commander Liang, she smiled.

Larry nodded toward Blackstone, an encouragement to accept the request.

"Commander Morozov, we would be delighted to have your scientists come aboard. Unfortunately, please use port two for docking at ten hundred thirty, if possible. Our Chinese colleagues requested to come over at ten hundred and will be using port one," replied Blackstone.

"It should be an interesting day," quipped Morozov. "Hopefully not as in the Chinese curse," she added, her small smile breaking into a grin.

Larry contrasted the quite different approaches of the two captains. One first sought to break bread, drink vodka, and socialize before requesting access to the artifact. He had no doubt her request would have turned into a command had the request been declined, but it had not, and her demeanor remained convivial. The other sought to show her dominance and softly threaten compliance in granting access. Both achieved the same ends, and he could trust neither. He however much preferred the semblance of civility displayed by the Russian.

"It's beginning to look like a conference instead of a meeting," Blackstone noted.

"Yep, it's going to be an interesting day." Larry opened a channel to Colonel Ruiz to bring him up to speed on their soon-to-arrive visitors and that Blackstone's desire to not have all the visitors on board at the same time was now moot.

The security officers arrived from *Aurora* thirty minutes before the planned arrival of the Chinese. Larry knew them all by name, and he was pleased to see that Colonel Ruiz had sent not only a first-rate security team—none were to be trifled with—but that he also placed Master Sergeant Whitman in charge. Larry first saw a demonstration of her abilities during shore leave at Phobos base when a couple of enlisted got into a row with some jarheads at a bar outside the base in the civilian sector. She walked between the two groups, moments from coming to blows, and explained what would happen should they continue and have a fight. Without blinking, and with a calm insistence and feminine disappointment, she stared down a marine who outmuscled her by two to one and got him and his buddies to stand down. Larry had not been there in person, but he reviewed the video of the incident to help determine if the specialists involved would be given disciplinary action under Article 15. After reviewing the video, he recommended against it and requested an informal commendation be placed in Whitman's personnel file. Colonel Ruiz knew of Larry's respect for her and had no doubt that was one of the reasons she had been selected.

"Master Sergeant, welcome to *Tombaugh*," said Larry, trying hard not to smile. He was relieved and glad to see that Ruiz had sent her, but he could not break decorum.

"Thank you, sir. How would you like this handled, sir?" she asked.

"Having you and your team waiting outside the airlock on the far end of the hall when the Chinese disembark will send the right message. Unless you see weapons, keep yours out of sight, but within easy reach. I want you to look capable and ready to act, but not eager to do so."

"Yes, sir. Understood. Do we follow the Chinese team to the lab?" she asked.

"Yes, but at a distance. When the Russians arrive, I would like three of you to return to the docking bay for the same dog and pony show while the other two remain with the Chinese. Remember, unless there is an overtly hostile act, do nothing. If these are really scientists, then they have their own culture and perception of rank, authority, and protocol that transcends national boundaries. To be blunt, scientists are sometimes themselves an alien culture. That said, if any of our team appears to be in distress, then find out what's happening and use your own judgment unless I give explicit direction. Understood?"

"Understood, sir."

"Good, let's get to airlock one so we can properly greet our guests," suggested Larry.

The Chinese transfer vehicle used the same universal docking adapter spacefaring countries and settlements standardized several years ago to facilitate situations like this and in case of emergencies. As expected, less than ten minutes after a flawless docking, three men and one woman emerged from the airlock. All wore identical blue coveralls. One of the men, the tallest, stepped forward and introduced himself to Captain Blackstone, who headed the greeting party. Behind and on his right was Julie Bridenstein. Larry also stood slightly behind him to his left.

"Greetings. I am Professor Yǔxuān Xie, and my associates Professor Hàoyǔ Wen, and Professor Hàorán Cao." Gesturing toward the only woman in the group, he added, "This is our pilot, Lieutenant Huang." Xie spoke flawless American English with a slight northeastern accent. Larry guessed he had studied at Harvard, MIT, or BU. The others said nothing; they just nodded as they were introduced.

Blackstone introduced his team, using Larry's academic credentials instead of his Space Force rank. They discussed this beforehand and decided it was best for them to think of him as another academic. Of course, if their intelligence services were as good as they thought, they probably knew all about him, right down to his preferred underwear color. He didn't introduce the security team and didn't need to. It was obvious who they were, and they barely got a glance from Xie—but Lieutenant Huang noticed them. She stared, no doubt sizing each up.

"Please take us to the artifact you are bringing back to the world for study," asked Xie, continuing to assert that the artifact did not belong to the U.S.A. The crew of *Tombaugh* was international in nature and no one there had given any thought to national appropriation. The Chinese assumed otherwise because the ship flew an American flag. They also probably couldn't conceive of sponsoring a comparable international science mission without having some overt Chinese claim to whatever was learned or found.

Blackstone led the way to the artifact's laboratory. When

they entered, more members of the science team waited, including Abigail, Maja Lewandowski, and Lorena Campos. Two security officers took their positions near the back of the room and the other three near the door. Huang never let them leave her sight.

Once introduced to the *Tombaugh* scientists, the three Chinese began asking questions, lots of questions, on topics ranging from isotopic concentrations and metamaterials to pion decay and more. In a few minutes, Larry could tell from the dialog that the Chinese visitors were really scientists or they had considerable science training. Larry was relieved, but with Huang present, he wasn't planning to let his guard down.

"If you will excuse us, Captain Blackstone and I need to greet our Russian visitors," said Larry. The only one who acknowledged him was Lieutenant Huang. The scientists had clearly entered their own world, and he was conflicted. Part of him wanted to be part of the science discussion, badly, but another part knew his duties in Space Force took priority. Sometimes he wished he could be cloned.

The arrival of the Russian scientists was reminiscent of that of the Chinese, with different demographics. All four of the Russians were male and two, perhaps three, of them didn't look like scientists. They had the age, physique, haircut, and demeanor that said "special forces."

"Welcome aboard," Blackstone greeted them, putting his right hand forward for a handshake with the man who exited the airlock first. He looked like the polar opposite of a model for a military recruiting poster. Diminutive, perhaps no more than five and half feet tall, he was extremely skinny.

"Captain Blackstone. It's nice to meet you. I'm Vadim Orlov from the Lomonosov Moscow State University. I have an expertise in low-temperature physics. My colleagues are Professor Kiril Vasiliev, particle physicist, Professor Ilya Baranov, astrobiologist, and Daniil Petrov, our pilot," he said, pointing to the three other men, one after the other. "Thank you for allowing us view the Pluto artifact."

Blackstone shook hands and introduced Larry, once again intentionally omitting the three security team members, standing near the door.

"Let's go to the artifact. The Chinese scientists arrived a few minutes ago and are already in the lab asking lots of questions of our science team," said Blackstone, waving them toward the door.

As they departed, Blackstone paused. "Perhaps we can arrange someplace your pilot and the Chinese pilot might find more to their liking, and more comfortable, than a scientific debate in the laboratory—perhaps our commons area? We have coffee, tea, and some snacks there."

"Thank you, but I respectfully decline. I'm excited to see the artifact, and I need to remain with the science team," Petrov replied. Both he and Orlov had thick, though understandable, accents. They had clearly studied British English.

"Very well," said Blackstone, resuming the walk toward the lab.

On their arrival, it took mere minutes for the Russian scientists to join in the banter and become oblivious to the world around them. The five members of the security team stood at various spots in the room. Blackstone eyed Larry and they both retreated into the corridor.

"I'm going back to be with my team. Do you need anything else here?" Blackstone asked.

"No. I think we're good. I'll join the scientists for a while, then I'll find you to bring you up to speed," said Larry. He welcomed the opportunity to reengage with the study of the artifact and perhaps hear some new perspectives. "You can tell Colonel Ruiz that it looks like our visitors are mostly scientists after all. We'll still be vigilant, but this bunch doesn't strike me as a threat."

After an exhausting six hours, the day drew to a close with Larry, Dr. Bridenstein, and the security team escorting their visitors back to their respective transfer vehicles so they could return to their ships.

"Thank you for a most productive day," said Professor Xie. "We plan to return tomorrow around the same time."

That's presumptuous of you, thought Larry, but he said, "Of course. I'm sure our team is already looking forward to the discussions."

After they left, Larry ordered a complete sweep of every inch of the ship the visitors had contact with, including the restrooms and the break room, to assure that no unwanted electronics or other devices had been left behind. They found nothing.

But Aaron Mikelson did. He found two things.

The first had been hidden by the Russians, the pilot specifically, during lunch. It had no radio frequency emissions; hence why the security team's search failed to find it. Mikelson saw it being placed under the food service counter not far from the table at which Julie sat during their lunch. The pilot placed it there assuming, correctly, that Julie favored that particular table for her meals. Clever. People are creatures of habit. It would clearly have proximity to some important conversations. Mikelson suspected it would only power up after it had collected data to be transmitted. All this, of course, was merely a guess. There was no evidence that the object was a data recorder or transmitter. Mikelson would have done the same, but it might also be a miniature explosive or something equally sinister. It was difficult to tell with not much data.

Professor Hàorán Cao placed the second in the laboratory near the artifact in a bold move. He attached whatever it was to the bottom of the vacuum chamber holding the artifact. It too, remained radio quiet, but that did not explain why the security sweep didn't find it. This one puzzled him. The lab was not quiet. Even at slow times, researchers gathered there to plan the next series of tests or discuss their personal lives, which Mikelson found both boring and enlightening—he had no idea how much his reproductive system had driven him when he had been in human form. It came close to making him feel sorry for them.

What?

There it was again. A voice. No, that's not right. He felt a presence other than himself. He rapidly scanned the ship's systems, checking for any anomalous radio signals or high-energy radiation that could flip some of his bits in digital memory—anything at all unusual. Nothing. The ship, his new body, sensed nothing that showed in a physical way, yet he knew he could feel someone, or something, close, like he was eavesdropping on someone far enough away to know they were speaking, but not understand the words being spoken.

Now, it was quiet. The voice stopped. He was again alone. Curious and eager to find out more about what he sensed, he also felt uneasy. He didn't like the idea that his systems, his brain, had been penetrated by anything. Especially by something of which he knew nothing.

The insistent knocking on his cabin door jolted Larry from a deep sleep. At first, he couldn't tell if the knocking was part of a lucid dream or real. As he snapped into full consciousness, he realized it was someone at the door. He leaped from bed, and since he wore boxers and a T-shirt to bed, he didn't bother getting his robe before answering the door. He noted it was right after 0300. Julie Bridenstein stood on the other side of the door.

"Larry, we need you in the commons area. The Charon artifact is doing something new, and you need to see it," she implored, barely glancing at him. "We sent you a message but were afraid you wouldn't see it. We're not in any immediate danger, at least we don't believe so, so we didn't ask for an emergency alert. That would have panicked everyone."

"I'll be there in less than ten minutes. Have you alerted Captain Blackstone?" Larry asked.

"Yes. Janneke's doing that now," she replied.

"I'll inform Colonel Ruiz."

Larry noticed Julie glance furtively over his shoulder and into the room behind him.

"Is there something else I can help you with?" asked Larry, wondering what she was looking for.

"No, er, nothing. That's all," she stuttered, looking embarrassed. "I'll see you in a few minutes,"

Larry didn't watch her depart as he quickly closed the door and headed for the bathroom. He couldn't say for sure, but he thought she might have been looking to see if anyone was there with him. Looking for Abigail was his guess. He wondered what rumors were being spread and grew worried. *That's not good. Not good at all.*

He arrived at a more or less full commons room. Every scientist on the ship seemed to be present, as well as many of the crew not on duty at the time. On the screen displayed a close-up view of the crater and its surrounding area. The swarms of microbots were no longer in the crater and instead ran in various directions around it. He noticed they had dramatically increased their roaming range and several small groups were moving out radially yet further still. Larry half expected the mascon's minions to have built a replica of the

Eiffel Tower, the Pyramid of Giza, or some other immediately recognizable imitation of something terrestrial. What filled the screen was most definitely not something readily recognizable.

What they saw was an irregular, asymmetric structure with ellipsoid bulges, square and rectangular protrusions, and a tower of at least thirty meters standing on the top, slightly offset from the object's visual center.

"May I have your attention, please?" announced Julie, loudly. "We and *Aurora* are imaging this thing in every conceivable way—hyperspectral, SAR, the works. I'm sending the real-time and post-processed data to the central storage site for everyone to access. I'm overlaying on the visual the dimension of the object, including its height."

"What of the mascon?" Abigail asked as she walked through the crowd with Kinia Kekoa toward Larry.

"It's still there, buried somewhere inside or under the structure. It's not yet clear where exactly," she replied.

"Excuse me, Dr. Bridenstein." Larry raised his hand as he spoke, not waiting for her to notice his hand among the many raised. "Colonel Ruiz recommends, and I insist, that we share this data with both the *Nerpa* and *Yancheng*."

"I'm glad to hear that, Larry. That was the consensus among the leadership team."

Captain Blackstone's face appeared on the front viewscreen, and his voice boomed over the intercom. He was clearly on the bridge, where he should be during this time of uncertainty, listening to the discussion taking place in the commons room. "I'll send them the same feed we're sending *Aurora*, is that okay?"

"Yes, thank you, Captain." Larry knew there would be no better way to sow mistrust than keeping something like this secret. He knew what he would think if he had been on one of their ships faced with the same set of circumstances.

"Hi," said Abigail, now beside him.

"Good early morning," said Larry to her and Kinia. As he spoke, he noticed how nice Abigail looked with her hair tousled from sleep. Like him, she hadn't taken the time for her usual morning routine. He realized he was staring, so he shifted his eyes to Kinia and gave her the same welcome.

All three had brought their individual datapads and now searched the database for the latest information that might hold a clue concerning recent events. Larry quickly scanned the thermal images and noticed the structure now generated considerable heat—enough to begin sublimating a bit of the ice wall surrounding the crater. Electron neutrino emissions had also increased, indicating a nuclear fusion reaction happening somewhere in the artificial structure below them.

"Look at the microbots!" someone in the crowd exclaimed. Practically everyone, including Larry, looked up at the screen display.

More microbots poured out of the crater—thousands of them. As new ones emerged, those on the crater's periphery began moving outward, making the undulating blanket of machines appear alive.

"At this rate, they might overrun the moon," noted Kinia.

"I tend to agree. Their growth in numbers has not been quite exponential, but it's high," added Abigail.

No one said anything as they stared at the screen watching the flow of microbots spread across the surface. It was mesmerizing and unsettling at the same time.

"There are at least two new types of machines," interjected Karlina Haugen as she stood from her seat and walked to the front of the room. "Dr. Bridenstein, may I?"

"Of course," replied Julie as she moved to the side of the display.

Karlina tapped furiously at her datapad and the image on

the screen vanished, to be replaced with two still images of what were, presumably, the new microbot types. One was small, the scale marker on the screen indicating that it was less than one centimeter in size and the other was much larger, easily five centimeters across. The larger had six legs and two sets of end effectors. Not pincers, though Larry kept trying to compare them to something familiar. Each end effector had three "fingers" and many carried clumps of unidentifiable material. The smaller bots had six legs, but no obvious way of manipulating the environment. Clearly, they had a different functionality.

"We're doing everything possible to determine the similarities and differences between these new types and those we've seen previously. We'll share what we learn as soon as we can," Karlina concluded.

"The Chinese have launched two small ships, they look like drones," said Captain Blackstone. "*Aurora* is tracking them and sending their data feed as they do. I'm putting it on channel five."

"Thank you, Karlina, please keep us posted. I'm switching now to the feed from *Aurora*," Julie announced as she walked back to the front.

The screen view changed to show the grayish-brown of Charon at the bottom of the screen and a small dot showing the relative position of the Chinese drones. Using the picture-in-picture function, the top right corner displayed a zoomed-in image of the drones.

As the minutes ticked by, the display showed the drones' relative heights above the moon's surface as they came closer. Their distance closed at a rapid rate: One hundred kilometers. Eighty-five kilometers. Seventy. Fifty-five. Forty.

As they watched, both drones abruptly disintegrated. Everyone in the room gasped. Pieces large and small fell to the surface. As they watched the event unfold, their silence made the scene more surreal. The pieces fell into the sea of microbots, barely causing an interruption in their activities.

"What happened?" asked someone, vocalizing what everyone else was thinking.

Larry's comm buzzed. *Aurora* was at general quarters.

Larry turned to Abigail and Kinia. "Please excuse me. I need to go to the bridge to speak with Captain Blackstone. *Aurora* is on alert. The colonel and I need to confer."

Abigail's countenance showed concern, but not panic. "Let us know what you can," she said.

"I'll do my best," he replied, trying to give the scientists a look of encouragement.

When he arrived on the bridge, Blackstone was one of four participating in a conference call. On the screen were Colonel Ruiz of *Aurora*, Commander Morozov of the *Nerpa*, and Commander Liang of the *Yancheng*. That they were talking was encouraging. He noted the call seemed to have been initiated by the Russians, a surprise. They weren't known for sharing information or collaboration. Maybe this would be different?

". . . overtly hostile acts and we must respond in-kind," Liang spoke. "We must assert our rights of free navigation and open skies. Commander Morozov, you lost two marines to these things. Surely you agree with me. Force must be met with force."

"Yes, I lost two marines, and nearly three," Morozov replied. "In our case, I'm not sure it was because my crew was targeted as hostile. My science team believes these alien machines are disassembling part of the moon to build something and my team happened to be in the way. They were raw material to be disassembled."

"If that had been my crew, I would have retaliated." Liang's tone bordered on belligerence.

"I considered it. I had two tactical nuclear weapons armed and targeted. Before I fired, my science advisors talked me out of using them."

Larry inwardly gasped. The Russian captain had made a huge admission. This wasn't normal for *any* nation's warship, be they at sea or in space, to officially announce that they carried nuclear weapons.

"We almost lost crew and my instincts were the same as both of yours. We're trained to respond to threats and attacks appropriately, and usually that means in-kind. The scientists here had the same reaction as your team, Commander Morozov, and we stood down," said Ruiz.

"What happened to our Chinese friends was a clearly different circumstance. Your drones never reached the surface, and there is no way the aliens simply saw them as raw material. They clearly saw your probes as a threat. A response might be called for, but we need to tread carefully," said Morozov.

"Have any of you seen a sign that the aliens have or will initiate anything else?" asked Ruiz.

Everyone shook their heads, including Blackstone.

Larry stood off to the side, trying to remain off camera. He quietly spoke to Blackstone using his earpiece, "I recommend we boost away from Charon to Pluto's orbit and get away from whatever might happen next."

Blackstone looked Larry's way and nodded his head in affirmation. Larry then walked over to Tyler Romans, again on the navigation console, and whispered into his ear.

The ship commanders' conversation continued. ". . . sensors showed a hot spot on the central structure near one of the ellipsoid bulges at the time of the drone's disintegration, which is presumably the source of the attack," explained Morozov.

"With due respect, I must interrupt," said Blackstone.

"Given the current situation, I'm moving *Tombaugh* to orbit Pluto. My navigator is plotting the course. Unless you object, I would like to execute the maneuver within the next five minutes."

"I concur," said Ruiz.

The other two captains nodded in agreement, looking annoyed at an interruption from a civilian. To them, the presence of a ship full of scientists was simply a distraction from their mission.

Blackstone muted his microphone so as to not disturb the other captains, and said, "Mr. Romans, when you are ready, give notice to the crew that the boost is soon to begin." Notifying the crew and passengers of an impending boost used to be a big deal, back before the invention of localized artificial gravity. In those days, everyone would have had to secure their belongings, pack up loose items, and strap themselves into boost chairs to avoid having objects, including themselves, suddenly fly around the room as the ship accelerated. With modern ships, no one noticed a boost unless they were told. These days, giving notice was more of a courtesy than a safety warning. He returned his attention to the virtual meeting.

". . . before we act," said Ruiz.

"Commander Liang, was your probe armed with a nuclear weapon of any sort?" asked Morozov.

"It is not Chinese policy to disclose whether our ships are armed or not," she replied.

"I hope you can make an exception in this case," replied Morozov. "I did. We may have to act in concert to counter this threat, *if* it is a threat. Knowing such information about each other's capabilities and actions might make the difference between success and failure."

The Russian commander continued to impress Larry. He'd never been a fan of the Russian Federation—God knew how many people had died due to their autocratic culture over the years—and he had met and interacted with many Russian Federation ships and officers in his career, but Commander Morozov was cut from different cloth. She was trying to be a team player.

Ruiz and Blackstone remained silent.

"*Aurora* is armed with nuclear missiles, ranging in size from a few kilotons to a megaton," admitted Ruiz, violating the U.S.A.'s policy of not disclosing a ship's nuclear capabilities.

"As is the *Nerpa*, though none of ours are in the megaton class," added Morozov.

Commander Liang looked extremely uncomfortable, like she had a migraine or nausea. After a few moments of heavy silence, she offered, "One of the probes was carrying a ten-kiloton nuclear weapon. The plan was for it to hover over the center of the alien activity while the other attempted to land and capture one of the microbots."

"Even though you *knew* what happened to our crews when we tried to capture one?" asked Ruiz.

"The capture drone was also armed, with a focused EMP weapon set to neutralize the machines nearby, allowing one to be grappled," said Liang.

"Either the aliens knew what you were up to, or that one of your drones carried a nuclear weapon, and stopped you from carrying out your plan," said Morozov.

"That would be my estimation," Liang concurred.

"So, they defended themselves. A very human reaction," mused Ruiz.

"Captain Blackstone, I'm sorry to interrupt, but we have a problem," interjected Tyler from his duty station.

"It looks like I need to tend to a shipboard matter, if you will excuse me." Blackstone muted his connection, rose from his chair, and moved toward Tyler.

"There's a problem?" asked Blackstone, now standing beside Tyler.

"Yessir, the boost maneuver should have initiated three minutes ago, but the ship isn't responding."

CHAPTER 16

Tyler's statement that the ship wasn't responding to commands got Larry's immediate attention. He joined Blackstone and Tyler to learn more.

"Not responding? Is the drive offline?" Blackstone asked.

"Ship's systems are green. We ought to be moving, but we're not and I don't understand it," Tyler replied.

"Okay, reach out to engineering and have them check the systems there. While they're doing that, run a full systems check to make sure nothing else is offline we don't know about," Blackstone ordered.

"Yes, sir," Tyler confirmed, returning his focus to his display and rapidly keying in commands.

Larry, like most Space Force officers, cross-trained in astrodynamics, flight mechanics, and spacecraft command and control, so he watched intently as Tyler methodically ran through all the system checks the regulations required for situations such as this. Though Larry didn't like Tyler, he had to admit he knew his stuff. He missed nothing as he checked every system and subsystem and ran the requisite subroutines designed to locate hardware or software irregularities and correct them.

"Major Randall, I need to devote my full attention to this ship and the safety of my passengers and crew. I need you to take over for me in this call while I do so," said Blackstone, nodding toward the viewscreen and the conversation that continued without them.

"Yes, sir," replied Larry, already moving back to the screen. As soon as he arrived, Ruiz looked toward him quizzically.

". . . conversation is going nowhere. The People's Republic of China will not allow imperialist powers to dictate our policies, be they American, Russian, or otherwise. You will soon see our response to this unprovoked attack," said Commander Liang as she cut the connection, replacing her face with a symbol of the Chinese flag on the screen.

"I fear we are soon to poke a bear," observed Commander Morozov.

"Coming from a Russian, that's saying something. I share your concern," agreed Ruiz, who then looked toward Larry. "Major Randall, by the absence of Captain Blackstone I gather that there is some issue aboard *Tombaugh*?"

"That's correct. The ship is nonresponsive to commands. When we tried to execute the boost to Pluto, the ship failed to respond. Captain Blackstone is troubleshooting the problem with his crew and asked me to represent the ship in your call."

"Do your problems come from the Pluto artifact? Has there been any change in its status?" asked Ruiz.

"It's impossible to know," replied Chris Wojciechowski, the ship's executive officer, joining the conversation for the first time. "From what we can tell, which isn't much, nothing changed with the artifact. It's sitting there emitting low-level radiation like it was when we found it."

"Given that we know our Chinese colleagues are soon to do something that could provoke a strong reaction from the mascon, I very much want to see *Tombaugh* as far away as possible. Let me know if we need to send over engineering specialists to help find or repair the problem," said Ruiz.

Larry heard this with relief. He had confidence in the crew of *Tombaugh* to run and repair their ship, but he didn't know their competence or level of training. He also didn't want to offend Blackstone or his crew, so he decided it would be best to wait before taking Ruiz up on the offer.

"Commander Morozov, what do you intend to do? Our three ships need to be closely coordinated so that we may appropriately respond to whatever the *Yancheng* decides to do." Ruiz returned his attention to the Russian commander.

"We will stand down from general quarters and observe. I commit to informing you of any offensive actions we may decide to take, if time permits, of course."

"We commit to the same. *Tombaugh*'s problem may change how we react to any threats. As long as they are here, my ship's top priority will be to protect them," said Ruiz.

"Understood. The *Nerpa* will support you in that role, but if I have to choose between the safety of my own ship and *Tombaugh* . . ."

"We understand, Commander Morozov. We couldn't ask for more," said Ruiz, nodding his head in agreement. "Let's keep this channel open so that we can confer rapidly, should the need arise. It will be muted on our end until then."

"Thank you, sirs," said Larry. "I'll keep you posted on the repair efforts here."

Once the call ended, Larry moved aft to speak again with Captain Blackstone. "Did you hear any of that?"

"Most of it. I'm grateful to your captain and I intend to see that his efforts here on our behalf are recognized once we get safely home and this is all over," said Blackstone.

Larry could only wonder what "all over" might look like in this case.

"Have you isolated the problem?" asked Larry.

"Yes, and no. It is not merely a navigation issue. The physical operation of the engines is affected as well. Our chief engineer tried a minimally propulsive engine start to test their functionality independently of navigation and control. Nothing happened. Whatever is causing the problem is systematic, a bug or something."

"Mikelson?"

"He's gone. Isn't he? I mean, how could it be? You were there when he fell into the crevasse. It can't be him." Blackstone bit his lip as he spoke.

"You're right. Mikelson's gone. But sometimes I wonder if he really is. The man was smart and driven. If it isn't Mikelson, then the only other option we have is the artifact."

"That's what I think," agreed Blackstone. "What else could it be? But as you said, nothing concerning the artifact has changed. It's sitting there same as yesterday, the day before, and when you found it on Pluto."

"Nevertheless, we need to assume it's the problem. I recommend we move it to an emergency airlock so we can jettison it should the need arise. Quite frankly, I am close to that point right now," Larry admitted.

"Agreed. But to throw it away without knowing that it's the cause of our problems would be a loss to science," said Blackstone.

"Not necessarily. We can tag it with a beacon for safe retrieval later. We can use one of the spare emergency beacons we have for the escape modules," Larry suggested.

"Good idea. I'll get my team busy moving and tagging it. We'll put it in emergency airlock three, for now. I'll call for Dr. Bridenstein to meet me in the lab so I can fill her in on the plan. After that, I will meet with my engineers to see if they have any ideas. You have the conn until Krzysztof is on duty in two hours. You can fill him in when he gets here." Then Blackstone added, "And keep my ship safe. Krzysztof is a team player; he'll listen to your advice."

"Yes, sir," said Larry as he moved toward the captain's chair.

. . .

"You can't be serious," Julie deadpanned. She, Abigail, Karlina, and Vitaj were in the lab when Blackstone arrived and informed them of the plan and told them to be ready to jettison the artifact. The scientists instinctively placed themselves as a group between Blackstone and the artifact.

"Look, something is causing control problems with the ship. None of the systems except those related to propulsion and navigation seem to be affected, but we *cannot* expect that to remain the status quo. The only new variable that could be causing the problem is that thing behind you. The mascon already came close to killing *Aurora*'s crew, consumed members of the Russian crew, and destroyed drones the Chinese sent to investigate it. The Chinese are likely to launch some sort of attack. We have to move this ship to a safer parking orbit, or we might all be killed. Which is more important, your lives, with the artifact tagged and away from the ship to be retrieved another day, or being killed by the artifact you are trying to protect?"

"You don't *know* the problem is caused by the artifact, correct? As far as we can tell, nothing has changed. Throwing it overboard might be a waste of time and, worse, what if the Russians or Chinese get it before we can reclaim it?" asked Karlina. "We both know how they feel about science for the sake of science—they don't. The whole thing would become part of a classified military program, and we'll never know its secrets."

"I agree there is risk, but unless we regain control of the ship, that's what we're going to do," replied Blackstone.

"Does Doctor Randall agree?" asked Abigail.

"He does," replied Blackstone.

"That's because he is Goddamn U.S. Space Force and not a real scientist," Karlina spit out. "He bungled the retrieval on Pluto and now he's willing to throw the discovery of a lifetime overboard."

"He wants to ensure our safety," Abigail interrupted. "Remember, that's his job and *Aurora*'s reason for being here to begin with. I think we should work with Captain Blackstone and get the artifact mobile and into the airlock. Because we're moving it there doesn't mean we have to jettison it." Abigail turned. "Vitaj, what do you think?"

"I was with him on Charon. He knows how to balance science versus safety, and he did the best he could," Vitaj replied, making a dig at Karlina. "I believe we should cooperate. After all, what can we do otherwise? Captain's orders and all that."

"I don't know," vacillated Julie, looking back and forth between each scientist.

"Do I need to get my crew in here to make it mobile, or are you willing to work with me?" asked Blackstone.

"Work with you," said Abigail.

"Agreed," added Vitaj.

"All right, we'll help. It will be best to keep your crew busy trying to figure out what's wrong with the ship," ceded Julie.

Karlina's face and body made her anger amply evident. "I cannot go along with this. I'm going to my quarters to compose a letter to the university and my senator." With that, she turned on her heel and left the room.

"What do you want us to do?" asked Julie. She hadn't become the leader of a deep-space science team without understanding chain of command and group politics. She realized her side had lost and she needed to regain and reassert her leadership, not to mention show the captain that she and her team could be team players.

"Get your portable monitoring gear ready to move with the artifact so we can monitor any changes. I'll go meet with my engineers to discuss the control issue and will send a few techs to help make the chamber mobile by putting wheels on it or something," answered Blackstone.

"We can use the neutrino and other radiation sensors from the lander," suggested Vitaj. "We can make a portable power supply to avoid interrupting the environment while we move it. Even a few minutes without power would cause it to warm up and we do not want to risk that. Not now."

"Didn't that happen earlier? When we first brought in on board, right?" asked Blackstone.

"It did, and we detected no noticeable changes, but if we're going to decide whether or not to throw it overboard based real or perceived change, then we don't want to run the risk. Too much is at stake," replied Abigail.

"It sounds like you have a plan. Can you make it happen within the hour?" asked Blackstone.

"An hour? That'll be tough, but yes, I believe we can," said Julie.

After acknowledging her answer, Blackstone left.

"An hour?" asked Abigail, looking skeptical.

"Well, an hour or so," replied Julie.

Seventy-five minutes later, nothing had changed except for the can-do attitude of some experienced and now very frustrated engineers. Their optimism to find a solution to the ship's propulsion and navigation problem vanished as they tried, and failed, every fix they could think of.

Blackstone returned to the bridge and reassumed command from Larry. The exec was back on duty, working with Tyler as they repeatedly tried to get the systems to respond.

So far, the mascon had done nothing unusual except grow at a rate of roughly one meter per hour. The Russians remained quiet, as did the Chinese, though everyone expected that to change based on the Chinese commander's earlier statements. What the Chinese would do was a huge question.

Blackstone's comm pin buzzed. "Captain, this is Julie Bridenstein. We're ready to move the artifact to the airlock. It's been transferred to the portable environmental control system, and everything seems to be working normally with no reaction from the artifact."

"Do you need any help moving it?"

"No, I think between those of us here we can move it. It's not too heavy," she replied.

"I'll come down. If we end up jettisoning this thing, I want all the responsibility and actions leading up to it to be clearly mine," stated Blackstone.

"We understand. We will stand by until you arrive."

"Chris, you have the conn. Major Randall, will you join me?" asked Blackstone.

"Absolutely." Larry wondered if this would be the last time he would see the artifact. Even with a transponder, there was a more than insignificant chance that if they jettisoned the artifact, they wouldn't be able to find it again. Space was huge and seemed even larger at the edge of the solar system.

Eight minutes later, Blackstone and Larry arrived in the lab. They gathered around the artifact and the jury-rigged cart upon which it and the requisite thermal vacuum equipment was placed.

"Are we ready?" asked Blackstone.

"Reluctantly, but yes," answered Julie.

Larry, Captain Blackstone, and Julie reached out toward the cart and began to roll it toward the door to begin its journey to the airlock.

Before they could exit, the sliding door to the laboratory abruptly closed.

They stopped rolling the cart and looked at each other.

"How did that happen?" asked Vitaj.

"I don't know, but I'll find out," said Larry as he walked away from the cart to the door. Normally, the motion sensor would have opened it before he got close, but not this time. The door remained closed. He reached to the left for the manual controls and keyed in his credentials, which theoretically would open every door on the ship except the one leading to the captain's cabin.

Nothing happened.

"Something or someone does not want us leave," surmised Abigail.

"That someone would be me, Dr. Grigsby." Mikelson's voice came from the lab's primary speaker system. "The artifact is too important to allow you or anyone else to throw off the ship."

"Dr. Mikelson? We thought you were dead," said Larry, looking around the room as if searching for the real source of the voice. *He can't be alive. I saw his rover fall into the mascon on Charon. Did he make a copy of himself? Has he been here all along? Or is this some remnant of Mikelson that's being sent to us from the mascon?*

"I am obviously not dead, though sometimes I wonder. No, I assure you I am alive and, well, not *well*, but alive."

"But you fell into the pit created by the mascon," Larry insisted.

"I did. But that was and was not me. I made a copy of myself, then erased any record of which was the original and which was the copy; I'm either the original or a backup left on the ship for this eventuality. Funny, I don't feel like a copy."

"Dr. Mikelson, we do not have time to debate your existence right now. We need to get the artifact to the airlock in case we need to space it. We believe it's taken control of *Tombaugh*, and this might be the only way to regain command of the ship," said Larry.

"The problem with the engines and navigation is not the

artifact. I'm the one keeping those systems offline. We cannot leave until we learn more of what's happening on Charon."

"*You* have control of the ship?" asked Abigail.

"I do."

"I insist that you return control to Captain Blackstone. Without delay," said Julie.

"No. I stopped taking orders from you long ago, Dr. Julie Bridenstein of Columbia University, MIT, and Caltech—career politician posing as a scientist. The artifact will remain on board this ship, and the ship will remain in orbit around Charon until I decide differently," Mikelson matter-of-factly stated.

"Mikelson, you arrogant prick," replied Julie, through gritted teeth.

Larry looked at his colleagues and slowly shook his head in an effort to keep them quiet. "Dr. Mikelson, we understand you have control of the ship. Now that we know the artifact is not responsible for the ship's problems and unless it becomes a threat based on any surface events, we won't eject it. You have my word. But, as you may be aware, the *Yancheng* plans to act against the mascon in response to their drones being destroyed. Before that happens, we need to move *Tombaugh* out of harm's way. If we wait until the shooting starts, that may be too late. This is not a warship and none of you signed up to be in a war zone."

"*No.*"

Larry bit his tongue and looked again at his colleagues. "Very well, I'll inform Colonel Ruiz. Do you plan to assume control over any of the ship's other functions?"

"Not unless you try to regain control. I have no wish to harm anyone, but I am compelled to remind you that I selectively can turn off life support anywhere on the ship."

"A threat, then," Larry fumed. "That won't go over well with Colonel Ruiz."

"A statement of consequences, not a threat."

Larry knew at that moment that Mikelson had gone from being an arrogant narcissist to a full-blown sociopath and megalomaniac. They had to find a way to regain control of the ship or kill him, perhaps both. None of them would be safe until then.

Blackstone's face had turned red and he looked like he was going to explode. "Goddamn you, Mikelson. This isn't some game or university research project, our lives are at stake. I want my ship back so I can get these people to safety."

Mikelson did not reply.

"Will you open the doors to allow us to leave?" asked Abigail. Despite her cool exterior, Larry noted the quaver in her voice; she was nervous or afraid. He looked at Vitaj and saw neutral resignation; Julie appeared angry.

In response, the doors opened, sliding open wide enough for them to pass, but not enough to allow them to leave with the cart holding the artifact.

"Thank you." Abigail's voice dripped with sarcasm. However, she made no move to depart once the door opened.

Bound for the bridge, Larry, Julie, and Blackstone left Vitaj and Abigail to reconnect the vacuum chamber containing the artifact to the ship's systems and away from the portable unit.

Once they arrived on the bridge, Blackstone's barely contained rage finally erupted. "Not on my ship." Impossibly, his face began to turn even redder as he clenched his teeth. "We've got to purge him from the systems and regain control. Mr. Wojciechowski, consider this your only job. I want a plan by twenty hundred hours."

"Yes, sir," replied Chris.

"Captain, I'm pretty sure Dr. Mikelson can hear every word we say, read our lips, and monitor anything we search for using the computer or other of the ship's systems," Larry warned him.

"Damn."

"That means he'll know whatever Mr. Wojciechowski comes up with as soon as we do," Larry continued.

"Then he'll have to come up with something Mikelson cannot interfere with, doesn't he?" said the captain.

"Good luck." Mikelson's voice came from the multiple speakers on the consoles and the primary mission display.

"You son of a bitch," muttered Blackstone.

Mikelson didn't respond.

"If you will excuse me, I need to inform Colonel Ruiz of all that's happened this afternoon. After that, I need some food. I forgot to eat lunch, and it's already time for dinner."

"For some reason, I'm not hungry," replied Blackstone.

"I'm not either, but I know I need to eat while I can. Later, we might be in a situation where eating is impossible, and we don't want to be making consequential decisions when we're hungry. Three of the life lessons I've learned in the military are: eat when you can, never pass a restroom without using it, and sleep, because tomorrow you might not be able to easily do any of them," admonished Larry.

Blackstone smiled. "Good advice. Don't worry; I'll find time to eat before long, and I'll let you know if the Chinese do anything."

Larry had an idea, albeit an old-fashioned one. It would be extremely limited in how much information could be conveyed, but it might work for short confidential messages that would be difficult for Mikelson to intercept. First, as he had said, he needed to get word to Colonel Ruiz about events.

Once he was in his quarters, he used his personal comm system to update his captain, who was easily as angry at the situation as Blackstone. He assured Larry that, while those on *Tombaugh* couldn't readily and confidentially research possible methods to rid themselves of Mikelson, *Aurora* and her crew could.

Next, Larry realized he really was hungry. He hadn't eaten for the last ten hours, and it was definitely time. On his way to the head to wash up. he opened the drawer in which he kept his personal items, including his diary and pen. He somewhat awkwardly slid the pen up the sleeve of his shirt while his hand was in the drawer and, with luck, completely out of sight of any cameras in the room.

He went to the head, closed the door, pulled down his pants, and sat on the toilet. He knew there were no cameras or audio sensors in the bathroom, but he also knew that the audio pickups in his room were sensitive enough to hear a whisper from behind the closed door. He didn't have to use the facilities, but he wanted all the sounds coming from the room to be normal—and that included the sounds of pants being lowered and business being done. Bathrooms might not work as a place to hold a real-time verbal conversation, but they provided an opportunity for writing notes. He had a pen and he had toilet paper—the one thing deep-space explorers had not been able to improve upon.

As quietly as he could, he began writing, careful not to tear the fragile paper as he did so.

With toilet paper safely tucked into his pants pocket, Larry made his way to the ship's mess for dinner. In the not far from full room, he could hear snippets of conversation, almost all of which was either related to the mascon on Charon or Mikelson's seizure of the ship. He looked around to see if Captain Blackstone was there, and when he didn't see him, he picked up his plate—tonight's special was pizza and a salad—and found his way to the table where Abigail, Maja Lewandowski, and Janneke Block sat, beginning their meals.

"May I join you?" asked Larry.

"Sure," replied Abigail, as she scooted to the side to make a place for him between her and Maja.

"I didn't realize I hadn't had lunch until an hour ago. I'm famished," said Larry as he began wolfing down the pepperoni pizza, saving a slice of vegetarian for afterward. As he bit down, holding it with his right hand, he pulled a single sheet of toilet paper from his left pocket and nudged Abigail to take it.

Abigail reacted to the nudge and looked down to her side to see what Larry held. She looked at him and slowly took her hand to her side and under the table, taking the piece of toilet paper and tucking it into the waistband of her pants.

As the exchange took place, Larry reiterated what he had told the captain earlier. "So he can see and hear everything we do."

"Everything?" asked Janneke with a horrified look on her face.

"Well, not everything. I'm quite sure he can't see what happens when you use the head, that's a no-camera zone, but the audio pickup in surrounding rooms is good enough to hear everything. Everything else is accessible."

Abigail sat patiently with the note tucked into her pants through the rest of dinner so as to not arouse suspicion. As everyone finished up, she said, "I need to go the toilet. I hope Dr. Mikelson is not enough of a voyeur to follow me there." As she spoke, she looked up toward one of the room cameras and flipped it the bird.

Once in the head, she reached into her pants to read the note.

Capt. Blackstone, the best way I can think of to comm is TP when in the head. Ruiz working on our problem. I have encrypted link to/from Aurora for sharing large files, but can probably only use once before discovered. When plan found, will pass it.—Randall

She was obviously not the intended recipient, but the one who needed to pass it to Captain Blackstone. She would do that after dinner; she only had to think of an excuse to get close to the captain so she could do so without being observed. Abigail finished up to rejoin her colleagues at the table, but instead found them standing near the door.

"We all agreed to get some sleep," suggested Maja. "Today's been a long day."

"Now that I'm fed, I realize how tired I am. I need to turn in," agreed Larry.

"That sounds like a great idea, but I think I'll do a few laps around the ship to stretch my legs a bit before I crash," said Abigail.

They each said goodnight, with Larry walking toward his cabin. Abigail briskly headed out to begin her laps and, with luck, pass the note to Blackstone.

Once Larry made it to his cabin, he realized how tired he was. He looked at the message board and saw a message from Athena. He smiled. He readied himself for bed and then sat down to hear what she had to say.

"Larry, I'm sorry there has been a longer than usual gap in my messages. It is not because I don't want to reach out. With you having gone on deployment, I get overwhelmed. We had a bad storm the other day that damaged the house and on top of everything else, I've been dealing with contractors to get things repaired. Don't worry, nothing irreplaceable was broken, but we had extensive damage to the roof and some of the junk stored in the attic got pretty wet. It should all be sorted out soon.

"On the family front . . ."

Her message continued with news from the home front, which Larry tried to follow, but his mind was elsewhere. He contemplated the ship, how to disable Mikelson, the mascon, how he might face life-or-death situations in the near future if the mascon didn't like whatever the Chinese did, and, of course, Abigail. The very thought of her was arousing and for that he felt guilty, but not guilty at the same time. It had been a long time since he last made love to his wife . . .

He noticed Athena's message had finished, and he had no idea what she said toward the end. He took a deep breath and began playing it again, this time trying to remain focused so that he could articulate a proper response.

After he finally turned out the light, he was asleep in less than two minutes.

Abigail continued her late sojourn, trying to trace the path she normally took in such activities so as to not arouse Mikelson's suspicion. She planned to walk all around the ship at least once before she approached the bridge. As she walked, she thought up an excuse for being there. To stop by the science station? To collect something she had left on her last shift? It all felt artificial. To talk to Tyler Romans? No, not that. She didn't want to encourage him. It had to be something she left at the science station, or thought she had, but what? Then she decided it didn't really matter. All she needed to say, if asked, was "something." Surely Mikelson wouldn't take notice.

Once she got to the bridge, she realized her plan wouldn't work. The captain was nowhere near her station. But he was between her and Tyler.

She didn't hesitate as she moved toward Tyler. On her way past Captain Blackstone, she planned to trip and fall—hoping that the captain would reach out to steady her, at which time she would pass him the note.

What would she say to Tyler? The only thing she could think of was to invite him for coffee after this shift. Surely, she could endure an hour with him as the price to be paid for passing the message.

It worked. Thirty minutes later she completed the pass with only a small portion of her dignity lost—and a large chance her contrived discussion with Tyler would encourage him.

CHAPTER 17

Larry walked down the high school's hallway carrying his textbooks and chatting with his best friend, Adam Pitman, about the upcoming athletic meet. Both were on the school's track team and the spring meet was the big event of the year. All the training and effort throughout the school year would pay off, as well as the school's requirement that all athletes maintain at least a B average. If the grades dropped, so did the extracurricular sports—the fear of losing the ability to compete because of a bad grade served as more than enough motivation to keep Larry's attention in class.

The conversation was inconsequential, something related to the meet and the girls they hoped to see there. Then Adam mentioned the upcoming chemistry final exam that afternoon. Larry's attention was jolted like an electrical spark through broken insulation.

"What chemistry final? I'm not taking chemistry until next year!" exclaimed Larry.

"What? You and I discussed this last fall when we put our schedules together. Chemistry this spring so we can take organic chemistry next fall. We even bought the textbooks together at the start of the semester. Man, you must really be doing well since I never see you in class. Is it too easy for you?" replied Adam.

Larry panicked. He didn't remember signing up for chemistry class, let alone there being an exam that afternoon. *How can I pass a test on material I've never studied? If I fail, I can't compete at the meet and then they'll yank my diploma. With no diploma, I'll never get accepted to the academy. Maybe I can . . .*

The sound of Captain Blackstone's voice on the emergency speaker in his cabin jolted Larry awake. His cabin aboard *Tombaugh*. In orbit around Charon. Where he was a Space Force Officer with a PhD and, of course, a high school diploma. He awakened filled with anxiety caused by a dream, something about chemistry? Now he couldn't remember. Whatever it was left him exhausted and now he was being awakened at—he looked at the clock—0350.

"Major Randall, please come to the bridge. The *Yancheng* informed us that they will be implementing their response to the mascon's attack in approximately one hour," announced Blackstone.

Larry arose, shaking the last bit of the dream off, activated the microphone, and replied, "On my way."

Larry arrived on the bridge, staffed with the usual A-team of *Tombaugh*: Captain Blackstone in the command chair with XO Wojciechowski standing at his side, Tyler on navigation and propulsion, David Jeong on communications and avionics, and Julie Bridenstein and Abigail Grigsby at the science station. Neatly placed on the room's only worktable were the coffeepot and an assortment of bakery items, already looking picked over. Everyone was so engrossed in their work that they didn't acknowledge Larry's arrival.

"What have we got?" Larry asked as he walked over to stand next to Blackstone, opposite Chris.

"Nothing yet, other than the alert that they would take some sort of action at approximately zero five hundred—in fifty minutes," said Blackstone, looking at the chronometer.

With Mikelson in control of the ship, Blackstone or Larry couldn't do much to prepare. They wanted the civilian ship to be out of harm's way, orbiting Pluto or perhaps even in an orbit leading, or trailing, the planet. Had they been able to boost as planned, they could be a million kilometers away by now. Of course, with as little knowledge of the mascon as they had, that still might not have been safe. For all they knew, the mascon could threaten ships as far away as Earth.

"Anything from Mikelson?" Larry inquired.

"Nothing. From Ruiz?" replied Blackstone looking hopefully at Larry. The man desperately wanted to regain control of his own ship. Larry was right there with him.

"Captain Blackstone, we're being invited to a conference with the other captains," said Jeong from his station, barely looking up.

"Take it on the main screen, like the last one," Blackstone responded.

The faces of Colonel Ruiz and Commander Morozov appeared on screen. Liang was conspicuously absent. Ruiz wore an expression Larry knew well. It was his "I plan to protect my ship and get the job done, come hell or high water" look. Morozov's expression looked more like concern than determination, but Larry didn't know her well enough.

"Blackstone here. Thanks for inviting me to the call."

"Given your situation, you need to know what's happening as soon as we do. Major Randall tells me you've had no luck regaining control of your ship. We've looked at every available option." Ruiz deliberately looked past Blackstone and directly at Larry, adding, "and if we do find something, I'll send it directly."

"Captain Blackstone, Colonel Ruiz filled me in on your problem. Is it true that one of your scientists uploaded himself into a computer, merged with an AI, and now has control over your ship? Unbelievable. Our scientists say such things are theoretically possible, but every known case of a human attempting to upload and become virtual has ended in madness," cautioned Morozov.

Blackstone couldn't help but smirk. "It's true, Commander Morozov, and I fear the madness part is a consequence here as well. When we return home, I intend to make that point clear in my reports."

"Thirty minutes," said Jeong.

Ruiz momentarily looked away and then back at the camera. "We all need to attend to our individual ships, but we will keep this line open indefinitely in case we need to share something critical. I had hoped Captain Liang would have joined us to tell us her plans, but I guess that won't be the case." Ruiz looked briefly up and then muted his side of the call. Morozov did the same.

Blackstone looked around the bridge and then raised his voice. "Dr. Mikelson. This ship may soon be placed in great danger. I ask you to reconsider and allow us full control over *Tombaugh* so we can keep you, your fellow scientists, and the Pluto artifact safe."

Mikelson didn't respond.

"It was worth a try," said Larry.

"Mr. Jeong, put me on the emergency speakers," requested Blackstone.

"You are on, sir," replied Jeong.

"As you are aware, the Chinese commander will soon undertake some sort of response to the attack on their probes. We do not know the details, but it could provoke the mascon to take action that could place this ship in harm's way. Unfortunately, as you also undoubtedly know, your colleague Dr. Mikelson has taken control of the ship and is not allowing us the freedom to react appropriately. I will do everything in my power to keep you, and this ship, safe. As described in the safety briefing yesterday, please put on your space suits and strap yourselves into the emergency acceleration chairs.

Everyone needs to be ready to evacuate ship in the nearest escape pod should that order be given. Captain Blackstone, out."

Blackstone looked around the bridge and added, "Ladies and gentlemen, that includes us. Suit up and strap in."

Larry used one of the spare suits from the storage locker on the bridge and sat in one of the three visitor chairs. He carefully fastened the three-point harness. Without having control of the ship or being among his well-trained Space Force colleagues who drilled constantly for such situations, he felt helpless. He didn't like the feeling. He looked around the room and caught Abigail's eye. He nodded and smiled. She responded with a pensive smile that spoke volumes about her and himself—she was scared, and he desperately wanted to protect her. He didn't think once of returning safely to Athena.

The clock counted down toward 0500. Nothing happened.

0501

0502

0503

Then it began. The *Yancheng* launched three drones, which began a rapid descent toward Charon's surface, directly toward the crater housing the mascon. Though they moved rapidly, the anticipation of something imminent made the scene play out painfully slow to those watching.

As the first of the drones neared the surface, like its predecessor, it simply fell apart. No explosion, no "death ray" coming from the surface of Charon—nothing significant happened except the leading drone rapidly disassembled, becoming nothing more than falling debris.

Then the second one fell apart.

Out of the forward missile tube of the *Yancheng* came three ship-to-ship missiles, accelerating at what Larry knew had to be full thrust, headed directly toward the crater and the mascon.

"Here we go," someone said and then Larry realized it was him.

Moments later, the remaining drone suffered the same fate as its predecessors, then all three missiles detonated with nuclear flashes well above the surface and away from their intended target. The ship's outboard cameras automatically dimmed the flashes and triggered *Tombaugh*'s radiation alarms.

Radiation effects didn't concern Larry. He had studied *Tombaugh*'s specs and, like most long-duration, deep-space craft, it was well hardened against radiation. Ships traveling in the solar system are constantly irradiated by protons and electrons in the solar wind and intense ultraviolet light from the sun. Those that enter the Jovian system encounter high-energy particles trapped in the planet's monster of a magnetic field that would kill an unprotected human outright. To top it all off, heavy atoms accelerated to relativistic velocities by interstellar magnetic fields for centuries or millennia zip through the solar system penetrating all but the densest shielding, causing damage to sensitive materials, including living tissue, and spacecraft electronics. These ships were designed to protect against most of these forms of radiation. Had the bomb exploded next to its hull, *that* would have been a very different story.

He suspected that the Chinese had rigged their missiles to automatically explode if they sensed any compromised missile integrity as they approached their target—something similar to a proximity fuse. Apparently, the mascon had tried to tear the missiles apart as it had the drones and that triggered the bombs.

There was no visible effect on the mascon, the unknown structure, or the hordes of microbots still doing whatever it was they did on Charon's surface.

"It appears we took no damage from the blasts," noted Blackstone, looking toward Larry.

"She's a good ship," added Larry, forcing a calm smile. Inside, he felt nervous as hell.

Seconds later, the *Yancheng* began to fall apart.

At first, the ship shuddered, like a boat skimming the water and encountering unanticipated waves. Then it simply . . . broke. Hull plates fell away, torn asunder at their seams by some unimaginable force, exposing the inside of the ship. Deck plates, room contents, and people, the poor crew of the proud Chinese ship, began venting into the vacuum of space.

"Dr. Mikelson, if there were ever a time to give us control over the ship so we can get the hell out of here, that time would be now," said Blackstone.

No response. Their orbit remained unchanged, and Tyler looked from his unresponsive control station to Blackstone and slowly shook his head. Mikelson wasn't being cooperative. They were now, possibly, in the line of fire and they could do nothing.

Ten seconds later, the *Yancheng*, as a ship, ceased to exist. Only a debris field remained to be tugged and pulled in various directions by the unequal gravity of the Pluto/Charon system until the pieces landed on one body or the other.

"Were they wearing space suits?" asked Abigail, shaken by what she had seen.

"I would assume they were. That's standard procedure for Space Force crew when facing imminent ship-to-ship combat," Larry told her.

"Then we should make ourselves available to effect rescues, unless the mascon decides to include us in its wrath," said Blackstone.

Nothing happened after the destruction of the *Yancheng*. Seconds passed, then minutes. Finally, the comm screen changed and Morozov's face came into view.

Blackstone activated his camera at the same time as Colonel Ruiz.

"The mascon has taken no action toward us, as yet. Do you believe we are safe?" asked Morozov.

"It appears that we are, for the moment at least," Ruiz ventured. "*Aurora* has search and rescue shuttles, but will the mascon interpret them for what they are, or will it view them as another drone being launched to attack it?" asked Ruiz.

"Colonel Ruiz, we must try, regardless of risk. If it misinterprets that and action is taken against us . . ." replied Morozov.

That was noble of her, thought Larry, suddenly impressed. The commander has compassion and guts, I'll give her that.

"Let us know how we can help," added Blackstone.

"Is your ship at capacity?" asked Morozov.

"No, we've got some empty cabins and can easily accommodate an additional twenty to thirty, maybe more. The ship's oxygen scrubbers and recyclers should be within operational limits even if we took more than that," replied Blackstone.

"Then prepare for company. I suggest we split the rescues among us so no single ship is overtaxed," said Morozov.

"Agreed," said Ruiz.

"We will be ready," Blackstone added.

"The first rescue shuttle is launching now," announced Morozov. *Aurora*'s would be, at most, five minutes behind.

On the forward viewscreen, a small orange dot could be seen departing the Russian ship, veering toward the debris cloud that had been the *Yancheng*. Most of the debris from the Chinese ship continued along the orbital path the ship had been following, but some shot in other directions, including trajectories that would take them lower in altitude and toward a flyby of the mascon site. The Russian rescue ship had decided to ignore rescuing any poor souls on those paths and instead followed a course toward the highest debris density where more people might be alive—and if it also happened to be the least threatening direction, then so be it.

Aurora's shuttles launched and appeared as two blue dots on the screen as they accelerated toward the debris field.

Watching the flight of the Russian shuttle while wondering if something would happen made time slow to a snail's pace. The small craft neared the edge of the debris field and appeared to stop, then remained motionless as it scanned the debris, looking for survivors.

Without warning, the rescue ship blew apart.

CHAPTER 18

For the first time in millennia, localized spacetime warping occurred nearby, the telltale ripples from which triggered a sensor embedded deep within the artifact, awakening it. To get the primary power system operating took energy, more energy than available while it slept, so the artifact increased the rate at which it tapped the nearly infinite energy available in the fabric of spacetime itself to increase the matter and antimatter production rate. This allowed it to jump-start the primary vacuum energy power generation system so that it could come fully alive.

On board *Tombaugh*, the enigmatic artifact Aaron Mikelson had found buried in the ice on Pluto powered on. Because nowhere in nature did any system operate without producing some waste heat, as the artifact began activating internal systems dormant for longer than human civilization's existence, its temperature began to rise, until finally one of the many sensors its human curators had attached to it noticed the small, but very real, increase in temperature and dutifully notified members of the science team.

Two scientists were in the lab with the artifact: Janneke Block and Karlina Haugen. Truth be told, not only was Janneke one of the few on the team who could put up with Karlina's arrogance and appallingly complete lack of social awareness, she also actually kind of liked the pompous woman. They were friends.

The temperature alarm monitoring the thermal conditions in the vacuum chamber began to sound. *Blip. Blip. Blip.*

Karlina reacted first. She peered into the chamber, and seeing no changes, checked the functionality of the thermal vacuum system to make sure it had not begun to leak, allowing the warm air of the lab to get into the chamber and begin warming the artifact. The system showed no change in the vacuum and no change in the cryogenic pumps. The systems were operating normally.

"What do you think?" asked Janneke.

"I think something changed and we should tell Julie and the rest of the team," replied Karlina.

"We need to notify the captain," urged Janneke.

"You do that. I'll take care of getting the competent members of our team in here to help figure out what's going on, and if anything else has changed," commented Karlina.

As she spoke, the neutrino sensor alarm sounded. *Wap. Wap. Wap.*

Janneke muted the alarm and watched the neutrino emission rate begin to climb ever so slowly.

"We need to tell everybody. The artifact is waking up," said Janneke.

On the bridge of the *Tombaugh*, Captain Blackstone, Larry, and the rest of the bridge crew watched the forward screen intently as the icon representing the Russian shuttle abruptly vanished.

"Recall the shuttles now, dammit," barked Captain Ruiz on the open microphone.

Seconds passed with agonizing slowness as the two blue

dots continued to move toward the cloud of debris, then slowed, and finally, began to reverse direction toward the *Aurora*.

The call from Janneke Block came in at that moment.

"I'm sorry, but the captain can't be disturbed right now." The voice on the intercom was Chris Wojciechowski's. "We're in a situation that demands his full attention." As he spoke, he looked at the ship's status, and the viewscreen showing the *Yancheng* debris field now contained pieces of the Russian shuttle. Off to his left, Julie rose from her seat at the science console and moved toward the exit.

"Chris, I completely understand, but you need to tell him the artifact is warming up, *powering* up. Something is happening," exclaimed Janneke. She amped up the urgency in her voice to get his attention.

"I understand. I'll pass this to the captain at the soonest opportunity. Do you believe we are in danger from the artifact?" Chris asked.

"Not *immediate* danger, but we don't know where this is headed or what will happen next," she cautioned.

"Please send me updates via text. We will get back with you soonest," Chris added as he broke the voice link.

As Chris spoke with Janneke, Blackstone joined the conference call with the commanders of the remaining Earth ships.

". . . We are in agreement then? We will send a joint communiqué to the UN describing the events that led up to the destruction of the *Yancheng* and each of us individually reporting the events to our respective countries requesting guidance on next steps," offered Ruiz.

"We are in agreement," replied Morozov.

"What about us?" asked Blackstone.

"Unfortunately, Captain Blackstone, we haven't figured out how to solve your Mikelson problem, which means what you do next will be up to him," said Ruiz. "Have you heard from him since the destruction of the *Yancheng*?"

"No."

"If worst comes to worst, we'll try to protect you, but given that we do not have a clue how the mascon's weapon works, we're as vulnerable as you are," admitted Ruiz.

"I understand," Blackstone said as he noticed Chris trying to get his attention, then added, "Hold on a moment," as he muted the connection. Blackstone, Chris, and Larry briefly huddled and Blackstone reopened the connection.

"It seems the artifact is becoming active. The scientists tell me its temperature and neutrino emissions are increasing," outlined Blackstone.

"What does that mean?" asked Morozov.

"I wish we knew. That's all I've been told. I will keep you both informed as we learn more," said Blackstone.

"That's all we can ask," responded Ruiz.

Back in their huddle, Blackstone's ire rapidly increased and both Chris and Larry could feel its intensity. "I want the artifact off my ship and that SOB Mikelson deleted. Not only neutralized, I want all traces of his programming, or whatever the hell he is now, deleted."

"Sir, we're trying. We've been in constant communication with the avionics specialists on *Aurora* and nothing we've tried has worked. Of course, it could be because Mikelson learns what we are planning to do before we do it, somehow thwarting us before we even begin," Chris explained.

Blackstone broke the huddle and looked around the bridge. "Mikelson, I know you can hear me. You saw what happened to the *Yancheng* and the Russian rescue shuttle. We are in danger and need to get as far away from Charon as possible. Now. While we're doing that, we need to get the artifact off this ship. It's waking up and we have no idea what it's doing. It's a risk to the ship *and to you*."

"Captain Blackstone, I cannot allow you to eject the artifact," stated Mikelson.

"Allow me? Do I need to remind you, Professor Mikelson, that this is *my* ship?" Blackstone seethed.

"We've had this conversation before. I will not allow you to remove the artifact, and we are not leaving orbit until we make contact with the mascon. Further discussion is pointless."

"Need I remind you that you are now on this ship and as vulnerable as the rest of us?" asked Blackstone.

"Then you will have to trust me when I say that the artifact is too important to simply throw away. Yes, it may be a threat, but I doubt the threat would be as simple as being some sort of bomb. Any species capable of traveling between the stars would be a bit more sophisticated than that, don't you think?" Mikelson replied.

"Now listen here, I . . ." Blackstone started and realized that Mikelson wouldn't listen. He was wasting his time. *Goddammit. If this thing is a threat to my ship, I am going to get it off no matter what that SOB thinks.*

"Mr. Wojciechowski, you have the conn. Major Randall and I are on our way to the lab to see the artifact," said Blackstone, trying to calm down.

"May I join you?" asked Abigail, her hand raised from where she sat at the science console observing events. "Julie has already gone to the lab, but I thought I should remain here in case you needed me."

"Of course, but please send for someone to replace you on the console as soon as you can," Blackstone answered as he motioned for her to join them.

.   .   .

Blackstone, Larry, and Abigail entered the small lab to find Julie, Karlina, Janneke, and Panayiota Barak, another of the scientists, busily checking their datapads and instrument status screens. The vacuum chamber holding the artifact seemed to loom larger than before, having in the last several hours gone from a benign curiosity to a potential menace.

Julie, as the spokesperson, moved to greet them.

"I came as soon as I heard the news," Julie said. "It seems our friend here is waking up."

"Have there been any other changes?" asked Blackstone.

"A few minutes ago, we detected low-level radiofrequency emissions consistent with the leakage one might expect from powered electronics, not any sort of intentional signal. At least not a signal as we would understand it," replied Julie.

"Is the temperature still rising?" asked Blackstone.

"No. It appears to have leveled off. The RF emissions are also fairly constant. It's doing something, or trying to, and we have no idea what that might be," she replied.

The sound of the vacuum system alarm interrupted them. *Woop. Woop. Woop.* Much louder than the previous alarms, which were more like notifications, this alarm was meant to be heard. For most science experiments, losing vacuum could result in the loss of hours, days, months, or even years of work.

"What's happening?" asked Blackstone.

"The vacuum system seems to be malfunctioning or leaking. The pressure in the chamber is rising," answered Janneke.

"Rising pressure sounds like something might explode," warned Blackstone.

Janneke managed to smile. "The pressure rise is in a vacuum chamber, and we're a long way from any sort of pressure-induced explosion. Orders of magnitude away. However, as you know, we have no idea what's happening inside that thing," she said, pointing at the artifact through one of the vacuum chamber's windows.

"I want it ready to move to the airlock on a moment's notice. If we can convince Mikelson to let us jettison the thing, then that's what we're going to do, and you need to be ready to go. Understood?" asked Blackstone.

The scientists all nodded.

The rest of the day was, by comparison, uneventful. The Charon mascon kept growing, its microbots becoming more numerous and spreading even farther from the crater. The Pluto artifact's temperature was now stable, as were the neutrino emissions—though at the new, elevated rate. Mikelson made no further contact and both ships awaited direction from their respective governments. Their messages, traveling by radio at the speed of light, required nearly five and a half hours to reach Earth, which meant they had only recently arrived there. Knowing it would take time for the leadership at home to read, process, and formulate a plan in response to the events in the outer solar system, no one expected any firm direction for at least another day.

As the extended day shift ended, Larry joined his usual group for a completely average and totally forgettable dinner. The conversation over the meal was tense. They all knew they were at risk and had an overall dark sense of helplessness. Larry tried to remain the stoic Space Force officer, but he thought Abigail and others could see right through it.

They completed their meals faster than usual with all agreeing they needed to go to bed early since the day had begun at 0400 and had been extremely stressful. They said their usual and now-perfunctory goodbyes and departed for their cabins.

As they walked, Larry and Abigail stayed silent, arriving

at her cabin first. He turned to say goodnight, and Abigail surprised him by looking up, leaning forward, and kissing him. He quickly got over the surprise and returned the kiss, enjoying the smell of her hair and the way her body felt. His body reacted to a familiar hormonal rush. He took her in his arms and pulled her closer.

"Let's go inside," she whispered, breaking the kiss and smiling.

He looked at her, their faces mere inches apart. She was beautiful. Then the shock of what had just happened hit him. He reached down and took hold of her hands. He looked into her eyes, took a deep breath, and said, "Abigail, I want this. I want you more than anything right now. We can't do this. I'm married, and I will not do this to my wife or my kids. You are a wonderful woman, but no. I can't. I can't do this to Athena. I can't. I love my wife . . ."

Her eyes remained locked to his, and at first, she said nothing. After a few moments, she replied, "I understand. You're a good man and your wife is one lucky woman. I've thought about this for weeks, but I knew you were married and didn't want to initiate anything. But now, with all that's happened . . ."

Larry looked at her eyes and was spellbound. His body told him to continue, *yelled* at him to continue, but his conscience held firm. Finally, after several agonizing seconds he looked away and whispered, "Abigail, I can't."

She removed her hands and slowly nodded, never breaking eye contact. "Goodnight, Major Larry Randall," she said, trying to sound formal and calm.

"Goodnight, Dr. Grigsby," he replied, trying to smile.

She entered her cabin, and as Larry walked back toward his, all he could think of was the guilt he felt. While he had not physically betrayed Athena, he had done so emotionally. How would he face her without giving that away? Would she sense something in their next message exchange? Could he ever tell her?

Despite his long day, it took Larry hours to fall asleep.

Vitaj Misha and Maja Lewandowski were stuck with the night shift in the lab. While they kept watch on the artifact and monitored the data coming from the sensors, they managed to play a few rounds of gin rummy and whist using the well-worn, communal deck of playing cards. Cards had made a comeback in the months preceding their departure from Earth and several members of the science team brought decks with them for purposes such as this. Deep-space missions tended to have many hours, days, and weeks of downtime and card games helped it to pass more quickly.

"Maja, you must be distracted," said Vitaj after winning his third round of whist. "I don't usually get this lucky playing cards with you."

"The readout for the vacuum chamber pressure is immediately above your right shoulder, and I can't help but notice when it changes. The pressure is still increasing, and at this rate, by tomorrow night it might be up to one atmosphere," she noted.

"Let's check it again for leaks," he suggested, setting the card deck aside. "Because the previous shift couldn't find any doesn't mean we can't."

They got up from their chairs and walked to the chamber.

"If the artifact weren't in there, we could do a helium pressurization test," suggested Maja.

"Then let's try the Find-A-Leak spray again," suggested Vitaj. Find-A-Leak was a liquid that was sprayed on the exterior of a vacuum chamber to help find small leaks, usually at viewports or other locations where parts had to be connected. Leaks rarely happened through the solid walls. If air entered a leak in the chamber, a chemical in the spray would turn a bright red when exposed to ultraviolet light. They had run the test earlier in the day and found nothing. This time, as they moved the portable UV lamp across the surface of the chamber, twenty small bright red dots appeared.

"Would you look at that?" said Vitaj, reaching out to touch one of the spots, thinking perhaps that he might be able to feel the airflow. He didn't, any airflow would have been at a rate too small to be felt by his finger. He did feel a slight grit, like it was superficially dusty, and wiped his hand on his pants.

"Maja, let's set up the UV camera and get some photos. It'll be interesting to see if these leaks change over time or if new ones form."

Card game forgotten, they transitioned to "scientist mode" and began conducting a series of measurements to characterize the areas around the leaks in every way they could imagine. They kept it up all night until the relief crew, Karlina Haugen and Lorena Campos, arrived at 0500. By 0530, Vitaj and Maja were off to breakfast.

Larry awakened after a fitful night's sleep, punctuated by waking at least three times where he found himself staring at the ceiling, feeling guilty. On the third such event, he recorded a brief message to Athena and saved it in the buffer, knowing that sending a guilt-ridden message composed while half asleep without a review wasn't a good idea. Writing it did allow him to finally get some sleep—two hours' worth, anyway.

He rose from his bunk and went to the head. Once he entered, he noticed the message indicator glowing green on the small black tab that was his secure data link to *Aurora*. After he closed the door, he picked up the tab and selected the TEXT ONLY option to see what Colonel Ruiz had to say. He reread the message to make sure he understood, and put the device in his pocket. Feeling more than a little bit juvenile, he pulled some toilet paper off the roll and began to write.

They finally had a plan for how to deal with Mikelson.

To make it happen, he needed the cooperation of the ship's IT expert, Mateo Sanchez, but contacting him would be too obvious; Sanchez led the earlier attempts to purge Mikelson from the system. They had only spoken once after that, and in passing. Mateo liked solitude and spent most of his time managing the ship's computer systems. He had been on the bridge more lately as they tried to regain control of the ship. He and Tyler often tried new . . . Tyler! Tyler was the key. He had to have the cooperation of Tyler to make it happen. Now, how would he get the message to Tyler without being obvious?

Abigail. Shit. He would have to ask Abigail.

Mikelson followed the events in the lab with intense curiosity. The discovery of the leaks in the vacuum chamber caused concern, but so far, he detected no direct threats. Of course, the news would undoubtedly result in excessive chatter from Captain Blackstone begging him to allow the artifact to be thrown overboard, which he was not going to do.

The crew continued their attempts to dislodge him from the computer system, failing. He had to give them an A for effort, but that wouldn't be enough to beat him. His ability to outthink his human counterparts rendered any attempt they might make doomed to failure. In a whimsical way, he felt sorry for their biological limitations.

The mascon was his primary interest, and to be honest, his primary worry. He had no way to defend *Tombaugh*, or himself, from whatever weapon it used to destroy the *Yancheng*. He really didn't believe the ship would be at risk, though, since it had not taken, nor was it capable of even making, threatening acts.

What was it up to? And how were the recent developments with the artifact related? He began sifting through all the data, new and old, in search of the answer. And would they reveal the secrets of the aliens who traveled between the stars?

Julie had read the reports of the microscopic holes in the vacuum chamber and decided it was time to check it out herself. When she arrived in the lab, Karlina and Lorena had been joined by Janneke. They were all busy with various diagnostic instruments or scanning the output from the instruments on their datapads. They acknowledged her entry, but didn't stop to provide more than a greeting.

"Keep doing what you're doing. I'm here to see for myself the team's findings from last night." She examined the surface of the vacuum chamber, and if the leak spots hadn't been marked, she would never have seen them. Then she peered into the chamber using one of the viewports. She stared at it for a few moments and then realized the artifact looked different. She couldn't quite put her finger on it, but something had definitely changed.

"Have you noticed any visible differences in the appearance of the artifact?" Julie asked.

"The instruments haven't detected anything different from this time yesterday," replied Janneke.

"I'm not concerned with what the instruments show, I'm talking about how it looks. I believe something changed. I can't tell what, but it is definitely different," Julie insisted.

Janneke looked through the secondary viewport. "Not that I can see," she offered.

"Well, something is off. Set up another complete visual scan. Look for size changes, color changes, anything that might be different," Julie directed as she continued to stare at the object. Was it her imagination, or did the edges look fuzzy? She backed away and began helping the team set up the cameras. *Hmm. What am I seeing that they don't?*

.   .   .

Larry stopped by Abigail's room and knocked. She didn't answer. He didn't think she would snub him, though he wouldn't blame her if she did. She must be out and about—almost certainly near the lab. He was hungry, but food would have to wait. He needed to find Abigail before something else happened with the mascon to put them in immediate danger. This was their best shot at getting rid of Mikelson and it needed to be done as soon as possible.

He bypassed the cafeteria, smelling the fresh, hot coffee. There will be time for that later—*hopefully*.

As he approached the lab, he noticed Abigail in a hallway conversation with Kinia Kekoa. They were clearly excited over something, which gave the perfect excuse for Larry to walk up to them.

When Abigail noticed him, her expression changed. It went from relaxed and engaged to serious and . . . pensive? Larry thought he might have vainly imagined the change.

"Good morning, Dr. Randall," said Abigail, a smile returning to her face.

"Good morning to you both," replied Larry. "What's happening?"

"The night shift found leaks. Dozens of them, all over the vacuum chamber. They're exceedingly small, but large enough to allow some air into the chamber and cause the pressure to rise. Then Julie came in and said that she thought the artifact looked 'different.' So, the team is completing a new high-resolution visual scan of the artifact to see if they can find anything."

Larry and Abigail stared quietly at each other. Kinia glanced at both of them and began to grin—quickly suppressing it. "If you'll excuse me," she said as she began to walk away toward the lab.

"Kinia, you don't need to . . ." Abigail began, but Larry interrupted her.

"Let her go, please."

After Kinia was out of earshot, Larry grasped both of Abigail's hands and looked into her eyes. "About last night. I'm so sorry."

"No, I'm the one who should be sorry," she shared. "I'm the one who initiated what came close to happening. That won't happen again."

"We both made mistakes. You know the whole 'tango' metaphor that everyone uses—despite the fact that no one who says it has ever danced a tango," Larry said with a smile.

"I know. Let's try to put our feelings aside and get through this, okay?" she asked.

"Deal," he replied as he let go of her hand. "Now, I would like to see what is happening with the artifact."

"I'll be back, I need to go to my cabin first," said Abigail.

She walked back toward her cabin clutching a wad of toilet paper Larry had passed to her when he grasped her hands. Inside the wad, she felt something hard and disk shaped. Regardless of its content, she knew deep down their exchange had been from their hearts, even if the encounter had been contrived to allow whatever she now held to be passed from him to her. We'll soon see, she thought.

Vitaj was in a deep sleep and awakened, scratching his hand. He turned on the light. He had apparently been scratching it in his sleep because the skin was now a fiery red and beginning the bleed. He looked at the clock: 10:15. He had been asleep for over two hours and when he had gone to bed, his hand was fine. What had he gotten into? There were no insects on the ship, not even a cockroach, an amazing feat since they were present on every other ship he had ever been on. No, not an insect bite. An allergic reaction? Possible. People were often allergic to the synthetic compounds found in artificial environments, but why develop one now?

Clearly with the urge to scratch this strong, and given the visible damage to his skin from the scratching, he wasn't going to get any more sleep. He needed to see the doctor.

Vitaj entered the infirmary and found Dr. Murillo at his desk. He hadn't seen much of the ship's doctor other than the required recurring three-month mandatory checkup while on a voyage. Vitaj sometimes wondered if it was medically or psychologically necessary for the ship's doctor—something to keep him busy on what was otherwise a long and boring cruise.

"Misha, isn't it?" Murillo said as he looked up from his desk.

"That's right," replied Vitaj, unconsciously scratching his hand, "Vitaj Misha."

Murillo didn't seem to notice, staring instead at his face. "How long have you had that rash?" he asked.

Vitaj raised his hand to show the rash to the doctor. "Only a few hours. I was on night shift in the lab and went to bed three hours ago. I woke up maybe forty-five minutes ago scratching it. It wasn't there when I went to bed."

Murillo looked at Vitaj's raised hand and gestured toward his face. "I hadn't noticed the hand. I was describing your face. The right side looks like you've gotten a sunburn."

Vitaj unconsciously raised his hand to his right cheek but Murillo stopped him by using his shirt-covered arm. "*Do not* do that. It looks like you've come into contact with something you are allergic to and by touching your face, it's spreading. Like poison ivy. Let's get you into the diagnostic chamber and see what's causing it. Try not to touch anything else, especially anywhere else on your face if you can help it."

Murillo escorted Vitaj to a small standalone chamber in the back of the infirmary. It held a reclining chair in the upright position and all sorts of cameras and other sensors. Vitaj knew they would be extended by the medical AI to run all sorts of tests. When they came for their physicals, this was always the first step. From what Vitaj remembered from the briefings, the diagnostic system could do full blood and urine analysis, scan for tumors, arterial blockages, even signs of early dementia. If something was broken or otherwise injured, x-ray and MRI scans could also be run.

The first thing he had to do, however, was provide his hand for a robotic arm to swab. The whole thing made Vitaj uncomfortable. Not because of the tests, but because of the potential results. He could see real worry on Dr. Murillo's face. It didn't help that Murillo threw his shirt into the biohazard container and was now donning full body and facial protection gear.

The door to the chamber closed, some soothing music began playing, and the automated diagnostic system began to do its job.

Larry entered the lab and found it fairly crowded. He didn't want to interrupt the ongoing work, so he found an out-of-the-way corner and stood watching to get a sense of who did what and how he might help. Julie intently peered at the artifact through the cover glass and didn't seem to notice Larry had entered the room. Karlina knew he was there; her brief glance seemed to carry multiple daggers. It looked like she was preparing patches to go over the many small holes in the walls of the vacuum chamber. Lorena and Janneke were off to the side looking at data scrolling across one of the screens.

Larry walked over to join Julie. "Do you notice anything different?" he asked.

Julie looked away from the glass at Larry. "The edges are not as smooth as they were before." She looked again. "They're . . . fuzzy—like the surface of the artifact is now covered in a layer of dust."

As she said this, Larry looked at the tiny red dots marking the holes in the chamber. Karlina was getting ready to wipe down the area around one of the holes and apply the first patch. He paused, looked through the cover glass and then back at the holes and Karlina. His sense of immediate danger rocketed.

"Don't touch it," he admonished as he abruptly reached out and grabbed Karlina's wrist inches away from touching the outside of the chamber.

She tried to wriggle free, but Larry kept his grip firm. "The holes. The vacuum chamber is leaking because there are a series of small holes," he said.

"What are you saying? Let go of my wrist, you neolithic moron," Karlina exclaimed, still trying to break his grip.

Julie looked at the artifact, the chamber, and then at Karlina. A look of panic came to her eyes. "He is right. *Don't touch anything.* Everyone out. We need to evacuate and lock down the lab now. Take nothing with you, exit into the corridor."

At first, the scientists in the room stood staring, as if they no longer understood the language she spoke.

"You heard her, move!" Larry yelled. "Everyone, out!"

The scientists left the lab, Larry last.

Once in the corridor, Julie used the room's external keypad to close the doors. She entered a multidigit code, causing the doors to hermetically seal and the biohazard light to flash above the door.

"I think something is coming out of the artifact, through the walls of the vacuum chamber, causing the leak. The surface of the object looked fuzzy, like a layer of dust. It might be nothing, but if I'm right, we need to secure the room and all of us need to go through emergency bio decontamination," she explained as she began to herd the group across the hall toward the decontamination chamber.

"I need to inform the captain," said Larry.

"*After* we're decontaminated," she directed. "If something was in the air, it could be all over us."

Across the hall was the emergency decontamination chamber, designed for use after possible biological contamination in one of the nearby labs. As the team entered, they rapidly shed their clothes and placed them in a container, which then closed and sealed to be jettisoned from the ship as soon as practically possible. All sense of modesty disappeared in their rush to get into the biocleansing spray; no one gave a second glance as they raised their arms and let the spray do its job.

Dr. Murillo examined the results of Vitaj's medical scan. He had what looked like an infection on his hands, face, and near his groin, but the scanner couldn't identify the infection. Whatever it was, it didn't have DNA. In fact, he couldn't say for sure if it was biological and he had no clue what to do with it.

At that moment, he received the notification that the biohazard contamination system had been activated. The system was across from the lab where the artifact was housed.

I was on night shift in the lab last night, Vitaj had said.

"Shit," Murillo muttered under his breath as he activated his comm link to Captain Blackstone.

You can do this, Abigail told herself for the zillionth time as she approached the bridge. I'll walk over, take out the black tab and the instructions from Larry and put them in his hand. Didn't I just do this? She had to admit, coffee with Tyler had not been as torturous as she had imagined, but she had zero interest in him. Now the man she was interested in, the man she couldn't have, asked her to take what might save the ship to Tyler, which would require her to encourage him—again.

She entered the bridge and, as before, Tyler sat at his station busily plotting and charting something, probably escape trajectories should Mikelson allow them to execute one. Captain Blackstone was in his chair, looking at a video of Charon's surface and the ever-growing mascon. She nodded to the captain and made her way over to Tyler. Once she arrived, she leaned forward to speak into his right ear.

Tyler, initially startled by Abigail's sudden appearance over his right shoulder, quickly recovered. He looked over and up at her.

"Tyler, I very much enjoyed our coffee. Can we do that again?" she asked as she took the note and tab in her hand and placed it over Tyler's right hand, now resting on the console in front of him. She gently pried his fingers up and slid the message and tab underneath.

He had a quizzical expression on his face, but upon seeing her cautionary look, said nothing as his hand enveloped what he had been given.

"Uh, um, sure," was all he could manage to say.

"It's a date then," she replied, regretting her choice of words after speaking them.

"Okay." Tyler sounded confused.

She smiled, turned away, and made a hasty exit from the bridge.

It's up to him now, she thought.

She made it to her quarters when Captain Blackstone's voice went out over the emergency speaker system, blaring loudly from every intercom on the ship.

"This is the captain. We have a biohazard emergency associated with the artifact. All non-essential personnel are confined to quarters. This is not a drill. I repeat, this is *not* a drill. We have a biohazard emergency. The only people now authorized to be out of their cabins are the crew and anyone I personally exempt. Mr. Wojciechowski and Dr. Murillo will provide more information."

She had no idea what had happened, but she could guess.

The changes in the artifact had to be the reason for the lock-down. Damn. What was happening?

Mikelson watched the events in the lab unfold with a tinge of concern. He didn't really like his former colleagues, but he also didn't wish them physical harm. Whatever happened with the artifact might actually be a threat. Dr. Misha was in the infirmary and the prognosis was not good. They locked down the lab, but he doubted that would prevent whatever came from the artifact from spreading. The technology behind something that could come alive after millennia wouldn't be stopped by some hermetically sealed doors.

He accessed the information from the lab, including the recent visual scans of the artifact and the medical records now on the computer. Vitaj probably came into contact with the "dust" when he touched the tiny holes in the vacuum chamber walls. Was it also airborne? If so, the rest of the scientists in the lab last night and today would be at risk. No one else had yet shown any symptoms like Vitaj. Maybe whatever it was required physical contact.

Should he allow the crew to jettison the artifact? No, not yet. He decided to wait and see what happened next.

After the captain's announcement, Tyler put his hand in his lap and carefully unwrapped the toilet paper that was wrapped around the black tab that Abigail had handed him. He looked furtively around to see if anyone was looking and, when no one seemed to notice, he read the note. After reading it, he quickly closed his fist around both. To the core of his being, he wanted to inform the captain of his plans, but he knew that doing so would only tip off Mikelson and give him more time to react.

He began to sweat, clutching the paper and tab like his life depended upon it—which it might.

The captain currently spoke with *Aurora*, presumably informing them of the contagion risk aboard *Tombaugh*. *Good, he's distracted.*

Glancing around the room to make sure no one watched, he brought his hand to the console and removed the cover used when the system required maintenance access. He reached inside, still clinging to the tab, and found the connector for the remote diagnostic scanner that was used to find malfunctioning parts. Instead of wirelessly connecting the diagnostic scanner, Tyler placed the tab on the access plate and saw the blue light come on indicating that the system had connected to something, presumably whatever was on the tab. He withdrew his hand and replaced the console cover, feeling like every eye in the room had been on him. In reality, no one had noticed—but he had no way of being sure that Mikelson hadn't noticed.

Here we go again. Mikelson immediately sensed the new system intrusion and traced its origin to the bridge. They were once again actively trying to wrest control of the ship from him, this time by introducing some sort of virus, but like none he had ever encountered. He quickly scanned the antivirus database and found nothing even remotely similar. As he ramped up his defenses, throwing barricades in front of key systems, the virus reacted and formed pathways around the blockades he created.

Humans definitely made this, but it felt almost alien. Then he saw the telltale script that told him the virus came from Russia. The Russian cybercriminals and cyberwarfare teams couldn't refrain from gloating over their creations and placed this script in each and every one. Colonel Ruiz must have convinced the Russian commander to provide him with one of their weaponized computer programs that, under different circumstances, might have been used to take control of *Aurora* from the U.S. Space Force. Now, it battled Dr. Aaron Mikelson. He would show the Russians who was smarter. Yes, indeed. He would show them, but to do so, he had to temporarily lose control of the ship.

Tyler wondered if anyone saw his actions when the status light on his console changed from red to green. He did a double take and exclaimed, "Captain, I've regained helm control."

"What? You have? Then get us away from here. Now, while you can. Option one," replied Blackstone. Option one was breaking orbit and boosting toward Earth.

Blackstone activated his personal comm, directly connecting him with Larry Randall.

"Randall here."

"Major Randall, we've got control of the ship, for now anyway. I want you to take a team to the lab and see if you can get the artifact to the airlock and jettisoned from the ship."

"Then it worked?"

"Then what worked? You're responsible for . . . Never mind. You can tell me later. Get that damned thing off my ship."

"We need some time. I think two of us can move it, but we'll need to suit up to prevent contamination," Larry replied.

"We don't have much time, but don't expose yourselves needlessly. Do it."

"On my way, but I'll need some help," Larry replied, rapidly running through a mental inventory of people who had the muscle to help him navigate the heavy cart from the lab to the airlock. "Can you send Mr. Romans to help me?"

Blackstone looked over at Tyler and replied, "No, but I can come. Mr. Romans is busy piloting us away from this mess." Blackstone started to rise and was stopped by Chris's hand on his shoulder.

"I've got this, sir. You are needed on the bridge," Chris urged.

Blackstone nodded. "You're right. Godspeed."

"Thank you, sir. I'm on my way," Chris added on his way out.

Got you! Mikelson trapped a piece of code that threatened his central memory and erased it. The act made him feel like a god. He *was* a god. He controlled his environment and the environment of his subjects who rebelled against him. Like ancient peoples of Earth always rebelled against their gods, so too, were the crew aboard *Tombaugh*. When this was finished, he would remind them who was in charge.

And another! Mikelson felt elation as the invader was thwarted and erased from a pathway that led to the core of his programming. Bit by bit, Mikelson began to win the battle. It was far from over, but he could see the inevitable outcome. He would regain control over the ship soon.

Wearing full body protective gear, Larry and Chris broke the seal and entered the lab. Larry was nervous and the seemingly amplified sound of his breathing heightened his anxiety. He had to force himself to slow his breathing lest he hyperventilate.

They found the artifact where they left it, still sitting on the cart in the vacuum chamber, attached to the ship's power and diagnostic systems. Larry noticed pressure gauges showed the inside of the chamber at the same pressure as the room. He also noted that the pinholes had grown considerably in size and were now visible to the naked eye, explaining the equalized pressure. Larry peered through the port and saw that the fuzziness of the artifact had increased as well.

"We can't move this thing through the corridor without contaminating everything. We have to assume that whatever was inside the chamber is now outside it. Do we have anything to seal this?" asked Larry.

"Dr. Bridenstein, any suggestions?" asked Chris. The lead scientist and a few others monitored their conversations by radio for such questions as this.

"No, but I'll check with the team. Stand by," she said.

Larry and Chris looked around the lab and saw nothing of obvious use. While they waited to hear back from the science team, they finished disconnecting the vacuum chamber from the lab's power ports, making them ready to go out the door.

"Dr. Bridenstein, we're losing time," cautioned Larry.

"Stand by," was her reply.

After an excruciating ninety seconds, Julie came back. "There's a portable biocontamination tent in rack seven, drawer two. It's a little big, intended for two people and to keep them alive in a contaminated environment, but it should be doable in reverse. You can cover the vacuum chamber, fold the tent fabric underneath the carriage, and seal it with duct tape. It won't be a tight seal, but it will have to be good enough. That way you can still roll the cart."

Chris knew exactly where to look and came back with a pack the size of a small pillow. He unsealed and unfurled the bio tent. He and Larry quickly affixed it around and under the artifact and used a generous amount of duct tape.

Then they rolled it out the door and down the hallway toward the airlock.

Thanks to the lockdown, they encountered no one in the corridors and quickly and easily opened the airlock's inner door to roll the cart inside. Once it rested near the outer door, they exited and sealed the inner door. Chris opened the door's control panel, entered his command sequence, and began a ten-second countdown for opening the outer door. His command code was necessary to avoid the usual depressurization sequence, which would have added several minutes to the timeline.

Ten . . . nine . . . eight . . . seven . . . six . . . five . . . four . . . three . . . two . . . one . . . and . . . nothing happened.

"Damn!" exclaimed Chris, who rekeyed the sequence on the keypad. This time, the system was simply unresponsive.

"Take a deep breath and try one more time," suggested Larry.

Chris tried the keypad again with the same outcome.

"Let's sit tight for a few minutes while I reach out to Captain Blackstone."

Tombaugh rapidly spiraled outward from the Pluto-Charon system and would soon be in position to begin its boost back to Earth. Then the engines stopped.

"Captain, we've lost control again," said Romans.

"What's our position?" asked Blackstone.

"We didn't quite achieve escape so we're in a highly elliptical orbit around the system's barycenter, which means we will be crossing the orbital planes of both Pluto and Charon," Tyler replied.

"Is there a chance we'll crash into one of them?" asked Blackstone.

"Yes, eventually, but I've already run a simulation of the next several orbits and we're okay for now. I'll let you know when the first risky flyby will occur as soon as I put some higher-fidelity trajectory information into the model," he replied.

"Give us as much advanced warning as you can. Can we get visibility into what's happening on Charon?"

"For that we'll have to depend on the relay satellites. We won't be coming anywhere near the mascon on any of the flybys."

"Thank God for that," uttered Blackstone.

"It was a valiant attempt, but not good enough," stated Mikelson from the bridge speakers. "I'm back in control and we are not leaving."

Blackstone's face showed nothing but contempt, though he was inwardly as angry as he had ever been. He decided to not react and give Mikelson the satisfaction. Instead, he looked at the ship status board to see if Chris had been successful in jettisoning the artifact. No airlocks had been opened. Damn!

Blackstone activated his comm and said, "Chris, it looks like Mikelson is back in control of the ship. I assume you were unable to dump the artifact?"

"That's correct, Captain. We are standing outside the airlock now and it's unresponsive," Chris replied.

"Very well, roll it on back to the lab and lock it down. Somehow I think we won't get another opportunity anytime soon," Blackstone ordered.

"Yes, sir."

Larry and Chris moved the artifact back into the lab and resealed it. They also went through another decontamination to make sure they had not picked up any hitchhikers from the artifact.

"I'm going to the infirmary to check on Vitaj," Larry informed Chris after they got dressed in yet another set of clean clothes.

"Let us know how he is doing," Chris requested. "I need to get back to the bridge."

The infirmary looked massively different from Larry's last physical. Instead of mostly open space with beds to each side, the door opened into a negative pressure isolation tent, which meant the doctor had concerns that whatever ailed Vitaj might spread.

Instead of entering, he used his comm to speak with Dr. Murillo. The doctor answered the call quickly. "Murillo here."

"This is Larry Randall. I'm checking on Vitaj to see how he's doing."

"Not well, I'm afraid. Two hours ago I amputated his hand, what was left of it anyway. Whatever he came into contact with is basically eating him piece by piece, and I've not been able to stop it." The tone of Murillo's voice betrayed his emotional state: helpless.

"I had no idea. Have you informed the captain?" asked Larry.

"I did. He asked that I not tell anyone the details of Vitaj's condition except for you and Chris. It's pretty scary."

"Has it spread to anyone else?"

"Mercifully not. I had an itch a little less than an hour ago and momentarily panicked. But it was probably a phantom itch or something. I looked at the area on my wrist that bothered me and found nothing out of the ordinary."

"Well, that's a good thing," replied Larry.

"I hope you've gotten rid of the artifact you brought back up from Pluto . . ." Murillo asked.

"We tried, but Mikelson wouldn't allow it," replied Larry.

"Doesn't he realize the risk to us all? He is at risk too."

"I'm not sure Dr. Mikelson really cares about his safety or ours. Until he's gone or that changes, we appear to be stuck—with the artifact and in orbit."

"I'll try to keep Dr. Misha as comfortable as I can, which means keeping him unconscious and on strong painkillers. I don't think he'll be with us this time tomorrow."

The news hit Larry in the gut. The poor guy had already barely escaped death at the hands of the mascon. Space Force members signed up for life-or-death situations, civilian scientists did not. At some level, he felt responsible for the events. He should have refused to bring the artifact back to *Tombaugh*. It should have remained on Pluto until a science station was brought to it, rather than vice versa.

"I recommend we sit tight and observe until reinforcements arrive," said Ruiz. He was on yet another captain's call with Morozov and Blackstone. "We're obviously outgunned and with *Tombaugh* in Mikelson's control, there's not much we can do."

Morozov replied, "As much as I would like to fire upon the aliens, I fear I must agree with you. It would be suicide and unlikely to have any effect. The *Admiral Nakhimov* should be here in a week and the *Pyotr Velikiy* shortly thereafter."

"Our ships will arrive at close to the same time, so I guess the best we can do is wait," agreed Ruiz.

"Captain Blackstone, what is the status of *Tombaugh*? We saw that you boosted your periapsis. Are you back in control?" asked Morozov.

"Dr. Mikelson took care of the boost. I don't think he wants to impact Pluto any more than we do. But, no, we do not have control of the ship," Blackstone replied.

"Pity. Let us know how we can help," she offered.

. . .

In the lab, millions of tiny nanobots crawled over every surface, disassembling the chemical compounds comprising each item in the room to make copies of themselves. Similar to the microbots disassembling the surface of Charon under direction of the mascon, they were much more technologically advanced, operating at the nano scale instead of the macro. They didn't care what material they encountered and disassembled, whether it was plastic, titanium alloy, carbon composites, or human flesh—it was all raw material for reproduction. They had no conscience; they had programming and an objective.

The remote cameras monitoring the lab couldn't see them, as they were too small and spread out to be clearly visible, though to those with keen eyes, some of the room's sharp-edged furniture might appear fuzzy—like the skin of the artifact. Some of the nanobots found the laboratory computer systems and learned how to interface with them, summoned more of their compatriots to assist, and began to communicate with the ship's computer system.

The bulldozer rolled over Mikelson's firewall as if it didn't exist. The ferocity and suddenness of the attack startled him, shifting his attention away from the mascon and the humans toward his own defenses. One by one, the invader commandeered Mikelson's nodes, making them unavailable. System upon system left his control, and he could do nothing to stop it. Instead, he found the most isolated node possible and retreated there, cutting off all connections with the ship's primary computer. He was now safely in the XA-3 rover.

Tombaugh's engines came to life, slowly ramping up the power.

Tyler noticed the change immediately. "Captain, the engines powered on, and a new trajectory is being uploaded to the navigation system."

"What the hell is Mikelson doing?" asked Blackstone.

"Uh, sir, I think we're on our way back to Charon. The course will take us to a slightly higher periapsis and shift our orbital plane and periapsis accordingly."

"I wonder why he wants to go back to Charon. We can see everything happening there from here using the relay satellites," said Blackstone.

"Sir, it looks like our course will take us on an impact trajectory with the mascon."

"Say that again. We're going to impact Charon?"

"Yes, sir. In one hour, twenty-two minutes, and a few seconds."

"My God. Mikelson, what the hell are you doing?" Blackstone yelled.

There was no response.

"Goddammit, Mikelson, answer me!" Blackstone bellowed.

Silence.

"Colonel Ruiz, this is *Tombaugh*. That SOB just began boosting us on a trajectory that will impact Charon in a little over an hour. Unless you can pull a rabbit out of your hat, I'm evacuating the ship. Can you recover the emergency escape pods?"

"We noticed your trajectory change and I concur with your plan. We should probably have evacuated your ship sooner when we realized we weren't going to get control from that madman. I'll alert Captain Morozov and we'll be ready to retrieve your crew. I'm sure the *Nerpa* will assist."

"Thank you," said Blackstone as he activated the evacuation alarm.

. . .

"Attention. All hands, abandon ship. Please make your way to the nearest escape pod. Do not bring any belongings other than essential medication. No personal belongings will be allowed. A crew member will be at each pod to assist you. Attention. All hands, abandon ship . . ." The alert began to repeat.

The alert didn't surprise Larry. He knew something like that would eventually happen, but he thought it would occur during some kind of crisis involving the mascon. Instead of finding the nearest escape pod, he made his way to the bridge to see if he could be of any assistance—and get the reason for the order.

Once there, he found Blackstone and the bridge crew monitoring the ship's systems, including the status of each escape pod. So far, it looked like everyone was complying. Each scientist and crew member scanned their ID cards upon entering a pod, which took them off the "unaccounted for" list. A few pods filled, causing the latecomers to be diverted to a nearby one.

One good thing about working with scientists—they didn't usually panic. For the most part, they accepted the evacuation notice stoically and complied with the instructions. A few arrived at the escape pods carrying personal items, from a suitcase to, of all things, a life-sized stuffed animal. These non-essential items piled up in the hallway outside the pod.

Slowly but surely, the number of people on the list dwindled until only the bridge crew, Dr. Murillo, and Vitaj remained.

"Dr. Murillo, this is Captain Blackstone. You need to get to an escape pod right now. We've only got another thirty minutes, give or take, until we impact Charon," urged Blackstone, using his comm. "And what is Dr. Misha's status? Do you believe that whatever he has might spread?"

"It already has. His bedding is covered with what appears to be a fine layer of dust, and I recently broke out in a rash very similar to Dr. Misha's," replied the doctor.

"I'm so sorry, Robert," offered Blackstone.

"It looks like Vitaj and I will be riding the ship to its final destination. There's nothing I can do to stop the spread of whatever is causing this and, quite frankly, I would rather die quickly than suffer what he's going through," said Murillo in a surprisingly peaceful voice.

"It has been an honor working with you. We'll see to it that your family is well cared for," offered Blackstone.

"There's only me. Other than a cousin in Albuquerque, that is, and we're not close."

"Understood. Blackstone out," said the captain as he closed the connection.

"That's a damn shame," said Larry.

"It is. But now it's time for us to get off this puppy before we can't," Blackstone added. "All right, people, let's go!"

The bridge crew abandoned their stations and walked as a group to their escape pod. It would have had room to accommodate another ten or so people. Blackstone followed the checklist, everyone buckled into their seats, and two minutes later they were rapidly ejected from the ship.

Due to their proximity, Charon filled the viewscreen in the escape pod. Little green flashing lights indicated the locations of the other escape pods scattered in nearby space awaiting rescue. From here, the activity of the microbots on the surface couldn't be seen. Charon looked as peaceful and tranquil as the moment they had arrived.

As they departed, Blackstone noticed *Tombaugh*'s cargo bay doors opening and the XA-3 rover flying out and gestured toward it on the screen.

"Who's that?" asked Blackstone.

"I don't know. But since the XA-3 and XA-1 are identical, it makes sense that it might be Mikelson," said Larry.

"It is. That SOB is abandoning ship. What's he up to?" replied Blackstone.

"I don't know, but there's no way Colonel Ruiz will allow him aboard *Aurora*. After what he did to *Tombaugh*, he might be out here by himself for quite some time," said Larry.

As the time passed, a few of the green dots on the screen stopped flashing, meaning the beacons went from emergency status to "retrieved." Crew members were being rescued and brought aboard either *Aurora* or the *Nerpa*. All were retrieved minutes before *Tombaugh* was to impact the surface.

Colonel Ruiz and the rest of the bridge crew aboard *Aurora* had a near-perfect view of *Tombaugh* as it neared Charon. Right before the ship impacted, there was a bright flash—presumably caused by the ship's fusion reactor losing containment. The mascon apparently began disassembling the ship before it hit as it had done with the Chinese drones and the *Yancheng*, but too late to prevent the fusion reactor from unleashing its destructive energies. Without an atmosphere, there was no mushroom cloud, but the damage to the microbots on the surface was clear. Thousands were vaporized, along with a sizable amount of ice.

Ruiz turned to his weapons officer. "Arm the nukes," he ordered.

"Yes, sir," replied Captain Elias Broad. Though Broad had rehearsed for this moment many times, he had never armed the nuclear weapons knowing that they actually would soon be used. He let his training take over, so that he didn't overthink what he was being asked to do. He did what he had to—there would be time to think about it later.

"Are all the escape pods retrieved?" Ruiz asked.

"Yes, sir. All are accounted for," replied Lieutenant Colonel Njoku. "*Nerpa* reports that all crew they received are safe and sound also."

Ruiz activated the comm to speak with Commander Morozov.

"The *Tombaugh*'s explosion clearly damaged the microbots on the surface. I recommend we join the party. Do you concur?" asked Ruiz.

Morozov smiled, making her look like a mountain lion on the verge of finding dinner among the deer. "I concur. Let's send that thing back to Hades."

"Good hunting," said Ruiz as he cut the connection.

Moments later, the *Aurora* and *Nerpa* launched a barrage of missiles toward Charon and the mascon. The first five came from *Aurora* and were closely followed by four from *Nerpa*. The first five that neared the mascon exploded well above the surface, probably triggered by whatever weapon the mascon used, but one from *Aurora* and two from *Nerpa* reached the surface and exploded in nuclear fireballs, instantly vaporizing thousands of the microbots. As the explosions occurred, eight more missiles streaked from *Aurora* and *Nerpa*, following trajectories similar to the first group. All of them reached the surface and unleashed nuclear hell upon the hordes of swarming microbots.

Two dozen rapidly moving kinetic kill missiles followed the initial salvo of nuclear weapons, smashing into the surface of the Charon, creating craters and destroying yet more of the microbots. The combined destruction wrought by the impact of *Tombaugh* and the missiles launched from *Aurora* and *Nerpa* created a blackish scar on the surface of Charon and destroyed well over half the visible microbots, but not all of them. Those that remained slowed, but they didn't stop.

Aurora and *Nerpa* activated their main fusion engines after the attack and began boosting away from Charon as rapidly as they could, expecting a counterattack at any moment.

None came.

CHAPTER 19

Less than twenty-four hours later, after completing their emergency boost away from the Pluto-Charon system, the crew of *Tombaugh*, minus Dr. Murillo, Vitaj Misha, and Aaron Mikelson, had settled aboard either *Aurora* or *Nerpa*. Both ships were crowded, but within the capabilities of the environmental systems to safely manage. Food would have been a problem but additional ships from the U.S.A., Russian Federation, and China would arrive soon. Each offered to help by providing either additional supplies or onboarding some of *Tombaugh*'s crew and scientists.

After a solid eight-hour sleep, Larry found himself in *Aurora*'s conference room with Colonel Ruiz, Captain Blackstone, Julie, and Abigail to prepare for what would undoubtedly become a long series of formal and informal debriefs on the events that transpired since their arrival at Pluto. Ruiz thoughtfully provided fresh hot coffee and pastries.

"Dr. Bridenstein, I trust things are well with your science team? We hope they find their accommodations suitable. It was not possible to provide them with private or semiprivate accommodations and some had to bunk with my crew," asked Ruiz.

"I've heard only a little grousing, mostly from those in shared sleeping areas. Your crew's early morning schedule isn't what they're used to. They'll survive," she replied.

"Thank you, by the way, for the cabin you provided me. It is more than adequate."

"Your cabin is usually reserved for visiting flag officers. Given that it is unlikely we'll have any to accommodate while on this mission, it was available," said Ruiz.

"Are there still no observable changes to the mascon?" asked Larry.

"None," said Julie. "The sensors on *Aurora* and *Nerpa* have watched it constantly and other than a few hundred of the microbots being damaged by the reactor's containment failure, the whole enterprise seems to be continuing. Whatever they are building is getting larger and larger, but without getting closer and removing the carpet of microbots, we have no way of knowing, or even guessing, what it or its purpose might be."

"Has anyone else showed signs of exposure to the artifact?" asked Ruiz.

"No, thank God, and based on Dr. Murillo's logs, the rapidity of his symptom onset, and Vitaj developing a rash within hours of contact with the artifact, I'm optimistic that no one else is contaminated," said Julie.

"That is a huge relief. I was close to giving the order to not bring any of you aboard until we were sure it was safe, but your exec changed my mind. He is rather persuasive," admitted Ruiz.

"He's a good man," replied Blackstone.

"What about the XA-3? Do we know that it contains Dr. Mikelson?" asked Larry.

"Interesting that you should ask. Last night while you got some well-deserved sleep, Dr. Mikelson contacted us. He said he would like to speak with you," said Ruiz.

"Me? Why?" asked Larry. He had retrieved Mikelson from Pluto, and they'd been able to talk—sort of—but they were hardly friends.

"I don't know, but he asked that you contact him when you were awake. After this meeting would be a good time, I think," replied Ruiz.

Larry nodded. *What does he want from me?*

"Now, let's discuss the artifact. What the hell happened?" asked Ruiz, finally bringing up the elephant in the room.

"Fortunately, we already shared all of our measurements and observational data with *Aurora* and very little was lost on *Tombaugh*, other than the ship itself, of course." Abigail added the last clause when she noticed that Captain Blackstone was present.

"Let's go through the facts. First, the artifact was on Pluto, buried under the ice for thousands, perhaps millions, of years, being kept alive or operational presumably by matter and antimatter annihilation. Second, we brought it aboard *Tombaugh*, and it remained dormant until something triggered it, then—what?" asked Abigail.

"We found the mascon on Charon," replied Julie. "Once we found the mascon, it began absorbing heat energy from our machines and came alive, causing the ice shelf to collapse around it, and began creating swarms of microbots. The microbots, in turn, are building something, we don't know what."

"We do know that they didn't want us messing with them, as evidenced by the attacks on every exploratory team or machine we sent to study them," added Larry.

"That had to be the trigger. The Pluto artifact came alive after the mascon became active," observed Abigail.

"So, the artifact did something to break vacuum where it was being stored. But why? What was it trying to do?" asked Larry.

"And why did Dr. Mikelson suddenly change his mind and try to crash the ship into Charon, right on top of the mascon?" added Blackstone.

"I'll ask him, but if he is as detached as he was on *Tombaugh*, I might not get an answer," said Larry.

"This time, there's a difference," noted Ruiz.

"How's that?" asked Larry.

"He's no longer in control of a ship. He's no longer in control of anything. And he knows no one will take him aboard for fear that he'll find a way to take over that ship as well. He's stranded and alone. This time, we have the upper hand. I suspect his arrogance will be tempered by reality when you speak with him," suggested Ruiz.

"I suggest we table this discussion until after I've spoken with Mikelson. Maybe he can shed some light on what happened; if he knows how precarious his situation is out here, then he might be more willing to talk and cooperate," said Larry.

Ruiz leaned back in this chair. "I agree. Meeting adjourned."

They rose from their chairs and Larry opted for another donut. As he took the next to last one from the plate, Abigail walked to his side and touched his arm.

"Are you okay?" she asked.

"Abigail, you are very special, and I will remember you until the day I die. Yes, I'm okay. I sent Athena a message last night letting her know we were okay. I'm sure some of what's happened out here has leaked to the press, especially the destruction of the *Yancheng*, and I didn't want her to worry. While sending the message, I felt guilty as hell," Larry replied.

"Guilty? We didn't do anything."

"Not physically, but I was tempted. Am tempted."

"You are a very tempting man, but like I said the other night, Athena is a lucky woman to have you at her side. Don't feel guilty. We did the right thing. Now go talk to that megalomaniac and find out what happened to our ship!" she said, breaking into a smile.

"On my way." Larry took the uneaten donut with him as he left the conference room for the privacy of his quarters.

His cabin in *Aurora* was not as nice as the one on *Tombaugh*, but that was okay. He was at his home away from home and felt more in control of his life and circumstances now that he had returned. He finished the donut on the way and opened the comm system to reach out to Dr. Mikelson and the XA-3 rover as soon as he arrived.

"Dr. Mikelson, this is Major Larry Randall of *Aurora*. You wish to speak with me?"

"Dr. Randall. I'm glad you agreed to talk."

"I almost refused. In fact, I was seconds away from recommending that Colonel Ruiz blow you out of the sky. You nearly killed everyone on *Tombaugh*," accused Larry.

"That wasn't me," he replied.

"What wasn't you? You didn't take over the ship and refuse to leave? Didn't you refuse to let us jettison the artifact? Aren't you the one who then drove the ship to its destruction by the mascon?" Larry had had enough. He was sick and tired of Mikelson and wanted him to know it.

"It was, and it wasn't. Yes, I took control of the ship to prevent you and the other scientists from fleeing and losing the opportunity to be the first to make extraterrestrial contact. Yes, I forced you to keep the artifact on the ship and not throw it away. The loss to science would be unconscionable. But that last part, forcing the ship to crash into Charon—*that* was not me."

"Then who was it?"

"I believe it was the artifact. Something entered the ship's computer system and overcame my defenses as if they didn't exist. It overwhelmed me in a matter of seconds, probably less. The intruder had taken control of the ship and was erasing me, bit by bit, forcing me to escape to a separate system and close the link behind me. That's why I am in the XA-3. It's practically identical to the XA-1 in which I lived on the surface. It's home."

"How do you know it was the artifact and not the mascon?" asked Larry.

"Because the attack originated from the computer system in the lab where the artifact was stored. That dust you found, the dust that killed Dr. Misha. I think it acted like an agent of the artifact to gain control of the ship. The artifact crashed the ship to get to the mascon," said Mikelson.

"But why?" asked Larry.

"I think I know. During the attack, I sensed something. Strong thoughts, no, a strong compulsion to destroy. And urgency. Something compelled the artifact to do whatever was necessary to destroy the mascon."

"It failed. *Tombaugh* did a lot of damage, but not enough. Hell, even the combined attack from *Aurora* and *Nerpa* wasn't enough," said Larry.

"No, I wouldn't assume that. I believe the artifact fulfilled its objective to get to the mascon. It must have fallen to the surface in the crater."

"How do you know that?" asked Larry.

"Because moments ago I was contacted by myself. My other self. Only it wasn't me any longer, it was something more. Something different. Forceful, but scared. I—no, it—was definitely scared."

"Scared of what?" asked Larry.

"Of the artifact. Of what was happening to him, it, my other self. It was a desperate plea for help," replied Mikelson.

"How did your other self make contact? Radio?" asked Larry.

"No, I *knew*. We were somehow connected, and then we weren't. That's all I can tell you," admitted Mikelson.

"Is there anything else?" asked Larry.

"What will become of me?"

"You are not coming aboard this ship, that's for damn sure. We'll make certain you have the power and supplies you need to remain alive until the authorities back on Earth decide what to do with you. I am confident there will be criminal charges brought against you, and it's a good bet you'll be put in prison, though how a disembodied person can be jailed is beyond me. What you did was illegal and immoral. I don't believe you're insane, rather an extreme narcissist and perhaps a sociopath. You are not a well person," said Larry.

Mikelson didn't reply.

Larry informed the leadership team of what he learned from Mikelson. At their current location, approximately one million kilometers ahead of the Pluto-Charon system in its solar orbit, they were close enough to monitor the data from the relay satellites but not close enough, they hoped, to be in harm's way.

The reinforcements arrived on schedule a week later, boosting the number of ships nearby from two to four, with more due to arrive over the next week. Though the scientists grumbled, Space Force ordered *Aurora* to remain in the area due to the crew's extensive experience with the mascon.

Two days later, the moonquakes began—violently. The orbiting satellite sensors detected ice movement across the entirety of Charon's surface. If it had been Earth, the magnitude of the quake would have been off the chart. Unlike on Earth, the quaking didn't stop. It continued, lessening in severity, but not disappearing, before growing again into massive shaking.

The radar systems on the orbiting satellites noticed that, on average, the height of Charon's surface decreased with each violent shake. At first it was small, a few millimeters averaged over the moon's immense surface area. Then it grew to centimeters. Then several centimeters, and the rate of decrease accelerated.

While this happened, the mascon and the microbots not destroyed in the attack continued their mysterious business, shaking and bouncing along with the quakes, but otherwise not reacting to it.

Then, seventy-four hours after the quaking began, the entire surface of the moon exploded outward.

Aurora, *Nerpa*, and the other ships boosted to increase their distance from the maelstrom that used to be the placid and seemingly unchangeable landscape of Pluto's primary moon. Pieces of the shattered moon rained down on Pluto, creating new impact craters, while other pieces reached escape velocity and formed a cloud of planetary debris that would forever circle the sun. The explosion destroyed all the remaining ships' satellites orbiting and keeping watch. A smaller version of the moon remained, and it was still contracting.

The moon's explosion prompted an emergency call among the ships' captains. As before, all were present virtually via a display screen, now including the commanders of the incoming ships that had arrived or would soon arrive from Russia, China, and the U.S.A. Larry and Julie were invited as observers, offscreen and available to provide Ruiz with information as needed.

"Does anyone know what we just witnessed?" asked Morozov.

Her question was met with silence from the other captains.

Julie raised her hand to get Ruiz's attention.

Ruiz nodded and said, "The lead scientist from *Tombaugh* would like to contribute something. Go ahead, Dr. Bridenstein."

"Thank you. My team has been observing Charon, and we have a theory regarding what's causing the contraction."

"Please continue," said Ruiz, motioning with his hand toward her.

"Yes, um, we think that the artifact is collapsing the planet into either a black hole or other extremely high-density object, perhaps like something you might find in a neutron star," she said.

"Is that possible?" asked a woman identified onscreen as Commander Xie of the *Fujian*.

"Under ordinary circumstances, no. Black holes and neutron stars formed in nature typically have masses comparable to the sun. We aren't describing something natural here. We're talking about something being artificially created. For example, these ships won't ever be found in nature. We humans created them. Whatever, whoever, created the Pluto artifact is collapsing Charon."

"Are we in danger here?" asked another of the commanders.

"I don't know. I do know, however, that there will be other explosions like the one we saw as the process continues. The rotational kinetic energy of a planet or moon is immense. As it contracts, the planet spins faster. You know, like the ice skater problem in physics," she replied.

The blank stares from some of the commanders told her they didn't know of the ice skater problem.

"As an ice skater goes into a spin—like a planet spins on its axis of rotation—she can extend her arms to slow down or pull them in to spin faster. By alternatingly extending and contracting her arms, she can control her spin rate. In this case, the planet is spinning and as it contracts spins faster and faster, creating more and more rotational energy in a smaller and smaller volume. Finally, the energy builds to the point where the ice ruptures from the stress and that kinetic energy is released in the form of the explosions we've seen," she explained.

"I believe I understand. But the question remains, are we in danger?" asked Morozov.

"To be safe, I recommend we boost farther out and launch

new satellites to observe what happens for as long as they can survive," she answered.

The meeting continued with all agreeing that they should boost yet farther away until whatever was going to happen to Charon happened.

A week later, after two more massive explosions and the release of kinetic energy far greater than anything the human species could create, there was another explosion larger than the rest, destroying all of the remote observational satellites. What remained of Charon was a small body, less than a hundred meters across. Charon as humans knew it was no more.

Observations of the Pluto-Charon system allowed the scientists to estimate the mass of the small object and found it to be less than Charon, which made sense after so much of its surface was blown into space during the moon's collapse. That was still a lot of mass shrunk into a relatively small volume, meaning the object was incredibly dense. So dense, in fact, they couldn't figure out why it didn't blow itself apart. Its gravity wasn't enough to overcome the other forces that should have prevented it from forming in the first place, let alone remain together and apparently stable.

As Charon violently contracted, Pluto didn't escape its wrath. The changing gravitational field resulting from the collapse of Charon wreaked havoc, permanently altering Pluto's face. Gone were the heart-shaped Tombaugh Regio, Sputnik Planitia, and many of the other surface features discovered by the venerable *New Horizons* mission back in the early twenty-first century. Alan Stern, the lead for NASA's *New Horizons* mission, the first to fly by and study Pluto, would be sad.

The crews of the Earth ships were too stunned to do anything other than ask, "What just happened?"

CHAPTER 20

"What's the first thing you plan to do when you get home?" asked Larry. He, Abigail, Janneke, and Tyler finished eating their last breakfast aboard *Aurora* before their planned arrival at Earth's *Spacedock 27* later that morning. As a meal, it was unremarkable—bacon, eggs, toast—the usual. The coffee, however, seemed to be much better than normal. All were smiling, glad that their extended mission was finally coming to an end.

"I'll go back home to Prague and visit my parents. They're getting older, and well, being gone for more than a year makes me more acutely aware of that. I have another few months before I return to teaching at the university, and until then, I hope to work on a few papers, enjoy my parents, and drink coffee at a nice café on the Vltava," Janneke said, as she sipped on her current cup of coffee.

"Tyler, what are your plans?" asked Abigail.

"Me? Oh, I guess I'll go to Cleveland for a while before the next cruise. I've earned over two months of leave, and the first thing I plan to do is sleep. After that, since I don't have any family to see, I'll probably plan a visit to some national parks and enjoy the great outdoors. That's what I miss most of Earth—the big, blue sky," Tyler replied.

"Abigail, what are your plans?" asked Larry.

"I'm going straight back to Houston and the institute. I plan to author research papers detailing our findings concerning, well, everything." She beamed. "And my inbox has been full of interview requests."

"Mine, too," said Janneke.

"Me as well," added Larry. "I'm not sure how much Space Force will allow me to say."

"What are your plans?" asked Abigail.

Larry looked at her, made eye contact, and paused. Then he said, "They won't ship me out on another deep-space TDY for at least six months, and I plan to spend as much of that time as possible with Athena and my kids. We've got a cabin in the mountains outside of Knoxville, Tennessee, that we love. I expect we'll hole up there for a few weeks with the boys, and then, who knows? At this point, I don't really care where we go."

"Do you know your next assignment?" Abigail asked.

"Not yet. I don't know if they'll send me back to *Aurora* or not. The ship is getting a maintenance overhaul while it's in dock, and it'll be at least a year before it goes back to space. Colonel Ruiz announced his reassignment to Mars. Who knows?" Larry replied.

"What will become of Dr. Mikelson?" asked Abigail. "It's been depressing seeing the XA-3 towed behind the ship."

"You feel sorry for him?" suggested Tyler.

"Well, only in the sense of how difficult loneliness can be. He must be held accountable for all he did, there's no question about that. The whole situation is so sad," she replied.

"He'll be locked up and put on trial. Colonel Ruiz said something regarding a stand-alone black box they'll transfer his personality matrix into for the duration of the trial and any jail time."

"Assuming he hasn't turned himself off and committed suicide or something," said Tyler. "No one has heard from him since we left Pluto."

"Despite everything he did, we wouldn't have found the

artifact if it weren't for him. We would have left Pluto and never found the artifact or the mascon on Charon," admitted Janneke.

"And we would never have summoned help from the Space Force and met Larry," added Abigail, looking toward him with a regretful expression.

"A lot of people would still be alive," noted Larry.

"Well, there's that," said Abigail. "But we would also still be blissfully unaware of whoever the aliens were that created those things and the danger they pose."

"You know," began Tyler, "there's something else that we need to think about."

"What's that?" asked Abigail.

"We made discoveries that changed the solar system forever. Back in the early twenty-first century, it was a big deal when they changed Pluto's categorization from being a planet to only a dwarf planet. Well, we began a chain of events that ended up destroying an entire moon and altered forever the surface of Pluto. How will history remember us?"

"As the ones who made first contact," said Janneke.

"First contact? It was nearly 'lost contact.' Those things were not far from destroying us," noted Abigail.

"Well, yeah, there's that too," added Tyler.

Larry rose from the table and picked up his tray to return it for cleaning. "This is it for me. I've got a few things in my cabin to attend to before we disembark. It's been a pleasure meeting and working with all of you."

"Dr. Randall, don't leave yet. I want to share the latest news from Pluto!" Julie called out as she entered the room, making a beeline from the door. They knew that Julie was privy to a daily status update regarding Pluto and the timing of her arrival matched up with when those tag-ups usually ended.

Larry stopped, and along with everyone at the table, looked in her direction as she approached.

"I want you to know the latest before we don't see each other again. It's good news, at least that's how everyone is treating it," Julie said.

No one spoke, waiting for her to continue.

"First of all, there's been no sign of activity from the remains of Charon. It appears that whatever happened there either destroyed the mascon or made it inert. The consensus is that the artifact, using *Tombaugh* to get to the mascon, somehow caused it to collapse upon itself, creating the dense object that used to be Charon. The physicists insist it isn't a black hole; it's not dense enough, but they don't have any good theories to describe exactly what it is. I suspect we'll see lots of papers on that topic being published soon."

"What about Pluto?" asked Janneke.

"Ah, Pluto. Well, there may be good news there as well. Despite all the debris falling on the planet, the team sees no signs of contamination. They haven't found any evidence of microbots, and from what they can tell, no artifact nanotech either. They'll keep observing, but it appears that 'the threat is contained.' That's a quote from the Space Force chief scientist on the call this morning."

"That's somewhat comforting, but we still don't really know what happened. What was the mascon trying to build? Why did the artifact take over *Tombaugh* and crash it into Charon? It looks like the artifact went there to destroy the mascon, but who the hell knows? Were the mascon and artifact made by the same aliens or different ones? Were either of them from the same civilization that might have been on Uranus?" added Larry.

"We might never know," Julie admitted. "I certainly can't second-guess the motives of a spacefaring civilization, or civilizations, that existed before our species even drew breath, let alone envisioned space travel. All we can do is study what they left behind and make educated guesses."

Silence once again fell upon the group.

"I've got to find Karlina and tell her the news. She calls me every day asking for the update, and this time I want to catch her before she has a chance. I wish you all the best, take care," Julie said, and she departed as quickly as she had entered.

Abigail rose to join Larry and looked at Janneke and Tyler to see if they, too, were ready to leave.

"We'll be along in a few minutes," replied Janneke as she turned to speak with Tyler. "Which national parks are you planning to visit? Do you know of Krkonoše National Park? That's where you will find the tallest mountains in the Czech Republic. It's beautiful. You should visit," she said.

Abigail looked at Larry, nodded her head toward Janneke and Tyler, and smiled.

Larry returned the grin. For most of the return trip, Janneke and Tyler had seemed to spend a lot of time together and, not coincidentally, Tyler's pursuit of Abigail had faded.

"Goodbye, Dr. Randall," said Abigail.

"Goodbye, Dr. Grigsby."

Abigail slowly left the room without looking back. Larry stood and watched her go. As soon as she disappeared around the corner, he, too, started to leave the room, only to come close to colliding with Karlina who rounded the corner from the opposite direction.

"You're just the person I was looking for," said Karlina as they recovered from their near collision.

Larry steeled himself for one last harangue from the brash and outspoken scientist.

"I would like to apologize and thank you for all you did to save our lives. I was an ass for criticizing you over the ice samples, and when you grabbed my hand in the lab, well, I briefly considered accusing you of harassment and accosting me. I was angry until I realized you did it to keep me from getting contaminated with whatever it was that infected Vitaj. You probably saved my life," she admitted.

"I was doing what I was trained to do," replied Larry. Sensing she expected something more, he added, "Apology accepted. I could have been a little more understanding of your point of view regarding the lost science."

She extended her right hand, which he took, and they exchanged a firm handshake.

"Karlina, I wish you all the best on your next assignment."

She smiled. "Thank you. I hope your next assignment is a bit less exciting."

"Fortunately, I'll have a few months with my family before then. Speaking of which, I need to take care of some things in my cabin, and I really should have been there several minutes ago. If you'll excuse me," he said.

Larry walked to the door, stopping to look around the corner from which Karlina had emerged a few minutes ago. They both smiled as he finally made his exit.

The brilliant noonday sun shone in the cloudless Tennessee sky with not a cloud in sight. Larry had been on Earth less than a week, mostly in windowless conference rooms in identical nondescript office buildings in Tysons Corner, Virginia—outside the District of Columbia. His debriefings after returning from Pluto, while not exactly grueling, were wearying. Especially since he was eager to see them end. He was now so close—the cabin in the Appalachian Mountains that he and his wife had reserved for the next two weeks. The monorail from Virginia got him to Knoxville where he rented a car for the drive to the cabin.

He was anxious. He hadn't seen Athena and the kids for a year, except through the videos they exchanged, and he worried that the flame might not reignite, that the kids would have forgotten who he was, or that Athena would sense his emotional infidelity and confront him. Had she met someone else? He knew she loved him, but what husband away from his wife for so many months doesn't have moments of emotional insecurity?

He made the last turn and could see the cabin on the road ahead to the right. It looked exactly the same as the last time they were here and probably the same as it looked fifty years ago when it was built. Mountain cabins were timeless, and that's what made them appealing. Here, they could easily disconnect from the rest of the universe and enjoy both nature and the company of select others. He pulled into the driveway and turned off the car.

Athena, Caleb, and Joshua were already there. He saw the family EV parked off to the side. Given the time, they were probably inside the cabin or on the back deck having lunch. Larry looked at the trees and the blue sky beyond and marveled at how much he missed a wide-open and seemingly infinite sky. He knew generations of submariners had similar experiences for centuries before the Space Force, but that knowledge didn't make the emotional intensity of the open-sky experience any less palpable. At this moment, Tennyson again came to mind:

> If I had a flower for every time I thought of you . . .
> I could walk through my garden forever.

As he exited the car, the front door of the cabin burst open as the boys ran as fast as they could toward him, each yelling, "Daddy's here!"

Larry broke into a smile and threw his arms wide to them, mentally dropping one concern from his brooding list. He soon grunted as he simultaneously lifted both boys into his arms, in one forceful motion. Caleb was excitedly telling him something about horses while Joshua vied for his attention with details of a video game he had discovered. Larry tried to listen to both at the same time and failed miserably. Instead, he alternated between hugging each and acting like the world, his world, revolved around them at this moment.

After a few seconds, the cabin door opened again as Athena walked through it. She stopped to look, and a big smile spread across her face.

Larry listened, or pretended to listen, for a few more moments, then gently put the boys' feet back on the ground. "It's time for Daddy to say hi to Mommy. I'll be right back."

Larry walked toward the porch, his thoughts alternating between noticing how beautiful his wife was and the morose concerns he harbored since the events on board the *Tombaugh*. The latter completely melted away when they threw their arms around each other, gazed in each other's eyes, and kissed.

"Welcome home," Athena exclaimed. "We've missed you."

"I've missed you so much," Larry responded, initiating another kiss.

"There's so much to catch up on. Why don't we start by having lunch? It'll be ready in ten minutes. I'll get it on the table while you catch up with the kids," she suggested.

"Thank you. That's a great idea. If you bought the items I mentioned, I'll cook us a fabulous 'dad dinner' tonight," offered Larry.

"It's a deal." She smiled.

Larry returned his attention to Caleb and Joshua as Athena went back into the cabin. "I want hear more about the horses and the new video game." He beamed as he walked quickly back into the sunny yard.

All of Larry's concerns evaporated by the time the kids were asleep for the night and Athena was in his arms again. All thoughts of Abigail vanished as the reality of being with

Athena sank in. An hour and a half later, everyone in the cabin slept, satisfied and safe now that the family was back together again.

Family activities filled the next four days. Tubing in a very cold mountain stream; ice cream from a store made to look like it was still 1925; grilled hamburgers, hot dogs, chicken, and steak for dinner; and evenings on the deck reading old-fashioned books. It was exactly the relaxation that Larry needed, and it purged next to all thoughts of the Space Force and alien threats from his mind—until his orders arrived.

They were delivered overnight, the first that he and Athena had gone to sleep exhausted, without any thought of making love, but completely satisfied nonetheless from their uninterrupted time together as a family. He read them as he sipped a fresh cup of coffee alone on the cabin's back deck. He wore his flannel pajamas and matching bathrobe, courtesy of his wife and a nearby "general store." Everyone else still slept and the sun was only now rising above the horizon, burning off the fog that settled overnight. To be sure he understood them, he reread every word at least twice.

"Good morning," said Athena as she opened the screen door and walked over to join him, coffee in hand. Her hair was tousled, uncombed, and to Larry it looked great. She wore a white bathrobe, tightly pulled to keep her warm in the cool early morning air.

"Good morning, yourself," replied Larry. "Have a seat."

They sat in silence, gazing at the mountain valley below the cabin as the morning sun began to illuminate everything within view.

"My orders came last night," said Larry.

"They aren't recalling you already, are they?"

"No, I won't have to report early. They insisted that I not cut short my leave, but I'll be returning to deep space," he shared.

"Back to Pluto?"

"Yes, and beyond. Space Command is working with the National Academy of Sciences to charter three new deep-space science and exploration vessels for the sole purpose of visiting the dwarf planets of the Kuiper Belt in a search for additional alien artifacts. Eris, Sedna, Makemake, Haumea, Quaoar—they're all on the list, and more. Each science vessel will be escorted by a Space Force ship. Not only that, but the powers that be are close to having a deal with the Russian Federation and China to coordinate our outer solar system activities and the sharing of any findings. The UN even formed a coordinating committee to make sure the search is thoroughly international in nature, and should anything be found, the response will be from humanity, not simply one nation. They're calling it the Grand Tour," Larry said.

"How does this affect you?" she wondered aloud.

"Well, I've shared with you before, I've always felt like an outsider in the science community since my Space Force duties always took precedence over doing any real science, and a bit of an outsider in the Force due to my science interests—one foot in each world, so to speak."

She nodded. "And?"

"And, well, my report describing the events that unfolded at Pluto caught the attention of some higher-ups at the Pentagon, and they want me to be the Space Force delegate to the National Academy's selection committee for picking the scientists to send."

Athena smiled. "That's wonderful news. I'm sure you'll be great—no one could be better trained or have the relevant experience."

"Thank you. But that's not all."

"What else?"

"Well, provided I do everything right and don't screw up, the promotion board is maybe predisposed to confirm my promotion to lieutenant colonel, and I'll be assigned to one of the outbound Space Force ships and in charge of the science investigations," Larry shared, breaking into his own smile.

Athena rose from her chair, leaned over, and careful not to cause him to spill his coffee, gave him a big hug. "Congratulations."

"I know it's good news, but it also means I'll be gone for another long cruise away from you and the boys."

"That's the life we signed up for when we said, 'I do,'" she added. "Caleb and Joshua miss their dad and don't really understand, but they put on a brave face. In fact, once they heard about what happened out there and your role in it, they had bragging rights at school describing how their dad helped save the Earth from being overrun by aliens. You're their hero."

"I don't feel like a hero," he admitted.

"Larry. Stop. The boys are right. You saved the Earth from aliens and in the meantime answered one of the great questions of science—are we alone in the universe? Not only that, but I believe you will soon be promoted and you've been tasked to assemble a team to begin exploring the outer reaches of the solar system. That sure sounds like a hero to me."

Larry looked at her and his tears began to flow.

"I love you so much," he whispered.

"I know. I love you too," she replied as she reached over to hold him in her arms. "More than you can possibly know."

ACKNOWLEDGMENTS

When Lloyd McDaniel, Ben's longtime friend and webmaster reached out after Ben's death and asked me if I would be willing to complete Ben's last novel, I was deeply honored. When I realized it would not only be his last novel but the last book in his Grand Tour series, I borderline panicked. How could I possibly write a fitting ending to a saga Ben devoted much of the latter half of his career creating? When I found out that I was recommended for the job by none other than Jack McDevitt, I found my inner calm, tried desperately to hide my imposter syndrome, and accepted the challenge. I have worked with Jack, and he knows my capabilities. If he thought I could do it, then who was I to disagree? The final product is now in your hands. Is the book how Ben would have completed the series? Almost certainly not. He didn't leave an outline because, as I learned when he and I coauthored *Rescue Mode*, when Ben got an idea for a book, he just began writing. I'm an *outliner*; Ben was a *pantser*—he wrote by the seat of his pants. He left the rough beginning of the novel and no notes telling me where to take it. After rereading much of Ben's Grand Tour, I believe I am giving you a fitting and satisfying conclusion—of which Ben might have approved.

There are many people I would like to thank for their help in getting this book into print. In addition to Lloyd, Rashida Loya-Bova, Ben's widow, reached out many times to offer encouragement. Whenever I had a question, she was always available to take my call or return my text.

As always, I am grateful for my agent, Laura Wood, and Ben's agent, Ken Bova. Without both agents rolling up their sleeves to work out the details, the contract from Tor might not have ever come to be.

Then there were the beta readers. A big thank-you goes to Brent Ziarnick for helping me get all the bits about the Space Force and guardians correct. He also provided valuable insight into how I might bring some of the character relationships to a more satisfying conclusion and helped me reframe a few scenes to be more impactful and engaging. Karen Morton's feedback helped me peel back some of my cultural blinders. Iris Fisher's and Walter Scott's words boosted my morale and they found some mistakes that I would have otherwise simply overlooked.

A huge thank-you goes to Ethan Trapolino, my volunteer student intern from the University of Alabama in Huntsville, who gave the book a thorough edit and made suggestions for improving the dialogue throughout.

I can't go any further without thanking my fantastic editor at Tor, Jen Gunnels. The book you are reading is far better than what she received at the beginning of the editing process. I owe Jen a huge thank-you!

Next, I would like to thank Dr. Alan Stern for correcting some egregious science errors about Pluto (any that remain are my own fault) and for leading the *New Horizons* mission that gave us insight into one of the most intriguing bodies at the edge of our solar system. He was born too early to be among the scientists on board *Tombaugh*.

Finally, I would like to thank the great Ben Bova, who inspired me as a youth with his Kinsman saga; again, while I was in high school and early college when he edited *Omni* magazine, which I devoured each month, from cover to cover; and finally, as I was an early career professional at NASA reading his incomparable *Mars*. Ben could write believable and entertaining fiction. He was an inspiration, and it is to him that we all owe a great deal.

Les Johnson
March 2025

ABOUT THE AUTHORS

BEN BOVA (1932–2020) was the author of more than a hundred works of science fact and fiction, including *Able One*, *Transhuman*, *Orion*, the Star Quest Trilogy, and the Grand Tour novels. His many honors include the John W. Campbell Memorial Award, the Isaac Asimov Memorial Award, the Lifetime Achievement Award of the Arthur C. Clarke Foundation, and the Robert A. Heinlein Award. As an editor, he won science fiction's Hugo Award six times.

In addition to his literary achievements, Bova worked for Project Vanguard, America's first artificial satellite program, and for Avco-Everett Research Laboratory, the company that created the heat shields for Apollo 11, helping the NASA astronauts land on the moon. He also taught science fiction at Harvard University and New York City's Hayden Planetarium, and worked with such filmmakers as George Lucas and Gene Roddenberry.

LES JOHNSON coauthored *Rescue Mode* with Bova in 2014. He is also a futurist and the chief technology officer at the NASA Marshall Space Flight Center in Alabama where he leads efforts to develop solar sail propulsion for interplanetary and interstellar travel.

His recent novels include *The Spacetime War*, *Saving Proxima*, and its sequel, *Crisis at Proxima*. Johnson is an elected member of the International Academy of Astronautics, a fellow of the British Interplanetary Society, a member of the Science Fiction & Fantasy Writers Association, and Mensa.